This Time Around

KAY SHANEE

BLACK
ODYSSEY
MEDIA

WWW.BLACKODYSSEY.NET

Published by
BLACK ODYSSEY MEDIA

www.blackodyssey.net
Email: info@blackodyssey.net

THIS TIME AROUND. Copyright © 2024 by Kay Shanee

Library of Congress Control Number: 2023919188

First Trade Paperback Printing: April 2024
ISBN: 978-1-957950-37-2
ISBN: 978-1-957950-38-9 (e-book)

Cover Design by Ashlee Nassar of Designs With Sass
Photography by Bolarinwa Olasunkanmi
To the extent that the image or images on the cover of this book depict a person or persons, such person or persons are merely models and are not intended to portray any character in the book.

Manufactured in the United States of America

Distributed by Kensington Publishing Corp.

Dear Reader,

I want to thank you immensely for supporting Black Odyssey Media authors, and our ongoing efforts to spotlight more minority storytellers. The scariest and most challenging task for many writers is getting the story, or characters, out of our heads and onto the page. Having admitted that, with every manuscript that Kreceda and I acquire, we believe that it took talent, discipline, and remarkable courage to construct that story, flesh out those characters, and prepare it for the world. Debut or seasoned, our authors are the real heroes and heroines in *OUR* story. And for them, we are eternally grateful.

Whether you are new to Kay Shanee or Black Odyssey Media, we hope that you are here to stay. So please be sure to check out more of Kay Shanee's array of stories over at our sister and fellow publishing mate B. Love Publications. We also welcome your feedback and kindly ask that you leave a review. For upcoming releases, announcements, submission guidelines, etc., please be sure to visit our website at www.blackodyssey.net or scan the QR code below. We can also be found on social media using @ iamblackodyssey. Until next time, take care and enjoy the journey!

Joyfully,

Shawanda Williams

Shawanda "N'Tyse" Williams
Founder/Publisher

Prologue

TESSA HOWARD

"D AMN, TESS. YOU'VE been dancing with the same guy all night. You feeling him?" Brianne, my friend and roommate, asked.

"Do you see him? I don't think I've ever seen a man so fine," I replied as I used my hands to fan the sweat on my face.

It was the last night of our impromptu spring break trip to San Diego. We enjoyed our days relaxing on the beach, doing touristy activities, and spending our nights drinking and clubbing. Neither of us was old enough to consume alcohol, but the ladies we were traveling with were, and they weren't stingy with the liquor.

"He's definitely fine. You should do something crazy like fuck the shit out of him," Brianne dared.

"Are you crazy? I'm drunk but not *that* drunk."

"You know you want to."

"More than anything in this world," I replied quickly.

"Then do it. You know I won't judge. That dick print looks mighty big from here, and he looks like he knows what to do with it too."

"I bet he does. I almost came from him just rubbing it against my back. That man is blessed."

1

"Oh shit, here he comes," she warned because my back was facing the dance floor.

Seconds later, I felt his hands around my waist and his lips on my neck.

"Come dance with me," he requested before gently pulling me away from Brianne and back onto the dance floor.

I knew he was intoxicated, but he wasn't sloppy and obnoxious like most guys our age were when they drank too much. I knew the likelihood of me ever seeing him again was extremely low, so there was no need to exchange too much personal information. However, I at least wanted to know what to call him in my fantasies because there would be plenty of those once I was back in D.C.

"What's your name?" I shouted over the music.

With perfect timing, a slow song began to play. He pulled me close to his body and gently pressed his lips against my ear.

"Cy."

"Ty?"

"No, Cy, with a C."

"Oh, okay. I'm Marie," I told him, giving him my middle name.

"Marie? A pretty name for a pretty woman."

"Thank you."

"When are you leaving?" he asked.

"Tomorrow morning."

"How early?"

"Ten."

"Where is home for you?"

"I'm actually from a small town here in Cali that no one has ever heard of, but I'm a sophomore at Howard University."

He nodded. "I'm from Chicago and a junior at the University of Chicago."

"Nice."

"Are you drunk?" he asked.

I giggled, which should have given him a clue that I was a bit tipsy, but he didn't know me well enough to judge.

"I've been drinking, and I'm feeling good."

"Can you make life-altering decisions in the state you're in?"

I frowned because I wasn't expecting that question.

"Life-altering? What are you talking—"

"Spend the night with me. I promise I'll cater to your pussy in ways that will change your life."

"Okay," I replied before he could utter the last word.

Prologue

CYPRESS BOONE

I COULDN'T BELIEVE MARIE had agreed to spend the night with me. She'd caught my eye as soon as my friends and I walked into the club, and we'd been dancing with each other all night. I couldn't get enough of being in her presence and prayed she didn't think I was a creep monopolizing her time.

Our vibe was perfect, and if I chose to pursue her beyond tonight, I had a feeling we'd hit it off. However, I wasn't interested in a long-distance relationship, and I already had a situation back in Chicago. Kianna and I had been talking for about a month, and although we weren't serious yet, I wanted to see where we'd end up. In the meantime, I couldn't get the thought of burying myself between Marie's thighs off my mind. *Is it right?* Probably not. *Do I care?* Absolutely not.

After agreeing to leave with me, she left me on the dance floor and whispered something in her friend's ear. I was sure her friend would talk her out of going, and I wouldn't be upset. They didn't know me from Adam, and leaving with a stranger wasn't the smartest thing to do. I'd already begun thinking of ways to ensure Marie's safety when she returned to the dance floor with her friend.

"I need some assurance you won't kill or kidnap my friend," the woman said.

"Cy, this is my friend, Brianne. Brianne, this is Cy," Marie introduced us.

"Nice to meet you, but knowing your first name ain't enough. How can I be sure you're not crazy?"

"Here, take this necklace. It belonged to my great-grandfather, grandfather, and father; now, it's mine. I plan to pass it down to my son when I have one. It means a lot to my family."

I couldn't believe I was trading what my family considered an heirloom for sex, but it was what it was. I took the necklace off and gave it to her friend.

"All that I ask is that you leave it at the front desk of your hotel, and I'll pick it up tomorrow. We're here for two more days."

Her friend held up the necklace and inspected it. When she was satisfied, she put it in her tiny purse.

"Please don't lose it," I added.

"I won't. We're staying at the Best Western right down the road," Brianne told me before directing her attention to Marie. "Have fun and do everything I would do. I'm gonna head back to the room with the girls."

On the way out of the club, I told Rich, my roommate at the university and on this trip, not to come back to our room for the night. Of course, he talked shit, but he knew the deal. We'd done this many times in the past, and I was sure we'd do it again. He could stay in the room with the guys we were with.

Our hotel was across the street, so it only took us a few minutes to get to my room. The door had barely closed before my mouth was on hers, and she welcomed my tongue inside. I'd never kissed a woman so passionately, and I could do this for hours. Begrudgingly, I pulled away from her and looked into her eyes, thanking God when I saw no fear or hesitancy.

Her dress was made for easy access, with a single zipper down the middle. I grabbed it and pulled it down, exposing her supple breasts that weren't covered in a bra, flat stomach, and black lace panties. Once the dress was unzipped, I slid my hands under the material, caressing her shoulders, and slowly pushed it down her arms until it fell to the floor.

I pressed Marie's back against the door and couldn't stop myself from kissing her again. She took control of the kiss this time, and I allowed her. Our tongues briefly danced before I felt her lips wrapped around mine, sucking. That one action turned me on so much I thought my dick might explode. As she fumbled to unfasten my pants, one of my hands found her hot spot. Using my index and middle fingers, I moved the crotch of her panties to the side and slid them into her slippery domain.

"Do you have condoms?" she mumbled against my lips.

"Of course."

I had plenty of them, but the next morning, when I woke up alone in bed, the brand-new box of condoms hadn't been touched.

"Shit."

Tessa Howard

IT WAS TWO o'clock in the morning, and I couldn't sleep. I'd been staring at the ceiling fan for the past hour, thinking about my life and how I could make a change for the better. My life wasn't horrible, but I wasn't fulfilled. This feeling had haunted me for a while, and I couldn't shake it.

As a professor at the prestigious Black Elm University, I took the summer off from teaching for the first time. I thought the time off would give me some clarity, and I'd figure out why happiness eludes me. However, the fall trimester was due to start in a few weeks, and mentally, I was in the same place I'd been at the beginning of the summer.

I lived in a four-bedroom house with my nineteen-year-old daughter, who was headed into her second year at BEU. She was my greatest blessing and, quite honestly, my best friend, and most times, I felt like she was all I had in this world. Cyrah lived life to the fullest, and I admired that about her because it was something I wasn't allowed to do.

My mother was and remained one of the most overbearing and negative people I'd ever encountered. Even at thirty-nine years old, I couldn't live how I wanted because my mother's judgmental words were never far away. I loved my mother, but I didn't like her very much, and as each day passed, my tolerance for her lessened.

For three years, I'd been in an on-again, off-again relationship with MacArthur Gentry, better known as Mac. When I first met him, I was mesmerized by his good looks. Add to that his charming personality, and I was ready to walk down the aisle. However, he had no interest in ever getting married.

After a year of dating, I'd come to terms with never becoming his wife, but recently, I'd realized I'd settled. Whenever I toyed with the idea of permanently ending things with him, thoughts of growing old alone crept into my mind. During those times, I'd bring up the topic of marriage to Mac, which would undoubtedly start an argument, and we'd break things off for a week or two before one of us would come running back. It was a vicious cycle going nowhere; frankly, I was sick of it.

Becoming the youngest woman hired as a professor in the history of BEU was a blessing and a curse. The salary was generous, and I lived a very comfortable life with my financial and property investments and savings. My daughter was on a full academic scholarship, although she could attend the university for free since I was employed there. I was grateful not to have to worry about paying for her education.

From my first day on the job, I had to prove myself, which I understood somewhat. However, it had been ten years, and nothing had changed. I'd never felt like I belonged, which was unacceptable considering 90 percent of the staff was Black. I could never figure out why my colleagues weren't more welcoming, and the only thing I could attribute it to was my age. The few professors who did take me under their wings retired a few years after I was hired, leaving me to fend for myself. I was tired of the dog and pony show and craved something new.

My life was nothing like I'd imagined it would be at this age. I'd expected to be married for several years by now and have at least one more child. Cyrah was grown and could start having children of her own soon. I'd be crazy to start over now, not that I wanted to have children with Mac, anyway.

I needed a change, something to shake things up. *But what?* I contemplated what I would do until the sun came up. The only ideas that came to mind were drastic, but I didn't see any other way. Hopping out of bed, I threw on my silk robe and went to my office. I took a few deep breaths once I logged into my personal laptop. An hour later, after deleting and restarting several times, I'd resigned from my position as an African American Studies professor at Black Elm University.

Back in my bedroom, I grabbed my phone from the bedside table and found Mac's phone number. It rang a few times before he answered groggily.

"It's early, you good?" he asked.

"I'm fine. I just called to let you know I can't do this anymore."

"Do what?"

"Us. I'm done."

There was a short pause before he replied.

"Tessa?"

"Is there someone else that would be calling to break things off with you?"

"No, baby. I'm confused. It's barely six a.m., and you're on my phone, breaking up with me. What the hell happened since I left your place last night?"

"I decided I want to get married. You don't want that, so my only option is to move on. Have a great life."

I ended the call and blocked his number. Mac would let this simmer for a few days before he ended up on my doorstep. I prayed I was strong enough not to give in to his charm this time. He wasn't the one for me; I needed to accept it and move on.

Sitting on the edge of my bed, I released a deep breath. I had no idea what the outcome of my early-morning decisions would be, but it felt like a ton of weight had been lifted from my shoulders. That alone let me know I'd done the right thing.

Cypress Boone

"WE FAKED THE funk for too long, Emery. I've been happier since we called off the engagement than I have for most of our relationship."

"Wow, Cy. Tell me how you *really* feel," Emery said.

"I just did."

Emery and I were engaged for two years after dating for a year. I wanted her to be the one, but we apparently wanted different things. When I proposed to her, I didn't expect the engagement to last as long as it did. Most women started planning the wedding when they accepted the proposal, but not Emery. After two years, we didn't even have a date set and were no closer to getting married than we were on the day we started dating.

"We can set a date and start planning the wedding right now," she offered.

"Too little, too late. I shouldn't have had to break off the engagement for you to want to set a date. Our time has passed, and our relationship has run its course. We can be friends or never have to speak again, but you need to understand we aren't getting back together. Besides, it barely seemed like we were in a relationship for months before I finally called it off. Can you even remember the last time we had sex? I'm not talking about you sucking my dick. I'm talking about actual intercourse."

For about two months before I terminated our engagement, Emery sucked my dick more times than the law should allow. While I appreciated a good blow job, nothing compared to sliding inside some good pussy. However, she used every excuse under the sun to keep me from penetrating her walls, and after being denied numerous times, I gave up and accepted the head she offered. It was either that or cheat on her, and I wasn't that kind of man.

Begging my woman for sex wasn't something I felt I should have to do. I'd asked her several times if something was physically, mentally, or emotionally wrong that caused her sex drive to decrease, but she never admitted to anything. I figured she'd come to me when she was ready to tell me what was wrong. Days, weeks, and finally, months went by, and we still hadn't had sex, but she was always ready and willing to let me bust one in her mouth.

"Damn, Cy. Did you even love me? How can you cut me from your life so easily? I've been dying without you," she cried, sliding right on by the topic of sex.

We'd met at a restaurant because I thought it was safer to do so. Until recently, Emery had been a reasonable woman, never violent, and carried herself in a respectable manner. However, she'd been acting out of character since we broke up. After she tagged me in several rants on Facebook and argued with some women in my comments, I blocked her from seeing my page. She'd popped up at my condo at weird hours, trying to catch me with the woman she assumed I'd left her for. I hoped the conversation today would put an end to her irrational behavior.

"I still love you, Em. I just love myself more. I want to get married and possibly have a family someday. You told me you wanted the same things, but after waiting so long, I gave up hope."

"But—"

"No, Em. You wouldn't even consider moving in with me until we were married, yet you refused to set a wedding date and never mentioned anything about planning a wedding."

"You're not being fair."

I admired Emery's beautiful face from across the table. There was a time when all she had to do was throw a sexy pout with those full lips my way and give me those puppy dog eyes, and I'd crack. That time was over. There was nothing she could do to make me take her back.

"I disagree."

Pushing away from the table, I stood and took some cash from my pocket, leaving enough to cover the bill and tip. When I walked away, I prayed I wouldn't have to have the same conversation with her in two days. Before I made it to the parking lot, Emery was blowing up my phone. I decided to block her, something I'd been trying to avoid. Aside from emailing and showing up at my place uninvited, which she'd already done many times, she no longer had a way to contact me.

Hours later, I was prepared to give up on my job search. For the past five years, I'd taught African American Studies at South Suburban College, a junior college in a south suburb of Chicago. I loved my job, but having earned my doctorate over a year ago, I'd been looking for a position at a four-year university.

"Maybe now isn't the time to leave," I said aloud as I clicked on a posting from Black Elm University.

I read the job description and was suddenly excited. The job duties and expectations were exactly what I'd been looking for, and to top it off, I met all the education and experience requirements. After applying for the position, I channel-surfed for a little while before eventually giving up on finding something entertaining to watch and going to bed.

"Okay, big bro, this must be serious if you called a family meeting," said Jade, my younger sister.

Being eighteen years older than my sister made me feel more like her father. I was positive she'd felt the same way for most of her life. My parents were twenty-one and twenty-two years old when I was born, compared to thirty-nine and forty when my sister was born. Neither of us was planned, but our parents loved us as if they'd been waiting their whole lives for us to join them.

After supporting each other through earning their degrees, they worked in corporate America for many years until retiring earlier this year. Since then, my father continued using his accounting degree by consulting with small businesses. Thus far, my mother had thoroughly enjoyed retirement, living a life of leisure.

This past May, Jade graduated from the University of Chicago, which just so happened to be the university that everyone in our household attended, with a degree in business. She had no idea what she wanted to do with her life, but our parents helped her gain employment through one of their connections. However, based on our conversations, she hated it.

"I picked up dinner since I kinda sprang this meeting on y'all," I said, ignoring my sister's observation.

"Oh, damn. You're making me nervous, son," my father, Robert, said.

"Nothing for you all to be nervous about, Pops. It's good news."

"Whew! That's good to know," my mother, Miriam, commented.

A few minutes later, the four of us sat around my parents' dining room table, eating pizza. I could tell they were anxious about my announcement, so I didn't make them wait any longer.

"I was offered a job as a professor at Black Elm University."

"Oh, my baby, I'm so happy for you," my mother said.

She stood and came around to where I was seated. Cupping my face in her hands as if I were still in elementary school, she kissed my forehead. My mother had always been my biggest cheerleader, and it didn't change as I got older. If nobody else was excited for me, I could count on Miriam Boone to be excited enough for everyone. However, I was unsure how she'd feel about me moving halfway across the country.

"Thanks, Ma."

"That's great, Cy. I've never heard of the place," Pops said.

"Me either," Jade added.

"It's not an HBCU, but 90 percent of the staff and 84 percent of the student body is Black or a person of color."

"Really?" Jade questioned. "Where is it?"

"In California," I mumbled lowly.

"What?" Ma said, stopping in her tracks on her way back to her seat.

"California," I repeated, louder this time.

"Cypress, that's *thousands* of miles away!"

"I know, Ma, but it's a great opportunity."

"It sounds like a great opportunity, son. However, if you accept this job, you're not giving South Suburban much notice."

"I've thought about that, Pops, but I'm not willing to let this opportunity bypass me just to save them the inconvenience of replacing me. If they wanted to fire me, would they give me time to find a job before doing so?"

"That's true, but you don't want to burn bridges. You may not like it in California and want to come back," my father pointed out.

"Yes, but it's a chance I'm willing to take."

"I can't believe you're considering taking a job in California," my mother said.

"He's a grown, forty-year-old man, Miriam."

"What does that have to do with anything? He's still my baby."

"Pop the titty out his mouth, woman. Don't make him feel guilty because you know he's a mama's boy, and he'll turn that position down if you don't want him to go."

My father was right. I *was* a mama's boy through and through. Seeing my mother sad, hurt, or in distress was hard, and I'd do damn near anything to keep a smile on her face.

"Please tell me you accepted the position so I can go with you," Jade pleaded.

"Calm down, everyone. I received the offer a few hours ago after a short phone interview. To be honest, I applied for the job on a whim and didn't do my research. I didn't realize until after they made the offer it was in Cali."

"So?" Jade pressed.

"I told them I'd reply with my decision by noon tomorrow. The university is on trimesters instead of semesters, so school isn't due to start for another few weeks. However, they need an answer immediately."

"Why are they in such a rush?" Ma asked.

"It's not really a rush. There's just a lot that needs to be done to make sure I'm prepared."

"Well, what did you decide?" my father asked anxiously.

"I'm going to accept the position."

"Yes! When do we leave?"

"You're moving to California?" Ma asked.

The sadness in her voice would've broken me down if I couldn't see her face, but the smile on her face matched the pride in her eyes.

"I have to be there in two days."

Tessa

"WOW, MOM. I can't believe you quit your job and dumped Mac. I can understand why you'd break up with him, but I thought you loved your job," Cyrah said.

It had been two days since I'd resigned from my position at BEU and ended my on-again, off-again relationship with MacArthur for good. Surprisingly, I had no regrets. I hadn't been able to share my news with Cyrah because she and two of her friends had gone to Miami for a couple of days, and she'd returned home late last night.

"I was sick and tired of being sick and tired, Cyrah. I felt like I was smothering and couldn't figure out why. My load immediately lightened when I pressed send on that email. I felt like a new woman when I ended the call with Mac."

"This was not the news I expected to hear first thing this morning, but I'm so proud of you."

Cyrah came to my side of the table and gave me the warmest embrace before kissing my cheek. There was a new breakfast recipe I'd been wanting to try, so I figured I'd share my news with her over breakfast. The mixed berry French toast came out great, and I'd definitely put it in our breakfast meal rotation.

"Thank you, sweetheart. I'm unsure what to do next, but I feel good about my decision."

"That was my next question," she said as she went to the stove to fill her plate with more food.

"I've been thinking about it, but there's not much I'm interested in doing."

"What about cooking?"

"Cooking? I enjoy it, but not enough to make a career out of it."

"Maybe not a career, but it'll keep you busy while you figure out what's next. I think you should focus on desserts and breakfast foods."

"Hmm, those are my favorite things to cook. I'll give it some thought. I'm not worried about money because the apartment units bring in enough to cover our living expenses, and my savings are nothing to sneeze at. I think I have a few weeks before they cut off our health insurance, so I'll have to find something for us right away."

"I know you'll figure it out, Mom. I'm not worried. What did Nana say?" she asked.

"I haven't told her."

She returned to her seat at the table before replying.

"I don't blame you. She won't have anything good to say. If I were you, I wouldn't tell her until it's absolutely necessary."

Cyrah had been the victim of Deloris Howard's harsh personality many times. Because I raised her differently than I was raised, my mother always found something to criticize. Cyrah was a free spirit; by the time she was nine or ten years old, she consciously decided to only deal with her nana on an as-needed basis.

"As I contemplated letting everything and everyone go that doesn't serve my spirit well, I considered the possibility of having to cease contact with her."

She shrugged before responding. "I've been telling you for years to protect your peace, but you're a glutton for punishment. I love Nana, but she's not nice, and I refuse to allow her to mistreat me because she's unhappy."

"You never built a solid relationship with her, so it's much easier for you to have minimal engagement with her. The woman raised me and—"

"She should be at the top of your sick and tired list."

We both laughed, something we could do because we were used to my mother's behavior.

"Before I decide about my future, I plan to enjoy a few weeks of me time. Even though I didn't teach this summer, I spent most of it researching and writing the curriculum for a new class. I don't want to do anything for at least a month."

"When was the last time you took a vacation?"

"Goodness, other than going to see Brianne, it's been years. You want to help me plan a little something?"

"You know I got you, Mom. I just heard about this Black-owned bed and breakfast in Sonoma."

"Ooh, that sounds nice. Is it new?"

"I think it's been around for a while, but I didn't hear of it until recently."

"Sonoma's only an hour's drive and I can walk along the beach, drink wine, and eat," I said, excited about the possibilities.

"You sure can. I think it has some spa services too. If not, I'm sure there's a place close by."

A vacation was the perfect way to start my hiatus. I prayed I'd come back refreshed and ready to start something new, whatever that might be.

"Uh-oh! It looks like you got company," Cyrah observed as she looked out the window above the kitchen sink.

"Who is it?"

"Mr. Mac. I'm going to my room to give you two some privacy."

"Dammit," I whispered when he rang the doorbell.

I hadn't looked at the time, but if I had to guess, I'd say it was close to noon. There was no need to make sure I looked presentable because Mac had seen me looking much worse than I did at the moment. I wore a pair of spandex shorts and a tank top with no bra, and my natural hair was covered in a bonnet.

Mac had his back to the door when I pulled it open. He turned around and smiled, showing all thirty-two of his teeth. I looked at him through the glass screen door and waited for him to state the reason for his visit.

"You're not going to invite me in?" he asked.

"Can I help you with something?"

"Seriously, Tessa, let's not do this."

"Do what?"

"Why are you pretending you don't know why I'm here? You called me at the crack of dawn and broke up with me two days ago, and I haven't heard from you since."

"We don't have any children or own any property together. I have no reason to continue communicating with you."

"Come on, baby. We do this song and dance every few months. It was unexpected this time, but we can fix it whatever it is. Can I come in?"

I sighed. Mac was speaking the truth, but this time would be different. I wanted a fresh start and couldn't do that if I continued wasting my time with him.

"No, Mac, you can't come in. I gathered your belongings and planned to drop them off, but since you're here . . ."

I opened the screen door and pointed to the box I'd put to the side. It was filled with all his things I could find around my house. Honestly, it wasn't much, considering we'd dated for so long. Mac stepped forward, peeked around the door frame, and then looked at me.

"You're serious?"

"I am. Get your box, please."

It was his turn to sigh, which he unnecessarily exaggerated. He picked up the box, and when he stood at his full height again, I could tell he was about to spew some bullshit from his mouth.

"You'll regret this, and when you do, don't come crawling back. You won't find another man like me, *especially* at your age."

"Good, because a man like you is the last thing I want. Have a great life, MacArthur."

He moved out of the way just as the door slammed shut.

Good riddance!

Cypress

TWO DAYS AFTER breaking the news to my parents, I hopped on a plane heading to California. With everything I thought I'd need in the near future in three suitcases, I was excited to start this new journey.

I had an early-morning flight, and because California was two hours behind us, it was still early when I arrived at the hotel. Since everything was last minute, the university booked me a nice suite to stay in as long as needed. I hoped it wouldn't be for more than a month, but I'd be comfortable if I did.

There wasn't much time to get settled before I had to catch an Uber to the university, which was about twenty minutes from the hotel. I had to meet with human resources to complete my paperwork, followed by a meeting with the members of the department in which I'd be working. We arrived on campus, and thankfully, the driver knew his way around because I couldn't direct him to the building. I stepped out of the car, and before going inside the building, I took in my surroundings.

The BEU campus was beautiful. There were fields of plush green grass surrounding distinguished-looking buildings. Tall trees provided plenty of shaded areas where students could hang out between classes. I hadn't been on campus a full minute and already felt more comfortable with my spontaneous decision.

I entered the building and eventually found the office where I was told to go. The woman was expecting me, and after I introduced myself, we got right to work. Most of the forms I needed to complete were done electronically while I was still in Chicago, so the meeting was over quickly.

My next meeting was located in another building. After asking a few people for directions, I found the building and the room where the meeting would be held. I entered the room and saw a Black man typing on a laptop at a large desk in the front of the room. He was probably in his early sixties, with his gray hair cut low and a short beard to match.

"Excuse me," I said.

The man looked up and smiled.

"You must be Cypress Boone," he said.

"I am. Are you Mitchell Stephens?"

"Yes. I'm the department chair for African American Studies."

We moved to the center of the room until we were within arm's reach. After a firm handshake, he offered me a seat in the front of the room and returned to the desk.

"Thank you for getting here quickly. I know there was a lot you had to do to prepare, so your efforts to meet our deadlines are appreciated," Mitchell told me.

"It wasn't so bad. I'd been looking for a position like this since I finished my doctorate over a year ago. Thank you for giving me the opportunity."

"I have to be honest with you. The woman who held this position quit on us with no warning. We had to act fast because, as you know, classes begin in a few weeks. Surprisingly, there were hundreds of applicants, but we didn't have time to sort through them all."

I frowned because it sounded like I may have been offered the job for reasons other than being the most qualified.

"Based on your expression, I guess you know where I'm going with this," Mitchell said.

"I was hoping I was wrong, but I guess not."

"Don't get me wrong. Your résumé and application stood out amongst the ones we viewed."

"Then what was the point of you telling me this?" I asked.

"A few of your colleagues had friends who applied and weren't happy when I went with you. Regardless of the short time frame, we didn't randomly choose you. You're more than qualified, but I wanted to give you a heads-up in case you hear some murmuring amongst your colleagues. Your hiring may come up in conversation, and I don't want you to be blindsided if someone says something that rubs you the wrong way."

This was not how I expected our first conversation to go, and I wasn't sure if I should thank Mitchell for the heads-up or take my ass back to Chicago. I inhaled and exhaled deeply before responding to my new boss.

"I believe everything happens for a reason. As you stated, I'm more than qualified for this job, so I won't let what you shared tarnish what I know is for me. Are there other people I—"

"Sorry I'm late," I heard behind me.

I turned around to see another middle-aged Black man entering the room.

"Hello, I'm Daven Curry. Nice to meet you."

Before I could return the greeting, two more people, a man and a woman, joined us. Introductions were made, and the meeting began. Everyone seemed anxious to hear my background. They listened intently while I shared, and then they did the same. Although my conversation with Mitchell alarmed me, the department members seemed like a good group.

About an hour later, Mitchell showed me to my office, which looked like it had recently been cleared out. After a few more directives, he left, giving me some time alone to get acclimated. There was a folder on the desk with keys on top. The folder contained the steps I needed to log on to the university-issued laptop, which, per the instructions, was located inside the desk.

When I finally left my new office, I no longer felt like a deer in headlights. I still had time to figure things out and planned to spend all my waking hours doing just that.

"I'm sorry, Ma. I was so rushed to get to campus for my meetings that I forgot to call. It won't happen again."

It was nearing eight p.m. on the West Coast, which meant it was almost ten in Chicago. I left campus, found a nice, quick spot to have dinner near the hotel, then returned to my room to get settled. Unfortunately, calling my parents didn't cross my mind, and my mother didn't mince words as she expressed how upset she was about not hearing from me.

"You haven't been there a whole day, and you're already forgetting where you came from," she fussed.

"Miriam, if you don't leave that man alone . . . He probably had a million things to do today," I heard my father say in the background.

I could count on Pops to remind my mother that I was an adult when she became overbearing.

"I don't care what he had to do. A text message would've sufficed just to let us know he arrived safely," she snapped at him.

"You're right, Ma. I'm off to a bad start, but I'll do better moving forward."

"I'm done fussing. You don't have to call me daily, but I expect to hear from you a few times a week. Do you want to talk to your father?"

Before I could answer, my father said, "Nope. I'm going to bed. Love you, son."

"Love you both, and we'll talk soon," I replied.

I could barely end the call with my mother before my sister called.

"What's up, Jade?"

"So, how is it?" I could hear the excitement in her voice.

"I haven't been here twelve hours yet. The only place I've been is my hotel room, campus, and a restaurant."

"Well, how was that?"

"Everything's been fine, Jade. Are you planning to call me every day to harass me?"

"Maybe not every day, but I'm ready to hop on a plane as soon as you say the word."

"I won't be saying those words for a while. I'm living in a hotel for the foreseeable future. You can't even visit until I find a place to live, let alone move here."

"Ugh! How long will that take?"

Jade was a bit on the spoiled side. I could hardly blame her because it was our father's and my doing.

"Hopefully, no longer than a month. Sit tight until then, and don't do anything stupid like quit the job our parents helped you get."

She groaned again. "What kind of place are you looking for, a house or an apartment?"

"I hadn't given it much thought. Cali is expensive, and although Black Elm is a small college town, I can tell nobody around here is broke."

"Okay. I'll send you some options. We're looking for three bedrooms, right? I want to make sure we have plenty of space."

"We, huh? You plan on helping me pay the rent?"

"I gotta go. I'll send you what I find. Love you, bro."

I shook my head as Jade ended the call. Allowing her to move out here with me might not be the right move, but I could count on one hand how many times I'd denied her in her twenty-two years.

The day had been long, and I was exhausted. It wasn't long before sleep overcame me, and I turned in for the night.

Tessa

"GIRL, CALM DOWN. It's really not that serious. You're more worried about how I'll pay my bills and where I'll get dick from than I am," I told Brianne.

It was early Sunday afternoon, and I was on the highway headed to Sonoma. When Brianne's name flashed across my dashboard, I was tempted not to answer it. I hadn't talked to her since I quit my job and broke up with Mac because she'd been on vacation with the man she was dating.

"You don't see a problem with that? I've never been one to worry about someone else's pockets or pussy—"

"Then don't start today. I thought about this long and hard—well, maybe not long and hard, but I did give it some thought. I'll be fine."

"Are you having a nervous breakdown?"

I laughed, but Brianne remained quiet.

"No, Bri, I'm not having any kind of breakdown or midlife crisis. I'm fine."

Brianne and I became best friends while earning our undergraduate and graduate degrees from Howard University. We'd found employment at universities in California but in towns a few hours away from each other. Typically, we saw each other twice a month, depending on our schedules.

"This is so unlike you. The Tessa I know is a planner and would never wake up in the middle of the night and quit her job. It was time for Mac to go, so I have nothing to say about you breaking up with him."

"I guess you better get to know the new Tessa, the one who's never felt freer than she does right now. The one who can finally breathe without feeling like a panic attack is brewing. The one—"

"Okay, sis. I get it. You haven't been genuinely happy for a long time, so I shouldn't be surprised. Text me when you arrive at your destination and periodically during the week to let me know you're alive. Enjoy yourself, and I'll come up when you get back."

"I will, and thank you, Bri, for understanding and not giving me too much of the third degree. As soon as my mother finds out—"

She gasped. "Mama Howard doesn't know. Oh my God! I should probably be there when you tell her so I can stop her from killing you."

"That's probably not a bad idea. I'll need your moral support because she won't have anything good to say."

"Let's plan on it. Have fun, be careful, and I love you, girl."

"I will, and I love you too."

After ending the call, the nineties Hip-Hop and R&B playlist I was listening to resumed playing. I turned up the volume and sang or rapped until I entered Sonoma's city limits.

The trip to Sonoma turned out to be the vacation I didn't know I needed. From the time I entered Truth Sanctuary, it was nothing but perfection. Not only did the Truth family own and operate the bed and breakfast where I'd be staying for the next week, but they also owned the ten acres of land surrounding it.

Before giving a tour of the land, the owner, Jacob Truth, shared how his family came to own the property, and I was blown away. The Truth family was brought to the Sonoma area by enslavers with the promise of freedom when they arrived. Unfortunately, that wasn't the way things went.

Joseph Truth, Jacob's great-great-great-grandfather, secured his freedom and was blessed to work for an elderly white couple who didn't condone slavery. The couple had no children, and when they passed away, they left everything to a young Joseph and his family.

By the grace of God, Joseph held onto the land, and generations later, Truth Sanctuary was one of the most profitable businesses in Sonoma. The story was heartwarming and inspiring, and I couldn't wait to share it with anyone who would listen.

On the vast property was a horse stable where they kept several horses that guests could use for horseback riding excursions, a barn where they farmed roosters and chickens, and a large pond where they cultivated a variety of fish. My favorite area was the small vineyard, where they harvested grapes for their wine.

I thought I was visiting a bed and breakfast, but it was much more than a place to eat in the morning and lay your head in the evening; guests could also choose to have dinner on the property. The icing on the cake was Truth Spa, where they offered all you'd expect from a spa, plus yoga and meditation. I was in complete awe when the tour was over and ready to enjoy my time.

I partook in everything they had to offer. Each day, I was served breakfast and dinner. Before I went home, I'd developed an appreciation for farm-fresh eggs and was pretty sure I wouldn't buy eggs from the grocery store again. At least three of my meals included fish, and the taste was impeccable. I couldn't compare it to fish I'd had in the past.

Horseback riding was so much fun I made it my business to experience it again before my time there ended. I'd never done yoga and had only dabbled in meditation, but it became a part of my routine each morning I was away. I felt such a deep connection to Truth Sanctuary that the thought of leaving saddened me, but I couldn't stay forever.

I felt like a new woman driving home. Although I didn't have a concrete plan for the future, I was excited about it. Unfortunately, when I arrived home, I was snatched from my high and found my mother in the kitchen talking to Cyrah.

My daughter looked at me with apologetic eyes when I entered. She knew I'd have something to say to her because she could've warned me of my mother's presence. Before interacting with Deloris Howard, I needed to prepare mentally; since I couldn't do that, this conversation wouldn't go well.

"Hey, Mom. I wasn't expecting you to be here," I greeted before bending to hug and kiss her cheek.

"I haven't heard from you in almost two weeks," she replied.

"You could've called."

"I'm the mother in this relationship. I shouldn't *have* to call you."

"Communication is a two-way street. If you wanted to talk to me, you could've called," I repeated.

"Have you lost your mind? Who are you talking to, young lady?"

"Is there a reason for your visit?" I asked, dismissing her reprimand.

"You're pushing it today, I see. How was your first week of classes?" she asked.

"I don't know. I quit last week."

"You *what*? I don't think I heard you correctly."

"You did, and I'm not going back and forth with you about it. It's my life, and it was my decision."

"Have you forgotten what your well-thought-out decisions have gotten you?"

"I haven't, but I'm sure you have them all on the tip of your tongue, ready to spew any chance you get."

"Mom?"

Cyrah's voice was filled with surprise. She'd never heard me speak to my mother this way.

"You damn right I do. We can start with the one-night stand that made you a single mother."

"We can start and finish with that because it's the only 'negative' thing you can say. You might think it was a mistake, but Cyrah is my greatest blessing, and I still haven't had sex as good as I did that night."

"Mom!" Cyrah exclaimed in shock.

"While we're at it, let's talk about my daddy and where he's been all my life."

"Our situations were entirely different. Me and your father loved each other. He just wasn't ready for a family."

"More like he wasn't ready to leave his, but that's okay. As soon as I get the results from Know Your Roots, I won't need you to tell me anything about my father."

My mother gasped at that little tidbit of information. I was sure she was shocked that I knew my father was married. I overheard her talking on the phone years ago but never asked her about what I'd heard.

"You did *what*?"

"You heard me, and I can't wait to get the results back. You've been feeding me the same lie all my life, but I've known my father was a married man with a family since I was ten. You're right. Our situations are different. I didn't have an affair with a married man, but you were a single mother, just like I am. At least I made something of myself, which is more than you can say. You should be happy Cyrah didn't see a string of men in and out of my bedroom like—"

"Mom!" Cyrah repeated, probably on the verge of a heart attack because this conversation had gone so far left.

"Say what you want about me, dear daughter. Those men you saw funded the lifestyle you enjoyed."

"Do you really think I enjoyed my childhood?"

"You always had a roof over your head and nice clothes on your back," my mother pointed out.

"Thanks to you always lying on yours. I'm going to my room. You can see your way out."

As wrong as it was to talk to my mother that way, it felt better than I'd ever imagined. There was so much more I could have said, but I was sure I'd get another opportunity. I'd lived my whole life doing what I thought would please my mother. No matter how hard I tried, she always found something negative to say.

Today was the first time I'd stood up for myself and returned to her the same energy she gave me. It was long overdue, and I didn't feel an ounce of regret. She tried to hide the shock on her face when I mentioned Know Your Roots, but I knew she was sweating bullets. I couldn't wait to get those results.

Cypress

I HAD NO IDEA who she was, but she looked familiar. I couldn't have seen her before she walked into my lecture hall on the first day of class and sat at the end of the front row. I'd only been to California once in my early college days, and she probably wasn't a twinkle in her parents' eyes way back then. *Why does it feel like I know this young lady?*

I shook off the thoughts and began to gather my things. I'd made it through the first few weeks of class as a professor at BEU and to another Friday. I didn't want to toot my own horn, but I'd say things were going well, especially considering the short time I had to prepare. It helped that I'd been teaching similar material at South Suburban College.

The weeks leading up to the start of classes were jam-packed. On top of going through the curriculum for the four courses I'd be teaching this trimester, I also did some apartment hunting. Jade held to her word and sent me dozens of places to view. She even went so far as to set up some late-afternoon and evening appointments. Unfortunately, none of the apartments were what I was looking for, especially since Jade was hell-bent on joining me.

It felt like I'd been on the go nonstop since I touched down in California, and I looked forward to doing nothing this weekend. It would've been nice to explore the city of Black Elm, but once again, I'd push that off for another time. There were a few apartments I'd made appointments to view, but other than that, I had no other plans.

I requested an Uber before I headed out of the building. The service was convenient, but I couldn't wait to have my own transportation. The university referred me to a company to get my car shipped. They were covering the costs. I simply had to contact them to set it up, which I'd be doing this weekend.

As I slid my phone into my pocket, I felt it vibrate. When I pulled it out and looked at the screen, I chuckled. It was one of my homies from Chicago. I hadn't told him, or anyone besides my family and former employer, that I'd accepted a job and was moving.

"What's up, Rich?" I answered.

"Shit. I was calling to see if you wanted to kick it tonight."

"It might be a minute before we can kick it again."

"Aww, hell. You got back with Emery's crazy ass?"

I laughed. "Naw, that's a done deal. I moved to Cali."

"Cali? As in California?"

"That's correct. I was offered a job as a professor at Black Elm University."

"Black Elm University? I've never heard of it, but that's dope. Congratulations, bruh!"

"I appreciate that, man."

"I know I ain't your woman or your parents, but you wasn't gon' tell a nigga?"

"I haven't told anybody but my parents and sister. Once I accepted the offer, I had to be out here two days later."

"How long you been out there? I know it's been a minute since we chopped it up."

"It's been a little over a month now."

"Damn, my boy moved to California. How's the job going so far? You like it?"

"It's not much different than teaching at South Suburban, but the classes are bigger. I haven't had a chance to do anything else, so I can't say if I like the city. I don't dislike it, but I'll update you once I find an apartment and get more settled."

"Cool. Well, congrats again. You know I don't have a problem hopping on a plane to kick it. Maybe you can hit up Sam and Omar, and we'll fly out there to celebrate your success."

"Most definitely. I'll talk to you later, though. My Uber is pulling up."

Rich and I were college roommates. We both grew up on the South Side of Chicago and attended the University of Chicago. He majored in finance and worked in the banking industry. Samuel and Omar closed out our friend group. I met them through a woman I dated several years ago. When that relationship ended, Samuel, Omar, and I remained friends. My circle was small, and I liked it that way. Men sometimes stirred up more drama than women, and one thing I hated was drama.

Once I made it to my hotel, I ordered dinner. After a quick shower, I threw on some sweats and a T-shirt before setting up my laptop at the workstation in my suite. Jade had emailed me the links to the apartments I'd be viewing this weekend, and I wanted to check them out beforehand to see if I should bother going.

My dinner arrived shortly after, and while eating, I perused the websites of the apartment communities and was particularly impressed with Tesrah Apartment Homes. The first thing I noticed was the size of the community. It was small compared to what I was used to seeing, with only three buildings, each with six units. The units had two or three bedrooms, with full bathrooms in two of the bedrooms and a half bath in the hallway.

The other positives that grabbed my attention were that the units came equipped with top-of-the-line stainless steel appliances, including a washer and dryer, hardwood floors throughout.

The property had a small gym with treadmills, stationary bikes, elliptical machines, free weights, other weight equipment, a pool, a clubhouse, and tennis and basketball courts. I was glad this viewing was scheduled first because I had a feeling I'd end up canceling the other appointments. Based on the websites of the other properties, they didn't hold a candle to Tesrah Apartment Homes.

After dinner, I called my parents, then my sister. I talked to them for about thirty minutes each. My parents were hounding me about what I planned to do with my condo. Things happened so fast that I didn't have time to think about it.

As confident as I was about my skills and abilities, I didn't want to jump the gun and sell my condo in case the university decided I wasn't a good fit. I figured I could rent it out for a while before I made a more permanent decision. My father agreed to help get the ball rolling in that direction.

Emery had apparently popped up at my parents' house, and my mother and sister were home. She told them she'd stopped by my place several times, claiming to be concerned about me, but the front desk person told her I wasn't home.

When they told her I'd moved, Emery turned on the dramatics, crying and saying I abandoned her and our relationship. Thankfully, Jade and my mother were hip to Emery and her stellar acting and immediately sent her on her way. She begged them to tell her my whereabouts, but they ignored her pleas. Although I'd blocked her phone number and social media pages, I was sure I'd hear from her eventually.

It felt great to sleep in the following day. I woke up feeling well-rested at about nine o'clock. My appointment to see the first apartment was at ten thirty. After using room service to order breakfast, I took care of my hygiene and dressed in a pair of khaki cargo shorts and a University of Chicago T-shirt.

Shortly after I finished breakfast, the Uber I'd requested arrived and took me to Tesrah Apartment Homes. I was surprised to see one of my students standing in front of the management office when I stepped out of the car.

"Ms. Howard? What are you doing here?" I asked as I approached the building.

"Professor Boone, good morning."

"Good morning. Do you work here?"

"One weekend per month, and this just so happens to be my weekend. My mother and I own the property. She works occasionally as well. The property manager, Tisha, and her assistants, Sharon and Mika, mostly manage everything."

"That's dope. I already liked what I saw online, but I'd love to see it in person."

"Let's get started. Since we're outside, I'll show you around the grounds first."

As we walked around the property, I was only half paying attention. I spent the whole hour trying to figure out where I might know Cyrah from but came up empty. Thankfully, she didn't seem to notice me staring. I'd hate for her to think I was a creep and have inappropriate thoughts about her. It was nothing like that. I just couldn't shake the feeling that she and I had previously met.

Before we finished the tour, I'd already decided to take the apartment. Cyrah took me to the office, and I completed the necessary paperwork. She promised someone would get back to me once everything was approved. As I was about to leave the office, she stopped me.

"Are you from the area?" she asked.

"No, I'm from Chicago. Why do you ask?"

I was curious to know if that was a random question or if there was something about me that was familiar to her.

"I feel like I've seen you around."

"It's funny you say that. I've been thinking the same thing about you."

"Do you visit the area often?"

I shook my head and replied, "My first time in Black Elm was a few weeks before classes started."

"Hmm. Maybe you have a twin somewhere. Well, I'll see you Monday, and when everything is approved, the property manager or I will reach out."

"Appreciate it. Enjoy the rest of your day, and I'll see you Monday."

As I went to the curb to wait for the Uber I'd requested, I couldn't shake the interaction with Cyrah. I didn't know why I felt connected to the young lady, but it would be on my mind until I figured it out.

Tessa

"**H**OW ARE YOUR classes going?" I asked Cyrah as we enjoyed dinner at a local restaurant.

"So far, so good. I'm still not close to declaring a major, but I'll figure it out soon."

"You got this year to figure it out, sweetheart. I don't want to pressure you, but I also don't want you to waste those folks' money."

Although I wasn't paying for her education, I didn't want her to waste her scholarships.

"I promise I won't. I'll figure everything out soon. Oh, I forgot to mention your replacement is one of my professors."

"Really?" I questioned, raising my brow.

When school started, I'd wanted to ask Cyrah if she'd heard anything about the professor who replaced me, but it kept slipping my mind. I hadn't talked to my former coworkers or department chair because my relationships with them didn't extend outside of work. If I'd thought we were friends, which I didn't, the fact that no one had reached out to me after my resignation confirmed what I already knew.

She nodded before saying, "I was surprised because weren't you and Dr. Smith the only two professors for Black Feminist History?"

"Yes."

"When I got my schedule a couple of weeks before class started, she was listed as my professor, so I was surprised to see Dr. Boone on the first day."

"Dr. Boone? That's his name?"

"Dr. Cypress Boone."

"Cypress?"

"Yes, ma'am. Do you know him?"

I knew a man who called himself Cy but had no idea his full name.

"No, that's a unique name. Is he Black?" She nodded.

"I've never heard the name before. Is he handsome?"

She pulled her head back. "Mom, he's old. I don't look at old men like that, and what does that have to do with anything?"

"Like what? All I asked was if he was handsome."

She released an exaggerated sigh. "He's actually very handsome, and he's not that old. He's probably around your age."

"Young lady, I am *nowhere* near old. Thank you very much."

"I know, but he's your age, and you're my mom, so—"

"Just stop right there before you make it worse. Anyway, how is he doing? Does he know his shit?"

"So far, so good. Based on the class name, I thought I'd prefer a woman as my professor, but he's good. I also forgot to mention he moved into one of our apartments."

"Dr. Boone?"

"Yeah. When I worked last weekend, I gave him a tour, and he applied immediately. He probably already moved in."

"A new tenant is never a bad thing. I'm glad we were able to help him."

"He's nice."

"Good. We don't need any riffraff living on our property."

"He's from Chicago, and—"

"How do you know that, and why are you telling me?"

"I asked him, and I'm telling you because he's new in town. Maybe you can show him around."

"Are you trying to play matchmaker?" I asked.

"I mean, you're about the same age and clearly have the same professional interests. Maybe you can even give him some insight on how to make the most of his role at BEU."

"Cyrah, I'm sure he'll be fine. He has plenty of colleagues that can help him adjust."

"Like they helped you adjust?" she said sarcastically.

I pondered her words and wondered if they would be more welcoming to Dr. Boone since he was older than I'd been upon my hiring and a Black male.

"I think it'll be better for him."

"Hopefully," she replied with a shrug before changing the subject. "What time will Auntie Bri be here tomorrow?"

"She didn't say, but knowing her, it'll be early."

"What kind of shenanigans do you have planned?"

"You know us. We just go with the flow. I'm sure she'll want to talk more about my resignation because I change the subject whenever she brings it up on the phone. I swear she thinks I'm going through a midlife crisis."

Cyrah laughed. "I guess that's understandable. Most people don't just up and quit a job like that one you had. It's a major move and not something anyone would expect from you. I'm still a little shocked myself."

"True, but I've repeatedly assured her that I'm fine. I guess she'll believe me when she sees for herself."

Cyrah and I finished our dinner and headed home. She had to study, and I had some series I wanted to binge-watch. I had no idea there were so many good shows out there, and I had a list of them I planned to watch before I put any thought into my future.

"Now that I know your ass hasn't lost your mind, what the hell have you been doing with yourself? I know this downtime is killing you," Brianne said.

She'd arrived at nine this morning, forcing me to get out of bed and dressed. We had a late breakfast, then found ourselves in and out of the boutiques in downtown Black Elm. It was after two p.m., and we'd stopped at the best smoothie shop in town. After getting our drinks, we found a table at the back.

"There's something you're not telling me," Brianne said. She'd always been able to read me like a book.

"What are you talking about?"

"Something's on your mind. What is it?"

Brianne was correct; there had been something on my mind since I had dinner with Cyrah the night before. I'd hoped it would pass, but my thoughts kept me up most of the night and lingered in the back of my mind all day.

"Cyrah's father," I said.

Brianne frowned before asking, "What about him?"

"Nothing, really. He's just been on my mind since last night."

"Why? What prompted this? You never talk about him."

"I can't talk about someone I don't know and barely have any recollection of."

"Then why are you thinking about him?"

"Last night, Cyrah told me a little about the professor who replaced me. His name is Cypress."

"Okay, I get it, but the odds of this being the same Cy are slim to none. Please tell me that's *not* what you're thinking."

"I mean, it *did* cross my mind."

Brianne shook her head. "I'm not trying to be a Negative Nancy, but don't get your hopes up. That man is probably somewhere happily married with two point five children, a dog, and a house with a white picket fence."

"I know, but when she said his name was Cypress—"

"You don't even know if that was his full name. I know not being able to give Cyrah the identity of her father has bothered you all these years, but this is a reach."

I nodded in agreement as I processed her words. I knew the odds of the man Cyrah spoke of being the man who impregnated me over twenty years ago were a long shot, but I couldn't stop my mind from going down that road.

Cypress

"**D**ID YOU NEED some help with something?" I asked Cyrah.

The class had just ended, and all the other students had left the lecture hall. She slowly gathered her things and was obviously in no rush to leave.

"No, but can I ask you something . . . personal?" she asked hesitantly.

"Umm, it depends on how personal."

"I was wondering, since you rented the three-bedroom unit .. . Are you married? Did you leave a family back in Chicago?"

"That's pretty personal," I replied with a chuckle.

"I'm sorry. I didn't mean to pry. I just—"

"It's okay, as long as you aren't asking for yourself."

Her eyes widened before she frowned. "*Eww*, that's gross. Absolutely not!"

I wasn't even offended by her reaction. Her disgust actually made me feel more comfortable answering her questions.

"I'm not married, and the only people I left in Chicago were my parents and younger sister, Jade. I got the three-bedroom because she plans to move out here as soon as she can convince our parents. She's probably a couple of years older than you. Maybe you can show her around."

"I can do that, but only under one condition."

"What's that?"

"I think you and my mother would hit it off, and—"

She stopped speaking when I began shaking my head.

"Are you trying to play matchmaker?"

"I am, and I think you and my mother have a lot in common. You'd make a great match."

"Really? How so?"

Cyrah let her head fall to the side and looked at me skeptically. "I think I'd rather you meet her and find out for yourself."

Now, I gave her a strange look. "You want me to agree to go out with your mother without knowing anything about her?"

She nodded as she spoke. "My mom is dope, make no mistake about it. However, I think it would be more authentic and genuine if you met her and allowed her to make a first impression without my biased input."

I folded my arms across my chest and took in Cyrah. She was a beautiful young lady with skin the color of copper, very close to my shade, and a head full of thick, dark, natural hair. Some days, she wore it in a curly bun on the top of her head; other days, like today, she wore it free and untamed. Her eyes were shaped like almonds, with full lashes, and the dimples decorated each side of her face reminded me of my own. Although her cheekbones were high, the fullness of her cheeks made them seem less prominent.

I wasn't inappropriately observing Cyrah, but I still hadn't figured out why she seemed so familiar. The feeling that I had known or seen her somewhere hadn't left my spirit.

"Okay, if she agrees to a date, I'll do it."

"Really?" she questioned with excitement. "Okay. Let me figure out how to convince her because she'll probably think I'm crazy for suggesting it."

"Are you sure you should be doing this?"

"I'm positive. I often go with my gut feeling, and my gut tells me you two are perfect for each other."

"You don't know much about me," I replied. "How can you make that declaration?"

She looked at me briefly before replying. "I told you when we did the apartment tour, I thought I'd seen you somewhere. It's strange, but I feel like I do know you. I mean, not all the intricate details of your life, of course, but . . . you seem very familiar."

With that, she left the lecture hall, leaving me a bit stunned. If she felt the same familiarity with me as I did with her, there had to be something to it . . . right? Hopefully, this date with her mother will give me an answer.

November had arrived, and it didn't feel like I'd been in California for three months. All my new furniture had been delivered, and I'd finally settled in my apartment. I would never claim to be an interior decorator and depended on my mother and Jade to help me, just as they did when I purchased my condo. I'd never been more thankful for FaceTime because they also helped me arrange everything.

It was close to the end of the first trimester, and I'd become more acclimated to the culture at BEU. My courses had been going smoothly, and my coworkers weren't as standoffish as they'd initially presented themselves, although I was still feeling them out. It'd be nice to have a friend or two in the city because there were days when I felt lonely.

The date with Cyrah's mom, whose name I still didn't know, was tonight. I wasn't sure what caused the delay because Cyrah presented the idea to me a few weeks ago. For some reason, she'd been very secretive about the details, which should've made me run for the hills, but it did nothing except intrigue me even more.

Not only did I not know her mother's name, but I also had no idea where we were meeting. Cyrah told me she'd email me the time and location by four p.m.

"You're going out on a date with the mother of one of your students?" Jade asked, her voice filled with doubt.

We'd been on the phone for about ten minutes. Now that my apartment was ready, Jade only called to press me about when she should put in her two-week notice and join me in California.

"Cyrah agreed to show you around town if I took her mom out."

"Ha! Don't use me as an excuse to spruce up your dating life. Have you gone out since you moved?"

"I'm not using you for anything. We don't even know when you'll be here."

"Whose fault is that?" she questioned with a slight attitude.

"Not mine. You better talk to your parents. Ma has never been on board with you moving out here. Hell, she barely let me leave. And Pops is cool with it, but he doesn't want you to leave your job on bad terms. You know how he feels about burning bridges."

"I have to hear about the bridges I might burn every day. I don't even like working in finance."

"Yeah, but you're good at it and don't know what else you want to do. It's not a bad look for now, and your salary is above average."

"Ugh! I hate it when you're right," she groaned.

"I'm always right. Have you checked to see if they have an office out here? Maybe Ma and Pops would feel more comfortable with that than you just quitting."

"That's a great idea, big bro. I'm gonna look into that as soon as we hang up. But back to this date with your student's mom. You don't think that'll be weird?"

"When it was presented to me, it didn't sound like a bad idea, but now that a few weeks have passed, it might be a little strange. I've already agreed to it, though, so I don't want to back out."

I wanted to share my thoughts about Cyrah with Jade, but it seemed weird to me, so I knew she'd feel the same. Instead, I'd wait until they met to see if Jade felt likewise.

"I guess if it gets you out and about, go for it. How's work been? It's been almost two months. Do you still like it?"

"I love the job itself. My coworkers are beginning to loosen up around me, so things are less tense when we run into each other. I've had lunch with them a few times, and some have invited me out for dinner and drinks after work."

"Did you go?"

"No, but I will eventually. I've been getting this apartment together and ready for your intrusion."

"Don't try to act like you don't want me to come. You're probably lonely as hell in that big old city all by yourself."

I laughed. "Black Elm is about the size of the South Side of Chicago."

"Okay, so it's not a big old city, but you're still lonely and miss your baby sister."

"I'm not lonely, but I do miss my family."

There were a few beats of silence before Jade spoke again.

"Speaking of being lonely, I ran into Emery a few days ago."

"I'm sorry."

"Why are you sorry?"

"I'm sorry you had to experience an interaction with her. I'm sure she behaved horribly."

"She tried to show her ass, but I told her I wasn't you and I'd beat her ass in that restaurant. She's still so adamant about you abandoning her with no warning. I don't know what you saw in her because she's not wrapped too tight."

I chuckled and shook my head. Jade had always been straightforward and never one to mince words to spare feelings.

"I agree; I dodged a bullet."

"You sure did. I will say, though, she must be eating her way through the pain of the breakup. It looks like she's put on quite a few pounds."

"Hmm, that's odd. You know how she is about her physical appearance."

"If you mean, I know how conceited and stuck on herself she is, then yeah. I was definitely surprised by her weight gain."

"She'll be fine. I'm gon' let you go so I can get ready for this date."

I checked my email while we were on the phone and had a message from Cyrah with the name of a restaurant and a time.

"Oooh, let me see what you're wearing," she requested.

"No, because if you don't like it, I'm not wearing anything else. I'll let you know how it goes."

I ended the call before Jade pressed the issue and kept me on the phone for thirty more minutes. I had just enough time to shit, shower, and shave before getting dressed and heading out.

Tessa

IT WAS LATE Saturday afternoon, and Cyrah and I were relaxing in the family room while we talked, with a reality TV show playing in the background. These were my favorite moments because many kids Cyrah's age avoided their parents like the plague. We'd been lounging around all day, and although I hadn't been doing much with my newly acquired free time, I welcomed the slow pace of the day.

Last weekend, when Brianne visited, we opted not to go bar hopping but stayed up late each night, drinking wine, eating, and talking about everything under the sun. I always enjoyed my time with my best friend, but the older I got, the longer it took me to recover from our weekends together.

Cyrah always made fun of me, saying I acted like an old woman, but shit, most of the time, I felt like one. My job had been very demanding and mentally exhausting, so I rarely felt like doing anything afterward. Mac, or whomever I may have been dating, took up any free time I'd been willing to give up.

When I told my mother I was pregnant, she would have bet her life that I'd become a failure. After having Cyrah, all I wanted to do was prove my mother wrong. I became focused on school, then work, then school and work, all while being the best mother I could be. While trying to become the success my mother doubted I'd ever be, I became a homebody.

"I know we've discussed this a few times, but tell me about my father."

Over the years, we rarely spoke of Cyrah's father. When she was old enough, I told her the truth about the circumstances surrounding her conception, but not much more. I was grateful she accepted what I told her and didn't ask many questions because there wasn't much information I could share with her.

"He was fine as hell and very mature for his age."

"You were the same age, right?"

"I was nineteen, and I think he'd just turned twenty."

"It's crazy to think I could have siblings out there somewhere," she said almost solemnly.

I didn't regret having Cyrah. She was my greatest blessing, but I hate it happened the way it did. I went through my entire life not knowing my father, and my irresponsible act caused the same fate for my daughter. The only difference was my mother knew my father's identity but refused to tell me.

"I'm sorry, Cyrah. One of the things that plagued me for most of my life was not knowing the other half of me, and I did the same thing to you."

"You don't have to apologize, Ma. We were dealt this hand, and I think we've handled it well, especially you. You're an amazing woman and mother. I'm still trying to find my way, but you've raised a dope human if I do say so myself."

"You're something else, but you're telling the truth. I don't give myself enough credit, but I did the damn thing. Raising you alone, with very little support, wasn't easy, but I'd do it all over again and wouldn't change a damn thing. It's probably selfish of me, but there were many times when I liked having you all to myself."

"Same. I loved not having to share you with anyone. I mean, if you'd had more children, I would've gotten used to it, but I enjoyed being an only child."

"Because you got all my attention, and I spoiled you rotten."

"Dang, Mom. You think I'm rotten. I always thought I was a pretty good kid," she defended, pretending to be hurt.

"I'm just playing with you, girl. You were damn near perfect, to be honest, although I have no one to compare you to."

"Do you or did you want more kids?"

"I'm almost forty years old and single as hell with no prospects. That ship sailed a long time ago. I vowed not to have any more children until I was married. I haven't given up hope on finding my husband, but my biological clock has probably stopped."

"Mom, famous people have kids into their fifties. You still got at least ten years."

"Girl, do I look famous? Nobody in their right mind wants to be taking care of a newborn at half a century old. At least I sure don't."

"What if you meet a man today and fall head over heels in love with him, and he has no children."

"Well, hopefully, he doesn't want any."

She laughed, but I was very serious. I hadn't started menopause yet, and my monthly cycle still came like clockwork. I still doubted I could get pregnant with these old eggs.

"Sooo . . ."

"I don't like the sound of that, Cyrah. What are you up to?"

"I kind of set you up on a date with my professor."

She said the words so fast that I almost didn't understand what she'd said. As a matter of fact, I hoped I heard her wrong.

"Excuse me?"

"Dr. Boone agreed to meet you. I made reservations at Elm Street Blues."

"You *what?*"

"Mom, are you losing your hearing?"

"I can hear you, little girl, but I can't believe what you're saying. Did you just say you set me up on a date with your professor?"

"Yes, at Elm Street Blues. Your reservation is for six, so we got two hours to get yourself together."

"Cyrah Nicole Howard, I am *not* going on a date with your damn professor. Are you crazy?"

"Mom, come on. I suggested it to him weeks ago and have been putting off asking you because I didn't know how you'd react. I wouldn't set you up with him if I didn't think you'd be a good match. You already know you have a lot in common with him—"

"I don't know anything, and neither do you. I can't believe you did this without talking to me."

"Would you have agreed had we discussed it beforehand?"

"Absolutely not."

"Then it doesn't matter. Stop being a prude and step out of your comfort zone for once in *my* life. All I've ever known you to do is go to school, work, and care for me. Even the few men you've dated didn't get to experience you fully."

I clutched my invisible pearls. "Well, damn, dear daughter. Tell me how you *really* feel."

"My bad, Mom. I'm not trying to be disrespectful. It would just be nice to see you start living. Quitting a job that made you unhappy was the first step, and I know it hasn't been very long, but since you returned from your trip to Truth Sanctuary, you've done very little."

"I'm taking my time to decide what I want to do."

"And that's fine, but a date with Professor Boone wouldn't hurt in the meantime."

"You've never tried to hook me up with anyone. Why him? Why now?"

"If I tell you something, you promise not to make fun of me or think I'm weird?"

"Sweetheart, I'd never—okay, I would, but this time I won't."

"I'm serious, Mom. What I'm about to say will sound crazy, but don't brush it off. Okay?"

"I promise not to brush it off."

"When I saw Dr. Boone at the front of the lecture hall on the first day of class, I felt like I'd seen him before."

"Didn't you say he's from Chicago? Where would you have seen him?"

"I don't know, but something about him is very familiar. If you met him, I was hoping you could tell me what it might be."

I frowned. "How can I tell you why it feels like you know someone I don't even know? Make it make sense, child."

"You may get the same feeling, and we can put our heads together to figure out why we feel connected to a man neither of us has ever seen. What if he's your brother?"

Considering I had no idea who my father was but knew I had siblings, it was very possible.

"Good Lord! You set me up on a date with my *brother*?"

We laughed about it, but the thought remained in the back of my head. I agreed to the date simply to rule out the possibility of Dr. Boone being my brother.

I wanted to see Dr. Boone as he approached our table, so I arrived about twenty minutes before our scheduled reservation at the restaurant. Luckily, I was seated immediately and sat facing the entrance. I ordered a glass of wine, and while waiting for the server to return, I texted Brianne.

Me: I let your niece play matchmaker.

Bri: What?

Me: She talked me into going out with her professor.

Bri: Your replacement?

Me: Yep.

Bri: What's his name again?

Me: Cypress Boone.

The server returned with my glass of wine and placed it on the table. As I lifted the glass to take my first sip, I caught a whiff of the most sinful and heavenly cologne, causing me to pause and enjoy the scent. When the figure appeared next to the table, I knew the sensual fragrance belonged to him. I raised my glass as my eyes traveled up his body, landing on his face as the chilled liquid met the back of my throat.

Not only did I recognize him immediately, but I also recognized the necklace he'd given to Brianne to ensure my safety on the night Cyrah was conceived. The shock of him standing before me, live and in the flesh, threw me into a coughing spasm. He quickly came to my aid, taking the glass from my hand and patting me firmly on my back. When the coughing ceased, I snatched my purse from the table and shot from my seat.

I moved as fast as I could, almost knocking down anyone in my way and not stopping until I was on the other side of the bathroom door. Pulling my phone from my purse, I was about to call Brianne, but her name was already flashing across my screen.

"It's *him!*" I said frantically, trying to refrain from shouting.

"It's who?" she questioned, understandably confused.

"Cyrah's father."

"What about him?"

"Dr. Boone is Cyrah's father!"

She gasped. "You're kidding."

"I'm not! What am I gonna do?"

"Did he recognize you?" she questioned.

"Not that I noticed. When I saw him, I choked on the wine I was sipping and had a coughing attack. When I recovered, I ran to the bathroom as fast as possible."

"I looked up his social media pages, and I was calling to tell you how fine he was. However, I need to go back and look closer because I didn't recognize him from that night."

"Bri, you were drunk."

"So were you," she countered.

"I wasn't *that* drunk. I—"

"Girl, stop! If you were anywhere near sober, you wouldn't have gotten your back blown out, and Cyrah wouldn't be here."

"Okay, maybe I was a *little* drunk, but I know who I slept with, Bri. It was twenty years ago, but I haven't had a man pleasure my body as well as Cypress did since that day. Plus, he still has the necklace."

"The necklace?"

"Oh my God. You were a lot drunker than I thought. You told him you needed something to ensure he wouldn't harm me. He gave you a necklace as security, I guess, and he still has it."

"Damn, I guess I *was* tipsier than I remember."

"And I guess I wasn't because I remember much more than you think. It's definitely him."

"I believe you. Now, you need to go out there and tell him that he has an almost twenty-year-old daughter."

"Are you crazy? I can't tell him that on our first date."

"Whenever and however you decide to tell him, he'll probably need to be resuscitated. You might as well get it over with. He's already missed out on enough time with his daughter."

"I need some time to process, so I won't tell him tonight. Let me get back out there before he thinks I fell into the toilet or something."

"Call me later. Love you."

"Love you too."

After ending the call, I did some deep breathing exercises to calm my racing heart. I had to go back out there and behave normally so Cypress didn't think I was a weirdo.

Cypress

I SPOTTED A GORGEOUS, brown-skinned woman seated at a table alone. Her natural hair was styled similarly to Cyrah's, and although I had no idea what her mother looked like, I was hopeful this was her. As the hostess led me toward the woman, I became excited. Even if we didn't hit it off, I'd undoubtedly enjoy my view for the night.

Just as I was about to introduce myself, our eyes made contact, and the woman had a coughing fit. I believed the wine she sipped on went down the wrong pipe. I did what I could to ensure she wouldn't choke to death, and when she gathered herself, she grabbed her purse from the table and almost ran to the back of the restaurant. As she jolted in the other direction, I couldn't stop my eyes from zeroing in on her backside. From the glance I managed to steal, she was thick in all the right places. *Just like I like them.*

I didn't like sitting with my back to the entrance, so I claimed her seat and waited for her to return. About ten minutes passed before I sensed her presence next to me. I looked up, caught the confusion in her eyes, and then explained why I'd taken her seat. She didn't seem to mind and allowed me to pull out the chair across from me. Once we were seated again, I spoke.

"Are you okay?" I asked.

"Yes, umm, the wine went down the wrong pipe. I'm fine."

"Good. I'm Cypress Boone, by the way." I extended my arm across the table to shake hers as she introduced herself.

"I'm Tessa Howard. Nice to meet you."

"Likewise."

We stared at each other for several seconds before the server approached our table, asking for drink orders. Tessa already had a glass of wine, so I asked the server to bring me the same.

"Have you eaten here before?" I asked, picking up the menu.

"Many times. Everything on the menu is delicious."

"What do you recommend for a first-timer?"

As I asked that question, I was looking down at the menu. When Tessa didn't respond after a few beats, I lifted my eyes and caught her staring.

"What do you recommend for a first-timer?" I repeated with a knowing smile.

Tessa's long gaze led me to believe she found me attractive, which was perfect because I thought she was one of the most beautiful women I'd seen in a long while.

"Oh, umm, how about we do this? I'll order a few different things, and we can share them. That way, you can taste multiple items on the menu. Are you allergic to anything?"

Are you on the menu?

"No, I have no allergies. Sounds like a plan," I said instead of what I was thinking.

When the server returned, Tessa ordered chicken nachos and spicy, crisp calamari as an appetizer. For our meal, she chose their world-famous chicken and waffles and some shrimp and fish tacos. I hadn't eaten much all day, so my mouth watered as she spoke to the server.

"I promise the food will not disappoint. I know I ordered a lot, but I have no problem paying for it all or splitting the bill," Tessa said when the server walked away.

"We just met five minutes ago, and you're already insulting me."

"I apologize. I didn't mean to insult you, but since I kind of took over with ordering the food, it's only right for me to offer. It's really not a big deal. In fact, I insist on splitting the bill."

Instead of responding, I looked into her eyes. I didn't know her, but she seemed nervous because she'd been rambling since she'd returned from the bathroom.

"Why are you staring?"

"Does my staring make you uncomfortable?"

"Oh, umm, well, I wouldn't say uncomfortable. It's a little weird, though."

"I'm staring for a couple of reasons. First, you're beautiful as hell, and I don't speak frivolously because I'm not one to dish out compliments like that. And second, I was trying to gauge whether you were nervous."

She cleared her throat. "Thank you for the compliment, and yes, I am a bit nervous."

"No need to be. Relax, and let's enjoy each other's company. Tell me about yourself."

Tessa took a deep breath. "As you know, I have one daughter. Cyrah is my only child, and I've never been married."

"I find that hard to believe."

"Why? There's a boatload of women deemed beautiful who never marry."

"That's true. Maybe all the pretty ones are crazy," I joked.

Thankfully, she knew I was kidding and didn't take offense.

"You may be on to something. I am a little crazy but not certifiable."

We had a good laugh before continuing the conversation.

"What do you do for a living?"

"Ha! Right now, nothing. I guess you could say I'm going through a midlife crisis and trying to find myself."

"Interesting. Would you care to elaborate?"

"Well—"

As she began to give more details of this "midlife crisis," the server returned with our appetizers. After placing the food on the table, she disappeared again. I said a quick blessing over the food, and we began to fill out plates. I ate some nachos and calamari, which were delicious.

"This food is good as hell, but it won't distract me from wanting to know more about this midlife crisis you claim to be having," I said, steering us back to the topic we were discussing.

She didn't speak again until she'd finished the food she'd been eating.

"One night, I woke up during the early-morning hours and couldn't go back to sleep. I'd been unsettled for a while but couldn't figure out what was causing me to feel that way. I ended up writing a letter of resignation and sending it to my employer, and breaking up with my on-again, off-again boyfriend. Immediately, I felt like the weight of the world was lifted from my shoulders."

"Wow! That's—"

"Impulsive, right? I know."

"It may have been impulsive, but it sounds like exactly what you needed."

"I haven't quite found myself, but I haven't felt this good in years. I have no regrets."

"May I ask what you did before you took that leap of faith?"

"Ha! Funny story. I taught African American Studies at BEU."

I heard her, but it took me a moment to process what she'd said. When I finally put two and two together, my eyes widened in surprise. When Tessa realized I'd caught on to what she'd told me, she began to nod.

"You're kidding," I said in disbelief.

"I'm very serious. I was a professor there for ten years."

"I guess that's what Cyrah meant when she said we had a lot in common. So, I have you to thank for this job," I joked.

"No, you have me to thank for making the position available, but I'm sure your education, experience, and skills are what got you the job. Now, enough about me. I want to know more about you, sir."

"Hold on, now. You can't drop something on me like that and move on. I got questions."

She laughed nervously before saying, "Ask whatever you'd like, but I can't promise to answer everything."

I shot off several questions about the job, the university, and my coworkers. She willingly answered all my questions about the former two but was hesitant to say much about the people she used to work with. I found myself mesmerized by her beautiful lips as she spoke, so I wanted to keep her talking, and I honestly didn't care what we talked about.

"I appreciate you being so open and sharing information about the school, my new role, and what's expected of me, but I noticed you're tight-lipped regarding your former colleagues. Why is that?"

"How do I know you won't run back and tell them everything I've said?"

"I know we just met, but that's not how I get down."

"That may be true, but I'd rather keep my thoughts to myself. Besides, your experience with them might be completely different, and I don't want you to form any preconceived opinions without getting to know them for yourself."

I nodded. "That's fair. I will say this, though. Initially, they weren't the most welcoming group of people, but they've invited me out a few times for dinner and drinks."

"Have you accepted their invitations?"

"I've accepted a few invites to lunch but nothing after work. I'm just now settled into my new spot, so I've been busy after work."

She didn't respond immediately and seemed to be in deep thought for a moment.

"Now that I think about it, the cold shoulders I received may have been my fault."

"How so?"

"When I started working there, Cyrah was only nine years old. I was a single mom and didn't have much of a support system. My mother wasn't always dependable, and when they invited me out, I always had to decline because I didn't have anyone to watch Cyrah. Eventually, they stopped asking."

"That could be, but I'm sure some of the other ladies had children and understood your position."

"Maybe, but I've always been a very private person. I never told them why I couldn't hang out, and they never asked. Although I wasn't ashamed about being a single mom, my mother sometimes made me think people would look down on me once they knew. Logically, I knew it was possible, but I also knew people didn't care that much. I had a couple of mentors during the early years, but I was on my own once they retired. By then, there was already a disconnect between me and the others. So, again, get to know them for yourself and decide how you want to move."

I appreciated her transparency and loved how she embraced the opportunity to reflect on her negative experience to see how she may have contributed. That alone said a lot about her character. I didn't know if anything would happen between us beyond this dinner, but I'd be sorely disappointed if she didn't want to see me again.

"I'll take that advice. At this level, we rarely get a chance to work with people who look like us. I can't lie and say I wasn't excited when I perused the website and saw so many Black faces. It's a shame your experience wasn't more positive."

"It is a shame, but sitting here talking with you, I realized I was a part of the problem, and I'd never even considered that until now. I'm sure you'll be fine. Enough about me; tell me about Cypress Boone."

Tessa

AFTER CALMING MYSELF in the bathroom, I returned to the table with my game face on. Within minutes of sitting down, it was evident Cypress didn't remember me. I should've been offended, but I'd be the first to admit I looked nothing like the nineteen-year-old girl he met all those years ago. Back then, I had shoulder-length relaxed hair and was thin with a round, plump ass. Today, I wore my hair naturally curly, and I was far from skinny. I wouldn't say I was fat, but damn sure would say the rest of my body caught up with my ass.

Besides the small amount of facial hair he sported, Cypress didn't look like he'd aged a bit. His hair was cut a little lower today than when we initially met, and he was a little less muscular, but his arms still looked like he wouldn't have a problem lifting me. He pretty much looked the same ... and Cyrah was his twin. She had the same copper-toned skin, almond-shaped eyes, dimples, and a birthmark on her inner arm in the same shape. I now understood why she felt like she'd seen him before. Looking at him had to be like looking in a mirror.

Not only was Cypress handsome, but he was also charming and could hold an intelligent conversation. I could've sat and listened to him talk all night. The sound of his voice, how his lips moved, and how his tongue slid over his lips every so often to dampen them had me crossing and uncrossing my legs repeatedly to relieve the pressure between them.

"Well, well, well, what do we have here?"

I cringed at the sound of his voice and couldn't believe it. Tonight of all nights, MacArthur decided to dine here. I slowly lifted my head, and when my eyes landed on his face, he looked angry.

"Mac, how can I help you?"

"Who is this, Tessa?"

Cypress stood and offered his hand to Mac. "Hello, I'm Cypress. You are?"

"MacArthur," he replied, looking at Cypress skeptically.

"Good to meet you, MacArthur. If you don't mind, we're trying to have a nice dinner."

"I do mind. Tessa, what the hell is—"

"Mac, our table is ready," a woman's voice called out.

The look on Mac's face was sheer embarrassment, and I had to cover my mouth to stop laughing. His apparent date approached our table and slid her arm through his.

"Baby, come on. I'm hungry. Oh, hello," she said.

"This conversation ain't over," he mumbled before walking away with the woman in tow.

I didn't know why I found what had just happened humorous, but I was tickled to death that Mac tried to check me about being on a date, and *he* was on a date. I couldn't wait to tell Brianne and Cyrah.

Cypress returned to his seat with a slight smirk on his face. I wasn't sure if it was because he found the situation funny or if he thought I was funny. I eventually composed myself and gave him my attention.

"So, I take it that was Mr. On-Again, Off-Again."

"It was, and I apologize."

"No need. Sounds like he feels you two have some unfinished business."

I shook my head profusely. "He might have some unfinished business, but I'm done. It took some audacity for him to approach me, questioning *my* moves when he's clearly here on a date."

"Yeah, that took some balls. Let me know if he does some crazy shit. I heard what he said as he walked away."

"I assure you, Mac is harmless, but I'll definitely let you know. Now, where were we before we were rudely interrupted?"

We eased back into our conversation, and MacArthur's interruption was a distant memory. Over two bottles of wine, we talked about politics and religion, two topics I typically avoided, and I was pleased when it seemed we agreed in most areas. We'd read many of the same books, watched many of the same television shows and movies, and listened to some of the same podcasts. It was as if this man was made for me, but I didn't want to get ahead of myself. Once he knew the truth about Cyrah, he'd probably never want to talk to me again.

From how he spoke about his family, I could tell he had a beautiful relationship with them. His parents' love story was one for the books, and from what he shared about his younger sister, Jade, she reminded me a lot of Cyrah. He pretended he was annoyed about his sister moving to California, but I could see the excitement in his eyes.

I assumed since Cypress still wore the necklace he'd planned to pass down to his son, either he didn't have one, or the child wasn't old enough to wear the necklace yet. I didn't like to assume, though, so I decided to ask him.

"I'm surprised a man with your good looks, charm, and accomplishments hasn't been claimed by a woman ready to have as many babies as you desire."

"The same thing you said about beautiful women can be applied to men deemed attractive."

"Touché."

"I was engaged for two years, but I don't think she wanted to get married, so I called it off."

"Really?"

He nodded and proceeded to tell me about his ex-fiancée, Emery. I knew there were three sides to every story—his, hers, and the truth, but it seemed as if he'd dodged a bullet with that woman.

"I believe everything happens for a reason, and what is meant to be will be. I haven't given up on finding love, but the dating waters are murky."

Our eyes connected during a moment of comfortable silence. The sexual tension was palpable, and if there were a way we could empty this restaurant, I'd let Cypress take me on the table, the floor, the counter, and in the kitchen on top of the stove. I had to force myself to look away before I climbed over the table and straddled his lap.

"So, um, how do you like your apartment?" I asked, attempting to discuss a neutral topic.

"Oh shit. I just remembered you're my landlord."

"That I am, and I like to make sure my tenants are happy."

It wasn't until I replayed what I'd said that I realized it could be misconstrued. Suddenly, his eyes were low, and he looked like he wanted to bury his face between my thighs. Well, maybe that was what *I* wanted him to do, but either way, what he said next led me to believe he took my response straight to the gutter.

"There's one thing I've been handling on my own that could use your immediate attention."

"I pride myself on ensuring all maintenance issues are personally handled," I replied, following him to the gutter.

"Check, please."

The sexual tension was thick in the back of the Uber headed to Cypress's apartment. We sat quietly, holding hands as I questioned my sudden spontaneity. The last time I was with Cypress, I did things I'd never considered doing, and two decades later, history was about to repeat itself.

"Have you been tested?" I asked.

Instead of a verbal reply, he released my hand and retrieved his phone from the cupholder between us. After swiping a few times, he gave it to me. It was a screenshot of the last three times he'd been tested over the past year, with the most recent test being two months ago.

"I haven't had sex since I was last tested," he shared.

Following his lead, I showed him my most recent test results from a month ago. He nodded after reading them, then took my free hand in his again.

"I promise to cater to your pussy in ways that will change your life," he said.

My heart almost stopped when I heard those words. *Does he remember me and is waiting to see if I recognize him? No, he would've said something by now.*

"I bet you say that to all the ladies."

"No, just you."

What kind of game is this man playing?

Our eyes connected, and I searched his to see if there was any level of recognition, but I saw nothing that led me to believe he remembered me. I shook off the thoughts and decided to deal with them in the morning. I wanted to enjoy the night as if I were nineteen years old again.

I felt a sense of déjà vu come over me when we entered his apartment, and Cypress pressed my back against the door. His lips found mine, and we kissed with an indescribable urgency. Our lips didn't disconnect as we undressed each other. He undid the knot on the belt of my wrap dress while I pulled the sides of his dress shirt from his pants.

My dress opened, and he moved us away from the door, cuffing my ass and urging me to wrap my legs around his waist. I did, and he carried me into his bedroom. It wasn't until he released me onto his bed that our lips parted ways.

"Take off everything but the shoes," he growled while he frantically undressed.

I followed his demand, slipping out of my dress and bra, then falling back on the bed to ease out of my panties. When they were around my ankles, Cypress lifted my legs, worked them around the heels, and tossed them behind him.

"Damn, you're beautiful," he whispered.

It was dark in his bedroom, with a few slivers of light shining through the blinds. I questioned whether it was enough light for him to compliment my beauty, but I knew it wasn't enough to show my flaws.

"Thank you."

"Your sweet aroma has invaded my senses. I want to lick every crevice of your pussy until you drown me in your juices. Can I do that?"

"Please."

"Please, what?"

"Lick me until I drown you. Please, do it now."

Cypress didn't hesitate to put my legs on his shoulders and bury his face between my legs. When his tongue made contact, I screamed to the high heavens. It had been a long time since I'd been orally pleasured because Mac couldn't eat his way out of a wet paper bag, so he wasn't allowed to partake of my goodness. I'd forgotten how the proper placement and flick of the tongue with the precise amount of pressure could quickly send me over the edge.

"My God, Cy," I moaned.

My hips pressed upward to feel more of him, and Cypress read my body language, wrapping his arms around my thighs to hold me in place.

"You want more, beautiful?" he asked, never moving his mouth away from my honeypot.

"Please."

My wish was his command because less than thirty seconds later, he used his tongue to send me to another planet, and he kept me grounded, using his fingers to massage my walls while his tongue continued to flicker like a rattlesnake against my clit.

"Oh, Cy. Please, stop."

"Nah."

Before he honored my request, I climaxed three times. I knew his face had to be dripping with my juices because the bed was soaked underneath me. I'd never been a selfish lover, but truth be told, I could've tapped out right then and there. I had no energy to please him as he'd pleased me, but I had to muster it up from deep within.

Cypress gently removed my legs from his shoulders, and I no longer felt his presence. My eyes were closed, but I faintly heard plastic tearing followed by a click. I opened one eye and was surprised to see he'd turned on the lamp in the corner.

Does this man like to have sex with the light on?

As he sauntered back to me, I noticed a condom covering his impressive manhood.

"Why the light?" I asked, barely above a whisper, because I hadn't recovered from the back-to-back orgasms he gave me.

"I want to see you, and I want you to see me. Is that all right?"

I nodded.

"Open your legs."

I didn't recall him being so demanding, but I liked it. When I hesitated to open my legs, Cypress spoke up.

"You scared of this dick?"

My head slowly went from left to right and then back again.

"You're a grown-ass woman, baby. Use your words."

"I'm not scared."

"Then do what I asked."

Cypress's sex appeal increased a hundredfold every time he made a demand. I was so turned on I could have released another waterfall on his face. I finally did as requested, and he blessed me with a sexy smirk.

"I've never seen a more beautiful pussy."

He placed a knee on the bed between my legs and hovered above me. Like magnets, our lips connected, and a slow and seductive kiss ensued. I could taste my flavor on his tongue and smell my essence on his face. As he ended our kiss, he took my tongue in his mouth and gently sucked on it before doing the same to my bottom lip.

My God! It would be beautiful to have kisses like this for the rest of my life.

Cypress released my mouth and moved down to my neck just behind my ear, and upon contact, my body shivered. He'd found one of my erogenous zones, and if he didn't bless me with his dick soon, I'd finish without him. Luckily, the wait was over. I felt the head at my entrance and opened my legs wider.

"You ready for this dick, baby?"

"Shit yes!"

With one deep stroke, he filled me to the brim, and oh—my—God!

Cypress

SURELY, I'D DIED and gone to heaven. There was no way Tessa felt so good wrapped around my dick. It had to be because I'd been having sex with the same woman for the past three years. *No, that isn't it.* Maybe it was because I hadn't had sex in a few months. *No, I've gone longer without sex before.* Whatever it was, I had to find a way to make this a permanent part of my life, at least for the near future.

Being with her felt like déjà vu in many ways. The way she moaned, arched her back, pushed me away while begging me not to stop. This didn't feel like our first get-together. With every stroke, I had an internal battle. I knew when I came, it would be the best feeling I'd ever had, but I didn't want to come because I wanted the feeling to last forever. However, when I felt Tessa's pussy pulse around me, I only had enough restraint to make sure she got hers before my volcano erupted.

"Good morning, handsome," Tessa greeted as she returned from the bathroom, still naked.

I appreciated a confident woman, and Tessa had proven to be very secure with herself. Based on some of the things she shared during our conversation the previous night, I could tell that hadn't always been the case. She had to grow into her confidence like many of us do.

"Good morning. How do you feel?"

"Better than I've felt in years. Thank you for last night."

She slid back between the sheets and cuddled up next to me. My arms went around her body once it was clear she'd found a comfortable position.

"Why are you thanking me?"

That was new. I didn't think I'd ever had a woman thank me after a night of passionate sex. I knew I'd done her body good, but I wanted to hear what I'd done that deserved verbal acknowledgment.

"Aside from the multiple orgasms you provided and how you made me feel, thank you for not being a selfish lover and making my pleasure equally important as yours."

"That would never happen," I assured her.

"I believe you. Also, thank you for not judging me for coming home with you on the first date and not kicking me out when we were done."

"You really have been with some whack-ass niggas."

"Let's just say this. You treated me better last night than the man I'd been dating for three years."

"That's too bad. I thoroughly enjoyed you too. I need to apologize for getting carried away that last time. I got caught up in the moment, and wrapping up was the last thing on my mind."

She angled her head to look up at me, and I lowered my chin, allowing me to see her eyes.

"We both got caught up in the moment, so I'm partially to blame too."

"Are you on birth control?" I asked, unsure if my question was appropriate.

"I'm not, but my eggs are old, and I'm not ovulating. We should be okay this time. However, if we plan to keep this up—"

"Hell yeah, if you're a willing partner."

"Then we need to be careful."

Tessa was right. We did need to be careful. However, what would be so bad about me having a child with a beautiful, intelligent, educated Black queen? If that was the worst that could happen, I was cool with that. *What am I thinking? I barely know this woman.*

"Does that mean you'd like to see me again?" I questioned.

She unwrapped her body from mine and sat up, resting her back against the headboard and pulling the sheet up to her chest.

"I'd like to do a lot of things to you again. Is it too soon to talk about what we're doing?"

I chuckled as I rolled onto my side to face her.

"I feel like we're too old to date without intention. So, I'm down to have that conversation. Do you have plans today?"

"No, but I should let Cyrah know I'm alive. I texted her on the way here last night and told her not to wait up for me, but I doubt she was expecting me not to come home."

"Why don't you call her, let her know you're safe and are spending the day with me? I'll hop in the shower, then make us breakfast while you shower."

"Are you sure? I don't want to impose on—"

"Tessa, you'll never be an imposition. Last night was not enough, and I'm not ready to let you go just yet. It's not like you gotta go to work tomorrow."

She gasped, grabbed one of the pillows, and hit me on the head.

"Oh, you got jokes, I see. Don't make me evict you."

"My bad, baby. I forgot you're my landlord. Do I still have to pay rent after that pipe I laid last night and until the wee hours of the morning?"

This Time Around   77

"Hell yes, and since you got jokes and want to point out the fact that I'm unemployed, I'm raising your rent."

"Damn, maybe this will change your mind."

I slipped underneath the sheet, pushed her legs open, and devoured her pussy. She kept talking crazy, but it was all the nasty things I liked to hear. Tessa came so hard she was barely coherent when I came up for air. I let her rest while I showered and made breakfast, as promised. She appeared in the kitchen just as I finished cooking.

"I guess you found the items I'd left for you on the bathroom counter." I was referring to the new toothbrush, set of towels, and the T-shirt she wore.

"I did. Thank you."

"How was your nap?" I asked with a smirk.

"You didn't have to do me like that. Watch your back because payback is coming."

She leaned against the counter beside me, where I'd just put the eggs in a bowl. After placing the skillet on the stove, I stood in front of her and trapped her between my arms.

"It sounds like you're threatening me with a good time."

"It's not a threat; it's a promise. When you least expect it, I'm gon' suck your soul from your dick."

My eyes widened in surprise. "You can't be talking like that, beautiful. This food will be long forgotten if you keep it up."

"You have a microwave, don't you?"

My dick twitched at the thought of fucking her against this counter crossed my mind, but I fought the urge and stayed focused.

"That sounds like a marvelous time. Can we schedule a day and time for this soul-sucking, or will it be a surprise?"

"It'll be when you least expect it."

She left a quick kiss on my lips, dipped underneath my arms, and began inspecting the food I'd prepared.

"Eggs, turkey bacon, and pancakes. Are the pancakes from scratch?"

"I don't make them any other way," I told her.

"Nice, I'm impressed."

"This is light work, baby. If you're impressed by this, just wait until I have more time to prepare. I actually love to cook."

"Oh, really? That's one of my favorite things to do, as well. Especially breakfast, and it's my favorite meal."

"No shit?" She nodded. "Mine too. That's wild."

"Well, since you made the food, how about you let me fix our plates?" she suggested, then began looking in the cabinets for the dishes.

"Nah, not today, baby. Let me serve you. If things work out how I hope, you'll have an opportunity to return the favor."

She turned around, holding two plates, and I winked as I removed them from her hands, placing them on the counter before guiding her to a chair at the kitchen table.

"I could get used to this," she said.

I made our plates, placing one in front of her and the other adjacent to her. Then I went to the refrigerator and removed the bowl of fruit and pitcher of mimosa, taking them to the table and placing them in the center.

"Fruit and mimosas? If you want to marry me, just say that," she joked.

Once seated, I leaned in her direction and looked into her eyes before saying, "A real man knows what he wants. I'm not saying you're my future wife, and I'm not saying you're not, but I am saying that not a moment of your time will be wasted once I know either way. Let me bless the food so we can eat. You'll need the nourishment for later."

Tessa

BY THE TIME the Uber dropped me off in front of my house, I felt like I'd known Cypress since we were children, and I had a strong feeling he felt the same way about me. We talked all afternoon and into the early evening about everything. I had several opportunities to tell him that Cyrah was his daughter, especially when he brought up his desire for children, but I didn't, and I knew I was wrong.

There was no legitimate reason for me to keep this from him at this point. It wasn't like I hid Cyrah from him for twenty years. When I found out I was pregnant, I had no way of contacting him. Even when social media became popular, I didn't know if "Cy" was his full or real name, and I didn't know his last name. I couldn't imagine Cypress would be upset with me about our unfortunate situation, so why was I stalling on telling him?

I sighed as I entered my home. The past twenty-four hours had been great, but this secret weighed heavily on me. I could barely get the door opened before Cyrah was in my face, interrogating me about my night. Although she was my best friend, she was my daughter, and I knew where to draw the line. We didn't discuss some things in detail, including our sex lives. We spoke about sex in a general sense, but I didn't need the nitty-gritty details of what she did, nor did I share those details with her. In this particular instance, Cypress was her professor *and* father, so there wasn't a chance in hell I'd share our intimate details.

"Well, well, well . . . you look freshly—"

"You better not say it," I warned while Cyrah was doubled over in laughter.

"Is this better? It looks like someone had a great night."

"That's much more appropriate. We're besties, but I'm still your mother."

"I know, but I still want to hear all about your date-turned-sleepover. Isn't he nice? Don't you think he's handsome? Did he look familiar to you? Are you gonna see him again? Wh—"

"Cyrah, please. Since I'm just now coming home, obviously, things went well. Regarding your other questions, let me get out of this dress and put on something more comfortable. We can talk over a glass of wine."

"I'll grab your favorite from the wine fridge, pop some popcorn, and meet you in the family room."

She disappeared around the corner while I went to my room. Today was one of those days when I was happy my room was on the main floor. The thought of going up a flight of stairs made me cringe because I was sore. My body hadn't been worked that well in the bedroom in ages.

After I changed into my lounging clothes, I checked my phone and saw I had two text messages. I unlocked it and smiled when I saw Cypress's name.

> **Cypress:** I enjoyed our time together and hope we can do it again soon.
>
> **Me:** You name the place and time, and I'm there.

He must have been holding his phone because the three dots immediately appeared.

Cypress: How about I make you dinner on Wednesday?

Me: Sounds like a plan.

I waited to see if he would send another text, and when he didn't, I moved on to Brianne's message.

Bri: You spent the night with your baby daddy?

Me: Who told you?

Bri: I talked to Cyrah. You know my niece can't hold water. I want details.

Me: You'll have to wait until tomorrow. I don't want to talk about it while Cyrah is home.

Bri: Ugh. Okay. Just tell me one thing.

Me: It was better than I remembered with your nasty ass.

Bri: TTYL

I left my phone charging on the bedside table in my bedroom and found Cyrah in the family room. A bottle of wine, two glasses filled halfway with the nectar, and a bowl of popcorn were on the table. Although she wasn't twenty-one, I'd allowed Cyrah to drink wine since she was eighteen, but only with me. She was instructed not to do so otherwise, but I wasn't foolish enough to think my daughter didn't partake in wine or other alcoholic beverages when she wasn't with me.

"Was I right about him?" she asked before I could sit down.

"Dr. Boone is very handsome and extremely nice, Cyrah. He was a perfect gentleman."

I took in her features as I spoke and smiled. I'd always known she looked more like her father, at least how I remembered him looking. Seeing him again only confirmed what I already knew: Cyrah was the spitting image of him. The familiarity they saw in each other was probably because looking at each other had to be like looking in a mirror. Although I'd only known for about twenty-four hours, I felt guilty for not sharing with Cyrah that Dr. Boone was her father, but I thought it was necessary to tell him first, and then we'd tell Cyrah together. *I have to tell him soon.*

"Mom, you were only supposed to go out on a dinner date, but you spent the night with him. I know you have more to say than how nice he is."

"There's a lot more, but that's grown folks' business. Dr. Boone and I have a lot in common and connect on many different levels. He wants to cook dinner for me on Wednesday."

"I knew you'd hit it off. You might want to pack an overnight bag next time, so you don't have to put on the same thing you had on the night before when you leave," she teased.

"Mind your own business, young lady. I had planned to come home, but we had good chemistry, and one thing led to another. That's all I'll say about it. What have you been up to?"

We spent the next thirty minutes discussing her activities since I'd left for my date the previous night. Cyrah's two closest friends went to college outside of California, and she had a handful of people she called associates. She refused to stop doing the things she enjoyed because her friends weren't around, so she was friendly with enough people to ensure she had people to do the things she wanted to do when the time arose.

Cyrah was much more social than I'd been at her age. At nineteen, I'd already lost contact with the one friend I had from high school. Thankfully, Brianne and I hit it off when we became roommates our freshman year, or I probably wouldn't have had a true friend while in college. Brianne became my rock during my pregnancy and those first few years of Cyrah's life. I probably would've given up had it not been for her encouraging me.

I was grateful that Cyrah had a more outgoing personality than I did. Growing up with my mother stifled my social growth. Every time I turned around, Deloris tore me down, telling me in several different ways I'd never be good enough. The result of hearing that so often made me walk on eggshells during my entire childhood and into my teenage years. However, when I got to Howard University, I was out of control . . . until I found out I was pregnant.

My pregnancy gave my mother a lifetime's worth of ammunition to put me down, and I vowed never to treat my child the way Deloris treated me. I allowed Cyrah the freedom to exist as she was, reminding her every step of the way that she was good enough. I gave her the space to become the person she was destined to be and promised to love her every step of the way.

When Cyrah finished talking my ear off, she tried to flip the conversation back to Cypress and me. Since I wouldn't be sharing anything else about my time with him, I turned in for the night, leaving Cyrah to do whatever people her age did on a Sunday night.

"Girl, I canceled my first class today just to hear about this date. Is Cyrah gone?"

I finally answered my phone after Brianne's third attempt. I knew it was her because she had her own unique ringtone.

"Yeah, I heard her leaving earlier. You couldn't wait until your lunch break?" I asked, annoyed to be awakened from my slumber.

"Absolutely not. I couldn't sleep thinking about what may have transpired between you two. Spill it."

"Oh my God, Bri. You're ridiculous."

"Call me what you will as long as you give me the tea."

I knew she wouldn't leave me be until I gave her the scoop, so I started when I realized it was him. Surprisingly, Brianne let me get through the story with minimal interruption.

"The dick was *that* good?" she asked after I'd told her how Cypress pleasured my body.

"I have no words to describe it. I've had decent sex over the years, but I'm here to tell you I've been settling."

"So, Mac—"

"Who?" I joked as if I didn't know my ex.

"Oh, it's like that?"

"Sis, Mac doesn't even compare to Cypress, and he was better than most."

"Damn! Do you plan to see him again, or was this just a one-night rendezvous?"

"He wants to cook for me and invited me over for dinner on Wednesday."

"Okay, so he can cook, huh? Are you going to tell him about Cyrah?"

"Umm, eventually."

She smacked her lips together. "Eventually? I meant on Wednesday."

Brianne quietly waited for me to answer her, but I couldn't because I didn't know if I would tell Cypress about Cyrah or if I'd chicken out.

"Tessa Marie Howard, you have to tell him, and it would be best if you did it sooner rather than later," she scolded me.

"I know, Bri. I'm going to tell him, but—"

"But what? You've been saying you wanted Cyrah to know her father since she was born. Now you have a chance to make that happen."

"I know, and it will. I just—I don't know. Now that it can actually happen, I'm scared."

"Scared of what? Cypress has no reason to be upset with you because you could not contact him."

"I'm not worried about him being mad."

"Then what's the problem, sis?"

How could I tell Brianne my true feelings without sounding like the most selfish person in the world?

"I'm listening, Tess. Whatever it is that you're afraid of, you can tell me. No judgment."

Another minute went by before I finally spoke.

"I've been Cyrah's only parent for her entire life. What if she forgets all about me once she knows? Besides you, she's my best friend. I grew up with her and—"

"Tessa, hold on. You know that's not possible, right?"

"Anything is possible. They've lost almost twenty years together and have a lot of time to make up."

"You're right, Tess. Anything is possible except Cyrah forgetting about the woman who sacrificed half her life for her. You know your daughter, and that's not how you raised her. Will she be excited? Will she want to spend as much time with him as she can? Of course. This is something she's always wanted. Don't take this opportunity away from either of them because if they find out you knew and didn't tell them, *that's* when you should be worried."

Another bout of silence passed before I finally agreed with Brianne. I had to tell Cypress the next time I saw him, and then we could discuss how we wanted to tell Cyrah. Whatever feelings I had about it would have to be put to the side. They deserved to know each other as father and daughter, not teacher and student, and I had to ensure it happened.

Cypress

JAZZ MUSIC PLAYED in the background as I prepared dinner for Tessa. I'd been looking forward to tonight since I extended the invitation. Over the last couple of days, we'd texted throughout the day and talked on the phone a few times. I thought the giddy feeling—the feeling I'd never admit to having about a damn thing—would fade when she left my presence. However, I'd been on a high since she returned from the bathroom after her coughing attack.

We clicked immediately, and the longer we conversed, the more I thought we were a match made in heaven. I didn't want to think about our sexual chemistry because I'd have to put the cooking on pause to give myself a release. Tessa was due here any moment, and I didn't want her to catch me with my hand in my pants.

On cue, my doorbell rang. I dried my hands on one of my kitchen towels and hurried to answer the door. Seeing her in the flesh for the first time since Sunday was like a breath of fresh air. Without speaking, I grabbed Tessa's wrist and gently pulled her inside. After closing and securing the door, I embraced her as if we hadn't seen each other in ages. Her body seemed a little tense at first, but she quickly relaxed.

As if they had a mind of their own, my hands slid down her back, past her waist, and stopped at her plump ass. She was wearing a long, flowing, yellow skirt, and as my hands caressed her backside, I could feel she wasn't wearing any panties. I didn't want her to think sex was the only thing on my mind, so I tried to control myself.

"Hey, beautiful," I greeted after pressing my lips against hers.

"Well, hello, handsome. Is that how you greet all the ladies?"

"Not at all, baby. I reserve this kind of greeting just for you."

"That's good to know. Whatever you're cooking smells wonderful," she complimented.

"I have a question for you too."

"Oh yeah? What would you like to know?"

I couldn't pull my eyes away from her. I'd never been so taken by a woman's beauty. Honestly, I was captivated by all that was her. We stared into each other's eyes for so long I never asked my question. Eventually, she cleared her throat and asked, "What's your question?"

"Did you forget your panties at home?"

As I asked the question, I slowly eased her skirt up her thighs.

"I didn't forget them," she whispered.

Dinner would have to wait a few more minutes. My dick was already screaming to be released from the joggers I wore, and I knew Tessa could feel it against her stomach. I didn't know what made me slip a condom into my pocket after showering and changing after work, but I was happy as hell.

Since Tessa arrived without underwear, I assumed we were on the same page. While our mouths and tongues reacquainted, I lifted Tessa's skirt above her waist as she began pushing down my joggers.

"Get the condom from my pocket," I mumbled against her mouth.

Once she had the condom, she pushed my joggers down just enough to release my dick. I heard the sounds of the wrapper opening before she covered my manhood with the condom. Not wasting a second, I lifted Tessa and pinned her against the wall, and she wrapped her thick thighs around my waist.

"Mmm," she moaned as I pressed my dick against her pussy.

Reaching between us, she guided my dick into her juicy hole, and we both sighed deeply. I'd never felt like a woman's pussy belonged to me more than I did right now. It was like Tessa's was made to fit snugly around my dick, and nobody else's. I already knew I wouldn't last long because that wasn't what this session was about. I needed a release, and clearly, Tessa did as well.

With each stroke, I had to talk myself out of filling the condom with my seeds. However, Tessa wasn't playing fair.

"Aww, shit. Fuck me, Cy. Make me come all over this big-ass dick."

Who was I to deny this beautiful woman? I made sure my feet were securely planted on the floor and deepened my strokes.

"Yes, Cy. Just like that, baby."

The more she encouraged me, the faster my strokes became. Her legs tightened around my waist when she climaxed, forcing me deeper inside her. Her walls contracted around me, leaving my nuts shriveled up and empty.

"Damn, baby. This shit is lethal," I praised.

"Ditto," she replied breathlessly.

With my dick still lodged comfortably inside her, I carried her to the bathroom in my bedroom. After placing her on the sink, I slowly pulled out. My seeds filled the inside of the condom while her juices covered the outside. I flushed the remnants from our lust-filled session and got a couple of towels from the cabinet above the toilet. We cleaned ourselves up and went to the kitchen.

"Why don't you have a seat, and I'll set the table?"

"You're not gonna tell me what you made?"

"Nope, but I'm sure you'll enjoy it."

I couldn't resist smacking her ass as she headed toward the table, causing her to giggle. After making our plates, I poured each of us a glass of wine.

"Wow! Everything looks delicious," she complimented as she sat down.

I'd prepared baked salmon stuffed with a spinach and cream cheese blend, garlic butter mashed potatoes, and maple bacon Brussels sprouts for dinner.

"How about I bless the food, and you can tell me if it tastes as good as it looks?"

We joined hands, and I said a short prayer over the food. I didn't eat until Tessa had tried everything on her plate. After each forkful, her head fell back. She closed her eyes and moaned, allowing me to assume she was pleased.

"Can I be honest with you?" she asked after swallowing a mouthful of food.

"Always."

"I'm generally not a fan of salmon or Brussels sprouts."

"Shit, I'm sorry. I should have—"

"No, please. Don't apologize. I've tried salmon several times, and it's never tasted this good. You'll have to give me this recipe. And you need some kind of reward for making these Brussels sprouts taste this damn good."

Tessa went back to her meal as I exhaled deeply. Her initial reaction made me think I'd messed up and ruined our date.

"My goodness! What did you use to whip these potatoes? They're so light and fluffy."

"I use Russet potatoes and a potato ricer instead of a masher. Oh, and Half and Half instead of milk or heavy cream."

"We haven't known each other long enough to get married, but this food is so good you may as well propose now."

She ate another heaping forkful of mashed potatoes and moaned. Watching her enjoy the meal I prepared was a stroke to my ego. I knew she was joking about me proposing but decided to run with it.

"Do you think it's too soon?"

She paused as she lifted the salmon to her mouth.

"Huh? What?"

"Do you think it's too soon for us to get married? Because I've never cared much about what others thought."

It took some effort to maintain the serious look on my face while Tessa's mouth opened and closed as she tried to respond.

"Cypress, I—um, we can't—I mean, I would marry you but—"

I decided to put her out of her misery and stopped her from trying to explain why we couldn't get married.

"Calm down, beautiful. I'm just fucking with you. I don't want to scare you away before you have a chance to fall in love with me."

Her breathing hitched before she cleared her throat. When she didn't respond, I let the moment pass and continued eating. After a few moments of silence, she asked me about my day.

"It was good. We had a great discussion in Black Feminist History. Cyrah is a firecracker and knows her shit. She shut down one of the white boys so good, I'd be surprised if he participates in another discussion for the rest of the term."

"She's always been very passionate about her beliefs. Sometimes, it could be to a fault, but whether she's right or wrong, she'll make sure you hear her point. I've always loved that about her."

"Does she get that from her mother?"

"Not at all. Unfortunately, speaking up for myself has never been one of my strong points. I'm working on it, though."

"As long as you don't allow people to run over you, and I don't see you doing that."

"In the past, I let people get away with way too much. I wasn't a doormat, but I wish I handled some things differently."

"Listen, every day is about being better than you were the day before. We're all works in progress."

"True."

We'd been eating while we talked, and our plates were clean. I asked Tessa if she wanted seconds, and she declined. She helped me clear the table, and while I loaded the dishwasher, she put the leftovers in plastic containers.

"I'm glad you didn't want seconds," I told her.

"Why? There would still be plenty left over for you to take for lunch and have for dinner tomorrow."

"Because I made peach cobbler for dessert."

She gasped. "Did Cyrah tell you peach cobbler is my absolute favorite?"

I shook my head as a smile spread across my face. The number of things I had in common with this woman was unreal, but I loved it.

"I was hoping you liked it because it's my favorite too."

"Wow, we have way too much in common. This is starting to get creepy."

"Nah, it's just the confirmation we need to allow ourselves to let our feelings flow without questioning them."

"I, umm, I suppose that could be it. How about we let our food digest a bit before dessert? There's, umm, something I need to talk to you about."

"This sounds serious. Everything good?"

"Can we go to the living room and have a seat?" she asked instead of answering my question.

I was a bit nervous as I followed her into my living room. We sat on the couch, and she angled her body toward me, so I did the same.

"I'm a little worried, Tessa. Did I do something wrong or—"

"No, it's nothing you did. I—"

My phone began to ring, interrupting her. I told Tessa I'd call whoever it was back and to continue once the ringing stopped.

"When I was a—"

The ringing started again, so I decided to see who it was.

"I'm sorry. Give me a second."

I returned to the kitchen to grab my ringing phone from the counter. It was Jade, which caused me some alarm because she knew Tessa was coming over tonight.

"This better be important," I answered.

"It's Daddy. He had a heart attack."

Tessa

MY HEART WENT out to Cypress because I could tell how close he was to his father by how highly he spoke of him. When his sister called and told him their father had a heart attack, Cypress began to panic. I ended up taking the phone from him and getting the details from Jade. While he packed a bag, I booked him a one-way ticket to Chicago that left in two hours. He didn't say much on the way to the airport, but when we arrived, he thanked me and promised to keep in touch. That was two days ago, which wasn't too long in the big scheme of things, but I'd expected to hear from him by now. He didn't even text me to let me know he landed safely.

I did my best not to worry, but I couldn't help it. I prayed a few times daily for Mr. Boone to recover fully and for the strength of those who loved him. I started texting Cypress several times but didn't want to intrude during this critical time. He'd contact me when time permitted or when his thoughts allowed him a moment of reprieve.

Over the past few days, I'd kept busy researching the history of African Americans in Northern California. I'd been toying around with the idea of putting together African American history tours since I'd returned from Truth Sanctuary, but research was necessary to determine if it was possible. I wouldn't share it with anyone until I had a plan, but what I'd discovered so far was very promising.

My doorbell chimed, and aggressive knocking on the door followed immediately. I looked at the time on my phone and frowned. It was close to noon, and I was still wearing my pajamas, robe, and bonnet. I wasn't expecting company, but I wasn't surprised when I recognized my mother's silhouette in the window.

"What does she want?" I whispered to myself.

I'd barely opened the door before she started griping.

"I guess I don't have to ask what you do all day. It's damn near noon, and you haven't even bathed," she pointed out.

"Is that the purpose of your visit, to point out that I haven't gotten dressed for the day?"

"Can I come in, or are you gonna make your mother stand outside?"

Everything in me wanted to slam the door in her face and leave her standing outside. However, my conscience wouldn't allow me to do so. I stepped back, giving her room to enter before securing the door. Deloris didn't wait for me to invite her further inside, so I followed her to the kitchen.

"Since you can't seem to call or visit—"

"There's no need for a guilt trip. I'll call or stop by when I feel like being verbally abused. Until then, get used to not seeing or talking to me too often."

"What the hell has gotten into you? This is not the Tessa I raised."

"Yes, it is. I'm just tired of being your doormat. I can't remember the last time I felt like you actually liked me. Most of the time, I dread being in your presence because I have to be perfect. If I'm not, you make me feel like the scum of the earth. You're only nice to me when your fake-ass friends are around, then you brag about everything I've accomplished like you're partially responsible for my success."

"It's because of me that you're the woman you are today. You should be thanking me for my tough love, but instead, you're mad and disrespectful as hell." She kissed her teeth. "I shouldn't be surprised; you never appreciated all that I've sacrificed for you to have a good life."

I exhaled deeply because what I didn't want to do was go back and forth with her about my upbringing.

"Why are you here?"

"Oh yes. There is a reason for my visit. I heard you and Mac had a run-in at Elm Street Blues while you were with another man."

"You can't be serious."

"If you're cheating on MacArthur, you must learn to be more discreet. This town isn't big enough for you to be so careless."

"First of all, I broke up with Mac weeks ago. Second, did you also hear that he was on a date as well?"

"That's neither here nor there, Tessa. Men will be men."

"Why am I not surprised by your response?"

"I also heard the man you were with is your replacement at BEU. If that's true, what will he think of you once he finds out who you *really* are? You're not a professor anymore, so you can't even use that to work in your favor."

"Dr. Boone is his name, just in case you and your friends want to do some digging with your nosy asses. Oh, and after one passion-filled night together, he knows more about me than Mac ever cared to know. Go tell *that* to your friends. You can leave now."

I turned and headed for my front door. When I didn't hear my mother's footsteps behind me, I stopped and looked back.

"If that's all you had to say, this conversation is over."

When I reached the door, I opened it and waited for her to make her grand exit.

"MacArthur has his issues, but he's probably the best you'll be able to find. This thing with this professor won't last long, and if you're smart, you'd beg Mac to take you back and try to build a life with him. A woman your age, who probably can't have more children, can't be picky."

With that, she stuck her nose in the air and swished out of my house. Instead of slamming the door behind her like I wanted to, I gently closed it before leaning against it. My mother had only been here for five minutes, and I was mentally exhausted. Whatever I had planned for the rest of the day would have to wait until tomorrow.

"I need a nap!"

"I am so sorry, Tess. You know how it is at these conferences," Brianne grumbled. "Between leading my group sessions, presenting, and networking professionally and socially, I've been tapped out at the end of each night. I had to turn down the dinner invitations tonight because I'm exhausted and still have one more day of this bullshit. On a damn Saturday, at that."

I'd been trying to talk to her since I dropped Cypress off at the airport on Wednesday evening. She didn't answer any of my calls but texted me that she'd call me when she turned in for the night, but she never called. It had only been a few days, but I desperately needed someone to talk to. Brianne was my only option since I couldn't speak to Cyrah about this.

"It's fine. I know you're working while my unemployed ass sits around the house twiddling my thumbs all day."

"That's probably only partly true, but what's the tea? I've been preoccupied but anxious as hell to find out how Cypress took the news."

"I didn't tell him."

"What?"

"I didn't—"

"I heard you. Why didn't you tell him? I thought we agreed you'd tell him on Wednesday."

"We did, and I tried. Just as I was about to tell him, he got a phone call that his father had a heart attack."

"What? Oh my God. Is his father okay? Is he okay?"

"Your guess is as good as mine. I haven't heard from him since I took him to the airport."

"Why haven't you called him?"

"I don't know if it's my place. We've known each other for less than a week. I'm not sure if—"

"Sis, you gave birth to that man's child. Her *grandfather* had a heart attack. Besides being a good person, you have legitimate reasons to be concerned. Call him. Or at least send a text."

Brianne was right. I would hate for him to return to California, thinking I wasn't concerned about him or his father.

"Okay. I'll send him a text as soon as we hang up."

"Good, and if he doesn't respond, call him," she suggested.

"I don't know about that. Anyway, how's the conference going?"

"It sucks without you. I ran into Mitchell and that woman who always looks surprised."

"Ha! Sentoria?"

Sentoria was the department chair for the Hispanic American Studies department. The way her eyebrows were arched made her look like she was surprised all the time. I could barely look at her without laughing.

"Yeah. I think she and Mitchell are messing around."

"What? *Eww*, Mitchell is old, and besides, they're married to other people unless they've gotten divorced. You know I didn't talk to them about anything unrelated to work," I reminded her.

"I met both of their spouses at that conference in Missouri last year. However, they give off vibes that lead me to believe they know each other intimately. Anyway, Mitchell asked how you were."

"Girl, stop playing."

"No, seriously, and I went off on his ass. I said he would've reached out if he were truly concerned about your well-being."

It had been several weeks, and still, no one from my department had contacted me.

"What'd he say to that?" I asked.

"Some mess about being busy and whatnot. Nothing but excuses. What else has been going on since we last talked?"

"Nothing much. I've been doing some research on this idea I have, but—"

"What idea is that?"

"I'll tell you when I've given it more thought. My mother and her negative energy visited me. I had to burn some sage when she left. I hate to say it, but I'm so sick of her."

I shared with Brianne how the conversation went, with her mumbling under her breath. When I finished, she shared her feelings.

"I know that's your mama, and I've never been one to disrespect my elders, but you should've been sick of her crazy ass. I'm glad you're finally standing up for yourself when it comes to her because how she's treated you since I've known you, and probably even longer, is unacceptable."

"Yeah, I know. It's been a long time coming."

"I've mentioned it before, and you didn't seem interested, but you should consider going to therapy."

Brianne had been suggesting I go to therapy for years. I'd never been interested, but maybe it was time I considered it.

"Maybe, but let me go so I can text Cypress before it gets too late in Chicago."

"Okay. Let me know how it goes. Love you."

"Will do, and I love you too."

Cypress

THE PAST FEW days had been mentally and emotionally overwhelming. Once I got the news my father had had a heart attack, I hopped on the next flight to Chicago. By the time I'd arrived at the hospital, it had been confirmed that my father had a myocardial infarction and would need coronary artery bypass grafting surgery. His condition was stabilized, but he'd remain in the hospital for a few days before returning home to rest and prepare for the surgery, which was scheduled for two weeks out. The doctors were adamant about my father taking it easy, which would be hard for him because he was a fairly active man. However, I had no doubt my mother and sister would ensure he followed the doctor's orders.

Thankfully, I only had to cancel classes for two days thus far, which was only one day for each class. There were two more weeks in the trimester, and I'd planned to come home and stay through the holidays. The visit was much needed because I had a lot of loose ends to tie up after leaving so abruptly in August. I knew I couldn't cancel all the classes leading up to exams, so I'd have to contact Mitchell to discuss alternative options.

Since I'd been home, my focus had been on my father's health, and it still very much was. However, since I knew he was stabilized and in good hands, I could direct my attention elsewhere. I picked up my phone, and as I went to my call log to look for Tessa's number, I received a text from her.

> **Tessa:** Hey, I didn't want to bother you, but it's been a couple of days. I hope you arrived safely and your father is doing well. Call me whenever you're not too busy.

I couldn't help but smile about how in sync we seemed to be. Instead of replying to her text, I FaceTimed her. The phone rang a couple of times before her beautiful face appeared on my screen. It was about seven o'clock in the evening in California, and her face looked fresh and vibrant, brightening my mood. I hadn't realized it, but I missed her. It had only been two days, but I'd already gotten used to her presence in my life.

"Hey, you didn't have to call me back right away," she said when she answered.

"Would you believe me if I told you I was about to call you when your text came through?"

"Why would you lie?"

"I wouldn't. You were on my mind, and I finally had a free moment. I apologize for not contacting you sooner. Things have been a little overwhelming," I admitted.

"I understand. You don't have to apologize. You speak very highly of your father, so I know you're very close. How is he, by the way?"

"He's still in the hospital but stable, thank God. He should be released in a few days but has to have surgery in two weeks."

"I've been praying for him, so it's good to know his health is moving in the right direction. I know the idea of him having surgery is scary to all of you, but everything will be okay. I'll continue to pray for him and your family."

"I appreciate your prayers. It means a lot."

"You're welcome. I don't want to hold you. I know you're probably busy with your family, and—"

"I wouldn't have called you if I didn't have time to talk to you. I need the distraction—I mean, you're much more than a distraction. I could use some good conversation from a beautiful woman."

"I'd be happy to provide that for you. Aside from the reason for your visit, does it feel good to be home?"

"Although I've spent most of my time at the hospital since I arrived, I didn't realize how much I missed my city. However, fall here can sometimes feel very much like winter, so it'll be nice to return to Cali." *And you*, I thought.

"The weather in Cali is why I don't want to live elsewhere. Are you staying in Chicago until after your father's surgery?"

"With it being so close to the end of the trimester, I'll probably stay until a few days before classes start again. I need to talk to Mitchell to make sure—"

"Your family should always be your priority. Considering the circumstances, I'm sure he won't mind if you teach your classes online for a week. It would be better than canceling the classes, and someone else can administer your exams."

"True. All I told him was that I had a family emergency and I had to come home. I'll give him more details and ask if—"

"Don't ask, Cypress. Tell him you will arrange to teach your classes online next week because you need to be with your family during this difficult time. Don't give him the option to say no."

Tessa knew Mitchell much better than I did. He'd been cool since our first meeting. I admit I was side-eyeing him at first, but he'd proven to be a decent person to work for.

"Pipe down, beautiful. I'll take your advice and tell you what he says when I speak to him. For now, tell me what you've been up to."

"Besides worrying about your family, nothing much. Remember, I'm unemployed."

"Oh yeah, you are jobless," he teased. "Since you're not busy, I need a favor."

"Sure, as long as it's something I can handle."

"I actually need two favors. One is easy, but you may have to give the other some thought."

"I'm listening."

"Can you stop by my apartment and throw out or eat the leftovers? If you go tonight or tomorrow, they should still be good. As a matter of fact, take any food with you that may rot before I return."

"Sounds simple enough, and I haven't eaten tonight, so that works for me. What's your second favor?"

I had no idea how she'd take my next request, but the answer would definitely be no if I didn't ask.

"Come to Chicago."

"Excuse me. What?"

"Come to Chicago," I repeated with more confidence.

"You want me to come to Chicago?"

"Is that asking too much?"

"Umm, I think it's kind of soon to meet your family, especially considering the circumstances. We've only—"

"It's never too soon if it feels right, but you don't have to meet my family if you're not ready. You'll be with me, and no one will know you're here except me. Unless, of course, you change your mind and want to meet them. I could use the company."

"Cypress, are you sure about this?"

"I wouldn't ask if I wasn't sure. I don't want to wait two weeks to see you again, and since you ain't got no job—"

"You just keep bringing that up. There might be an eviction notice waiting for you when you return."

"You brought it up first this time, and I know you wouldn't evict me. Dating a homeless man is *not* a good look," I joked.

"And dating a jobless woman is?"

"You may be jobless, but you got that real estate money coming in, so I know you're not broke. Actually, I'm trying to decide what to do with my condo. Maybe you can give me some tips."

"Maybe. I'm sure Illinois rental property guidelines and laws differ from California, but I can help you."

"Should I look for a ticket?" I asked.

"How long would you want me to stay? The holidays are coming up, and I don't want Cyrah to spend them alone."

"How about I get a one-way ticket for now, and you can leave when you're sick of me."

"One way?"

"And you leave when you're ready."

"I don't know, Cypress."

"No pressure. I know I sprang this on you, so think about it for a few days and let me know."

"Okay, I will."

We talked for a little longer, and I began to yawn. Tessa noticed and expressed that she could see how tired I was in my eyes. I wasn't ready to end our call, but she insisted so I could get some rest. It turned out she was right because I never made it to my bedroom. Instead, I fell asleep on the couch in the den.

Tessa

"I CAN'T BELIEVE YOU'RE going," Cyrah said. "But I absolutely love this for you. Honestly, I love this new attitude you've had lately. It's kind of 'YOLO' but still responsible."

We were in my bedroom, and I was packing for my trip to Chicago. My flight left early the following day, so Cyrah and I were having a last-minute girl's night. It was only six in the evening, but we'd already showered and had on our matching pajamas. She was lying across my bed, watching me go back and forth from my walk-in closet to my luggage.

"I don't know what's gotten into me these past few months. Maybe it's because I'm about to turn forty. The old me would never have agreed to accept a one-way ticket to Chicago to spend time with a man she barely knows. It honestly didn't take me long to decide. I knew I wanted to go seconds after he asked, but I didn't want to seem desperate, so I made him wait and wonder. I'm setting a horrible example for you. Don't be like your mom, Cy."

"You're a great example, woman. Besides, I have a good feeling about him, and my gut has never led me down the wrong path."

"Hopefully, your gut instincts work for me as well as they do for you. I'll be back in time for Thanksgiving."

"And if you decide to stay longer, I can fend for myself. Just know I won't be spending the holiday with Nana."

We both laughed because we knew that would be torture. I'd definitely make sure I returned so my baby wouldn't have to suffer alone. I stopped packing for a moment and looked at Cyrah. It was crazy how she had her father's whole face. I knew if I didn't tell them who they were to each other soon, one of them would figure it out. It was inevitable.

"Seriously, though, I have a good feeling about him too. Hopefully, he's having the same good feelings."

"Do you think he'd invite you to his home and pay for your plane ticket if he wasn't feeling you?"

"Men have done stranger things, sweetheart."

"I think Dr. Boone is different."

"What's going on with your love life since you're all up in mine?"

"There's nothing to share here. I haven't run into a guy I'd give the time of day in months," she commented, sounding disgusted.

"Is it that bad?"

"In my age group, it is. All they want to do is have sex, which is cool, but can we have a conversation and go out to dinner first? I'll even pay for my own food."

I laughed. "Hell, if you don't pay for your food, they'll expect something in return. So, I take it you're not into casual sex, huh?"

"That's the thing. I don't mind casual sex, but my attraction to someone tends to be more than just physical. At least let me pick your brain a bit before we hit the sack."

Her level of annoyance with the dating scene made me laugh. I knew Cyrah wasn't a virgin. She came to me before she gave her virginity to her high school boyfriend when she was seventeen. He was also a virgin, and I thought they'd be together forever. However, they called things off before he went away to college.

"I can understand that. Does the current dating pool make you miss Leon?"

"Sometimes, but I don't regret us breaking up. If we somehow find our way back to each other, at least we lived a little before making a lifetime commitment."

"How in the world did I manage to have such a mature daughter? At your age, I was doing exactly what you *don't* want to do. That's how I ended up pregnant with you by a man I didn't know."

"I guess I learned from your mistakes," she replied with a shrug.

"You know you weren't a mistake, though."

"My conception was not planned; hence, it was a mistake, but I know you don't regret having me, and I'm the best thing that ever happened to you."

"As long as you know. If you—oh, that's the doorbell. Must be the pizza."

"I'll go get it and meet you in the kitchen."

She disappeared to answer the door. I put a few more things in my suitcase before joining her in the kitchen. We'd ordered our favorite pineapple and bacon pizza, and as soon as the aroma hit my nose, I realized I hadn't eaten since breakfast.

"Oh my God. I'm starving," I expressed my hunger as I grabbed a paper plate.

"Me too."

We filled our plates with slices of pizza and sat at the breakfast bar. After taking a few bites, I asked Cyrah what she planned to do while I was gone.

"Did you forget Mariah and Kinsey will be here tomorrow night?"

"Oh, damn. I sure did. Are they still planning to stay here?"

Mariah and Kinsley were Cyrah's friends from high school. Neither came home for the summer, so this would be the first time they'd seen each other in several months.

"Is it still okay since you won't be here?"

"Of course. I trust you girls will be responsible. But you know how I feel about strangers in my house, so as long as it's just them, it's fine."

"You don't have to worry about us doing anything stupid. The three of us haven't been together in so long we may not even go out."

"I'll transfer some money into your account so you can get groceries. Oh shoot, this is Brianne calling. Let me run and get my phone," I said as I saw her name flash across my watch.

"What's up?" I answered.

"You sound out of breath. Did I interrupt something?"

"No, ma'am. I was in the kitchen, and the phone was in my bedroom."

"Oh, okay. I thought you may have left early, and I caught you with your ass up and face down."

"First of all, I wouldn't have answered if that were the case. And second, why are you so damn nasty?"

"At one point, I thought I had to be nasty enough for both of us. I mean, you have your nasty moments, but you can always count on me to be the nasty friend. With that said, I'm mad your little trip will delay your visit with me, but you better be walking funny when I see you again."

"Girl, stop," I said as I laughed.

"I'm serious. When a man flies you out, you know you gotta show out on that dick."

"I won't disappoint you, sis, because that's exactly what I plan to do."

"That's what I'm talking about. Okay, text me when you land, and I'll see you soon. Love you."

"Same and will do."

As I placed my phone on my dresser, a text from Brianne came through.

> **Bri:** I didn't want to say anything because I wasn't sure where Cyrah was, but make sure you tell that man he has a daughter.
>
> **Me:** That's the plan.
>
> **Bri:** Stick to it. Don't chicken out.

I walked out of the doors of Chicago Midway Airport and looked around. Cypress said he drove a black Mercedes-Benz. I spotted the car and began to walk toward it with my luggage dragging behind me. Before I reached his vehicle, he stepped out of the driver's side and met me at the curb near the trunk.

"Damn, you're a sight for sore eyes. Thank you for coming," he greeted before embracing me as if he missed me.

"It's good to see you too," I responded when he pulled back, leaving his arms around my body.

He moved his hands to cup the sides of my face as he leaned down and planted the softest, sweetest kiss on my awaiting lips. I was disappointed when the kiss ended. He stepped to the front passenger-side door and opened it.

"Get in, and I'll put your things in the trunk."

He grinned as I did as he asked, keeping his eyes on me until he closed the door. Less than a minute later, he slid behind the wheel and looked at me again.

"What?" I asked, blushing like a teenager.

"I can't believe you agreed to come. Thank you again."

"Cypress, I want to be here. You don't have to keep thanking me."

"I hear you, but I'll probably say it a few more times. It's only been two minutes, and I'm already starting to relax. I need you to know how much I appreciate you."

"Thank you for inviting me."

We probably would have stared at each other until the end of time had someone not tapped on the window and told us to get moving.

"Are you hungry?" he asked, finally pulling away from the curb.

He casually rested his hand on my thigh, and upon contact, even through my jeans, his touch sent shockwaves through my body. I rested my hand on top of his, causing him to look my way and wink briefly.

"Starving."

"What do you feel like eating? I know this dope breakfast spot—"

"Say no more. You know breakfast is my favorite."

I'd never been to Chicago, so I took in the sights as we drove through the city while Cypress pointed out different things. We pulled into the parking lot of a place called Peach's. Just by the name, I knew I was in for a treat. We were seated quickly once inside, and I was grateful because my stomach was scratching my back. We perused the menu, and so many items caught my eye that I had difficulty deciding.

"Everything sounds so good. What do you usually get here?"

"I've probably tried almost everything on the menu. What are your tastebuds saying?"

"Umm, the peach bourbon French toast, applewood smoked bacon, and cheese grits sound wonderful."

"What else sounds good?"

"The catfish and greens."

"Okay, I'll get the catfish and greens, and we can share. Is that cool?"

"Perfect."

The server approached our table, and Cypress ordered our food along with a Peach's Palmer for our drink, which he insisted I try. We conversed as we waited, and he commented that he couldn't believe I'd never visited Chicago.

"Chicago was never on my bucket list of places I wanted to visit."

"Being from California, I guess I could see that, but there's nothing like summertime in the Chi. You'll have to come back."

"Only if you'll stick around to be my tour guide."

"Thank can be arranged, beautiful."

"So, how's your father?"

"He should be home and resting. The surgery is scheduled for next Wednesday, and if all goes well—"

"*When* all goes well. Speak positively," I told him.

He nodded. "You're right. *When* all goes well, my mother can relax. She's been on pins and needles."

"I'm sure it's been as hard for her as it has been for him."

"It has, but he should be able to come home just in time for Thanksgiving. I know my mother won't be up to cooking, so Jade and I agreed to take on the task."

"Aww, that's so sweet. Can Jade cook as well as you?"

"She's still learning, but a few dishes have become her specialty."

"I love that. Holidays aren't a big deal in my family, but it sounds like they're very special in yours."

"You know, it's never been about the holiday itself. It's always been more about fellowship with family. You and Cyrah are more than welcome to join us."

His invitation caught me a little off guard, and I didn't know how to respond, so I changed the subject.

"You sure you're ready to spend the next several days with me?"

He chuckled, putting the dimples that matched our daughter's on display and reminding me of what I needed to tell him.

"I caught how you changed topics, but I understand. To answer your question, I think spending some time alone with you is just what I need. You'll take my mind off my worries and calm my spirit."

"The welcomed distraction, huh?"

He nodded as he said, "A perfect and beautiful distraction."

Our eyes connected, and it felt like Cypress could see deep into my soul. I sometimes wondered if he looked at me long enough, would he recognize me? He hadn't done or said anything to make me think he had any recollection of that night, so I felt it was safe to assume he didn't remember me.

We didn't tear our eyes away from each other until the server returned with our food. Once Cypress said the blessing, neither of us spoke for a good ten minutes unless you count the moaning I did after every bite.

"You should really stop that, baby," Cypress said.

"Stop what?"

"Your moaning is doing something to me. Please, stop."

"But this—"

He leaned toward me and lowered his voice to a whisper, saying, "I respect you too much to fuck in the bathroom or my car, but if you keep that shit up, you'll leave me with no choice."

At that moment, I had to decide if I wanted to be bent over the sink in a public bathroom or have my legs on the ceiling of his Mercedes.

"I can feel you over there thinking. If you moan again, I'll decide for you," he warned.

Suddenly, I was hot from head to toe and tempted to pour my glass of water over my head. Instead, I took a few large gulps, praying it helped. The whole time, Cypress didn't take his eyes off me. When I placed the glass of water back on the table, I cleared my throat and continued eating.

"Did you want the rest of those greens?" I asked, not looking him in the eyes.

He laughed as he handed them to me. It was a struggle to stifle my moans because the food at Peach's was just that damn good, but I managed. We finished our meal with minimal talking, and before we left, he promised we'd visit again before we returned to California.

Cypress

BEFORE HEADING TO my place, we stopped at the grocery store. I'd been home almost a week but had been eating out daily. There were a few things I wanted to cook for Tessa, and once I shared my plans with her, she decided she'd like to cook for me as well.

We weren't rushed, so we moved leisurely through the store. As we passed one of the aisles, I thought I recognized someone. When I was sure it was Rich, I hesitated to approach him because I'd been home for a minute and hadn't reached out to connect. He'd already given me a hard time about moving to California without telling our crew, so I knew he'd do the same if he knew I was in town and hadn't told anyone. However, when he moved to the side, allowing me to see the profile of the woman he was with before he leaned down and kissed her, I had to make my presence known. I abruptly turned down the aisle, catching Tessa off guard.

"What do we need down here?" she asked, oblivious to my anger and shock.

Unfortunately, I couldn't answer her because I was trying to process the scene before me. Her voice must have gained their attention, causing them to look in our direction. They noticed me immediately because they damn near pushed each other to the other side of the aisle, trying to put some space between them.

As I took in Emery's face, I noticed it was much fuller than I remembered. I couldn't tell what her body looked like because of the winter coat she wore.

"Is everything okay?" Tessa asked when I didn't respond to her.

"Everything's fine, baby. I thought I needed something down here, but it must be in the next aisle."

Tessa and I continued down the aisle, walking between Rich and Emery. I was sure to make eye contact with both of them, but I didn't say a word, refusing to do anything to embarrass Tessa or make her believe I still had feelings for my ex-fiancée. Tessa was no fool, though. She may not have known who Rich and Emery were, but she picked up on the vibes as we walked past them and began questioning me before we could get to the next aisle.

"What was that about? Did you see the way they were staring? Do you know them?"

I'd answer her but now wasn't the time. I was still processing that someone I considered a friend was sneaking around with the woman I once planned to marry.

"Not now, Tessa. Let's finish getting what we need."

"Umm, okay."

Thankfully, she picked up on my mood change and didn't press the issue. I knew I wouldn't get off that easily, though, and she'd circle back to it as soon as she had an opportunity. Hopefully, by that time, I'd be ready to discuss. We finished our shopping in virtual silence, but once we were in the car, Tessa turned to face me and said what was on her mind.

"I won't press you to tell me what happened in there, but if you're going to allow it to fuck up the rest of your day, let me know, and I'll keep my distance. I'm sure you have extra bedrooms."

My jaw tightened as I squeezed the steering wheel, trying to contain my anger. I hated that I'd allowed what I'd discovered to alter my mood, but who wouldn't? I had so many questions that would probably never be answered. *How long had they been seeing each other? Was* he *the reason why she wouldn't set a wedding date? Are there other men?*

"That was my ex-fiancée and friend—well, former friend," I finally admitted.

She gasped and slapped her hand over her mouth. When I glanced in her direction, her eyes were wide with surprise. Tessa has no connection to Rich and Emery, yet it took her a minute to process what I'd shared.

"Cypress, I am so sorry."

"It's cool."

"No, it's not cool. That man was your friend, and you were engaged to marry that woman. You should be devastated. How did you refrain from beating his ass up and down the aisles? Hell, if you had told me, I would've gladly taken care of her for you."

I would never put my woman in a situation that would cause her to exert violence on another woman because of anything involving me. Still, I appreciated how Tessa didn't hesitate to volunteer to defend my honor.

"I'm pissed, but it's not because I'm still in love with Emery," I explained.

"You have every right to be upset, regardless of the reason. You were engaged to her, which means, at some point, you thought you could spend the rest of your life with her. I would understand if you still had feelings for her—"

"I don't, Tessa. I don't have romantic feelings for Emery. Those feelings began to fade well before I called off our engagement. I'm more pissed at the nigga I considered one of my best friends for the past twenty years than I am at her."

"Twenty years? Oh, hell no! They both deserve your wrath. Let's go back inside and—"

"Calm your feisty ass down. We're not going back inside, but I appreciate your offer to ride for me."

"I'm still learning things about you, but from what you've shown me so far, I know you're a good man and don't deserve what they did to you. It was wrong on so many levels, but guess what?"

"What?"

"If this works out the way I'm hoping, you'll have a new woman and friend all rolled into one."

"I like the sound of that. How can we speed up this process? Do I need to fill out an application?"

"You're already beyond the application process., Dr. Boone. You got the job, but there's usually a thirty-day probationary period. However, your performance on your first day was exemplary, and we can look into fast-tracking you to a permanent position."

"In case you didn't know, Dr. Howard, I stay ready, so I don't have to *get* ready, which means I'll be ready when you are."

She gave me a sexy smile before adjusting her body to secure the seat belt. I did the same before starting my car. Within five minutes, we were turning into my driveway and pulling into my garage. I brought Tessa's luggage inside before we unloaded the groceries. Since she didn't know her way around my kitchen, I unpacked the groceries while she gave herself a tour. When she returned to the kitchen, she'd changed into an oversized T-shirt with thick, fuzzy socks. I couldn't help but wonder if she wore anything underneath.

"It seems you've made yourself at home," I commented, happy she felt comfortable in my space.

"Is this not *my* home for the next few days?"

"I hope you're staying for more than a few days, and you're welcome to do as you wish while I work. I'm finished here, but before I give you my undivided attention, I need to check on my father and make a few other phone calls."

"Okay. I'll go to the den and find something for us to watch. What kind of movies do you like?"

"I'm willing to try any movie with a Black cast."

My comment caused her to giggle, but she assured me she'd find something we both would enjoy. Before parting ways, I pulled her body into mine and stole a kiss as my hands caressed her ample ass. Thoughts of what I wanted to do with her later tried to fill my head, but I shook them away. There were a few things I had to take care of before I could get lost between Tessa's thick thighs.

"What's up, big bro?" Jade answered.

"Nothing much. Just calling to make sure you and Ma got Pops home okay."

"It's not like they had to carry me, son. I'm not handicapped," my father yelled from the background.

"Give the phone to the old man since he's not handicapped," I told Jade.

Seconds later, my father's face appeared on the screen. He looked only a few years older than me, even after the ordeal he'd gone through.

"Why are you calling *her* phone to check on me?" he asked.

"Because I didn't know if you were resting. I'm sorry I couldn't be there when you were released. I had to—"

"Son, it wasn't a big deal. Your mother and sister got me home just fine. I understand if you have things you need to take care of while you're home."

"Appreciate that, Pops. I'll stop by later to check on you. Do you need anything?"

"Now you know these two overbearing women made sure everything I needed was here before I was released from the hospital. You can wait until tomorrow to come by. It's no rush."

"Okay. I love you, Pops. Let me talk to Ma."

"Love you too, son. I'll see you tomorrow."

My mother's face appeared on the screen, and she was all smiles. I knew it was because she was happy to have my father home, at least for a few days.

"Hey, Ma. How are you?"

"I'm fine for now, Cy. Glad to have your father home."

"I bet. How's he doing?"

"Boy, I just told you I was doing fine. Why would I lie? You don't have to go behind my back and ask your mother," Pops shouted.

"Robert, mind your own business. Cypress is talking to me, *not* you."

I laughed at my parents' banter. They loved each other to the ends of the earth, but the fussing never ended.

"Well, you're talking about me, so he might as well be talking to me," he mumbled.

"As you can hear and see, your father is feeling fine. Jade and I will make sure he doesn't disregard the doctor's orders."

"I know you will. Do you need anything?"

"No, son. We're good over here. Call me before you stop by tomorrow, and I'll let you know if that's changed."

"Cool. Love you, Ma. Is Jade still around?"

"Duh, you called my phone. Where else would I be?"

Her face filled the screen, and I could tell she was moving through the house.

"Are you headed to your room?"

"Yeah, why? You got some tea?"

"Yeah, and I don't want Ma and Pops to hear it," I whispered.

"Okay. I'm in my room, and the door is closed. Spill it."

I told her about my encounter with Rich and Emery at the grocery store, and like Tessa, she was ready to throw hands.

"Nah, baby sis, they're not worth the bail money. Like I told Tessa, I appreciate the offer, but it's unnecessary."

"Tessa? The lady from Cali? She's here?"

Oh shit!

"Huh? Oh nah. I was talking to her on the phone, and she offered to fly here and take care of Emery for me," I lied, trying to cover up my blunder.

"You think I believe that? I'm coming—"

"Jade, no! She's not ready to meet my family yet. Chill."

"Tuh! She flew her ass all the way from Cali to Chicago, and she's *not* ready to meet the family? Boy, bye."

"Seriously, don't come over here. You're gonna scare her away," I warned.

"Look at you, big bro. You really like her. Aww."

"I do, so chill out. She'll be here until a day or so after pops' surgery, so I hope I can convince her to meet the family before then."

"Fine, I'll wait, but if she's still acting funny in a few days, I'm taking matters into my own hands."

For some reason, Jade made me think of Cyrah. Their personalities were very similar, and I was sure they'd hit it off once they met.

"I'm sure you will. I need to go tend to my company, and don't tell our parents she's here."

"Your secret is safe with me . . . for now. Love you, bro."

"Love you too."

After ending the call with Jade, I FaceTimed Samuel. I'd chopped it up with him and Omar a few times since moving to California, but I hadn't reached out since I'd been home.

"A FaceTime call? Aww, you miss my face," Sam answered.

"Nigga, please. Hold on. Let me get Omar on the line."

I placed Samuel on hold and FaceTimed Omar. He was just as surprised as Samuel that I'd called him this way. I merged the calls, and they appeared on my screen.

"Before I get to why I called, Pops had a heart attack. He's doing fine and is scheduled for surgery next week."

"Oh, damn. I'm sorry to hear that, but I'm glad he's doing all right," Samuel commented.

"Yeah, bruh. I'll be sure to say a prayer for him. Keep us posted on his condition and let us know if there's anything we can do," Omar added.

"Will do. I appreciate it. Look, I don't have much time, so I'm gonna get straight to the point. Did either of you know Rich and Emery were messing around?"

"Rich Davis and your ex, Emery?" Samuel asked.

The puzzled look on his face led me to believe he had no idea.

"Bruh, you bullshittin'. Don't y'all go way back? Wasn't he your college roommate?" Omar questioned.

"You both are correct. Did you know?" I asked again.

"Hell no. That's some foul shit," Omar denied.

"This is the first I heard of it, but Rich has never had much integrity. I just fucked with him because he was your friend," Samuel said.

"Yeah, Rich ain't somebody I communicate with outside of when the four of us are together. I'm only cool with him because of you," Omar admitted.

"When did you find out? How long has it been going on?"

"I don't have any details. I saw them hugged up at the grocery store, and I made sure they saw me, but neither of them said a word."

"You didn't knock his ass out?" Omar asked.

"I wanted to, but I refrained."

They questioned me about how I would handle the situation and were surprised when I told them I planned to do nothing.

"Don't get me wrong, I'm pissed because I thought that nigga was my friend, but I don't care enough to risk my freedom beating his ass."

"Yeah, because his punk ass would probably press charges," Samuel said.

We talked for a few more minutes before I ended the call. Samuel and Omar met Rich through me, so they were cool with one another but not extremely close. I didn't think they knew about the affair between Emery and Rich, but I had to FaceTime them to see their faces when I asked to be sure. My circle had gotten smaller, but it was good to know I still had a few friends I could trust.

Tessa

THE EARLY FLIGHT must have caught up with me. There was light coming into the small windows in the den, so I didn't think I'd been asleep too long. When I sat up, I saw Cypress sitting on the end of the couch, and I smiled. His eyes were already on me, and he returned the smile.

"Why didn't you wake me up?" I asked.

"Because you were obviously tired. Your flight was early, so I figured you needed a nap."

"What time is it?"

"It's still kind of early; almost three. Remember, we're two hours ahead of Cali."

"Oh yeah. So, what have you been doing besides watching me sleep like a creep?"

He chuckled as he pulled me onto his lap. I sat sideways with my legs extended and one arm around his neck.

"Nothing. After I talked to my family, I called a few of my homies to let them know I was in town. I came in here, and you were snoring, so I've patiently waited for you to wake up."

"I don't snore. Why would you say that?"

"Because it's the truth. I have no reason to lie."

"No one has ever told me I snored," I whined.

"Maybe because you've never felt comfortable enough to allow yourself to fall into a deep sleep around others."

"You're not kidding? I was *really* snoring?"

"Baby, calm down. I didn't say you sounded like a bear, but yes, you have a delicate little snore."

"Hmm." I wasn't sure if I believed him, but I was ready to move on to another topic.

"I guess I'll have to take your word for it. How's your father?"

"He's good. My mother is happy he's home. Oh, and Jade knows you're in town, so don't be surprised if she stops by."

"Oh goodness."

"Yeah, she's hardheaded."

I was trying to find the perfect time to tell him about Cyrah. "So, remember right before you got the phone call about your father, I wanted to talk to you about something."

"Oh yeah. I remember it seeming serious too."

"I—"

I was interrupted by someone frantically pressing the buzzer repeatedly.

"I told Jade you weren't ready to meet the family and not to bring her nosy ass over here. I'm sorry, baby. Stay here, and I'll get rid of her."

"It's fine. I'm sure she's harmless."

He lifted me from his lap, and we both stood before I followed him to the door where the intercom was.

"You haven't met Jade. She'll know your Social Security number, middle name, and birthday within five minutes."

I laughed, but Cypress didn't crack a smile.

"She has the access code to get in, but I'm glad she has enough respect not to just barge in."

Cypress pressed the button without using the screen to confirm it was his sister. A few minutes later, someone was pounding on the door.

"What the hell's wrong with her?" he griped as he opened the door.

Instead of Jade standing in the hallway, it was the woman from the grocery store.

"What are you doing here?" he asked angrily.

I touched my ears to ensure I'd taken my earrings off just in case Cypress changed his mind about me beating her ass.

"Who is she?" Emery had the nerve to question.

"None of your business. What are you doing here?" he repeated.

"I wanted to explain."

"There's nothing to explain. We aren't in a relationship, so you're not my concern."

"But I'm pregnant. What about the—"

"You're *what*?"

Emery unzipped her coat and caressed her stomach, showing her baby bump. Cypress looked like he'd seen a ghost while waiting for her to explain.

"This is why I wanted to try to work things out with you."

"I know damn fucking well you don't expect me to believe the child you're carrying is mine after I caught you with the homie."

"It's possible."

"No, the fuck, it's *not* possible. I'm a good man, Emery. God wouldn't do this to me. I don't deserve to be forced to raise a child with a woman who would fuck my best friend behind my back. You stopped fucking me months before I called off the engagement. Are you trying to tell me you've been pregnant *all* this time?"

She avoided his question and apologized again, adamant about the possibility of the baby belonging to him.

"I'm sorry it happened this way, but this baby could be yours. My period is irregular, making it hard for the doctor to determine a due date. She thinks I'm between twenty-eight and thirty-four weeks."

Emery was a petite woman, but from the size of her stomach, it was hard to believe she was that far along.

"How long you been fucking Rich?"

"It just happened, Cypress. I swear."

"How long?"

Emery's mouth opened and closed multiple times as she tried to come up with what I assumed would be a lie.

"How about I call Rich and see what *he* has to say? Baby, can you go grab my phone?"

"Baby? Cypress, who is this woman? You're mad at me, but it looks like you're in a full-blown relationship already. Were you cheating on me with her?" I heard her say as I walked away.

It would serve her right if he were, but he didn't bother responding. When I returned with his phone, she pleaded with him not to call Rich.

"Then tell me the truth," he demanded.

Crocodile tears fell from her eyes, but she said nothing. If she wanted sympathy from Cypress, she was barking up the wrong tree.

"Tell me the goddamn truth, Emery, because I'm telling you right now, if that baby is mine, I'm taking your ass to court and suing for full custody. I refuse to—"

"Me and Rich started sneaking around about a year ago. The baby could be either of yours, and that's the truth. I'm sorry, Cy. I don't want you to think badly of me."

"I already think you're as low as they come. I still don't believe your trifling ass. I want a paternity test ASAP."

Ouch!

"You'll have to wait until the baby is born. I'm too far along, and it's dangerous," she lied.

I was not a genius or well-versed in establishing paternity, but even I knew there were noninvasive tests to prove paternity that didn't put the mother or child in danger.

"You're just gonna keep lying in this man's face," I interjected. "There are tests out now that don't endanger you or the baby."

"Who asked you? This is none of your business," Emery spat angrily.

"I'll schedule a test and let you know the details," Cypress told her before walking away, leaving the door wide open.

Cypress was hurt and disappointed; I could see it all over his face because he didn't try to hide it. Emery didn't look ready to leave, so I decided to say a few words.

"Thank you."

She rolled her eyes and kissed her teeth before asking, "Why are you thanking me?"

"For fucking over a good man—no, a *great* man. He's mine now, and I promise you, I'm not letting him go."

"Cypress still loves me. You saw how hurt he was," she spat with confidence.

"Of course, he's hurt. He just lost a friend of twenty years over some pussy, and there's a possibility he may have created a child with the likes of you. That's why he's hurt, so don't get it twisted."

I slammed the door in her face and returned to the den, where I found Cypress seated in the same place he was before we were interrupted by an uninvited and unwelcome guest. His head was resting on the back of the couch, and his eyes were closed. When he sensed my presence, he reached for me. I took his hand and straddled his lap. The conversation I needed to have with him would be delayed once again.

Before I could get comfortable, he grabbed the sides of my face, lifted his head, and devoured my lips. I opened my mouth to welcome his tongue, and he weaved his masterfully around mine. His kiss was needy, and I knew exactly why, but I didn't mind. I'd allow him to use my body, just this once, to release the emotions he had yet to express today.

His hands slowly moved from the sides of my face, down my back, stopping briefly above my ass. Our tongues played a sexy game of cat and mouse, his around mine, mine around his, as we practically inhaled each other. He gripped the back of my T-shirt and pulled it above my ass. The thong I wore left my cheeks exposed until Cypress covered them with his large hands. He simultaneously caressed my backside as he pressed me against his growing erection.

"Mmm," I moaned.

I could feel a puddle forming in the crotch of my panties and knew my juices would soon cover the front of the gray sweats he wore. Our mouths disconnected long enough for Cypress to take off my shirt and toss it behind him. My naked breasts must have been calling him because he massaged one with his hand, using his thumb to fondle my nipple, while the other had the pleasure of being caressed by his tongue.

I wanted him inside me, so I reached between us and claimed his manhood, pulling it from his sweats. While his mouth went from one breast to the other, his free hand moved my panties to the side. Before I knew it, Cypress had stretched my walls with his girth, and I screamed with pleasure.

"Oh damn!"

"Shit," he groaned.

With my hands gripping the back of the couch, I bounced up, down, and around his dick like a rodeo queen. Flashbacks of the first time we were together came rushing back. I hadn't felt

this free with a man since then and didn't want the feeling to end.
Cypress held onto my hips to control my movements, but I gave
him a run for his money. My climax was nearing, and I chased that
feeling like an addict chancing a high.

"Damn, baby. Slow down," he pleaded.

"I can't, Cy. I'm 'bout to come."

He released his hold on me and let me do my thing. Seconds
later, I exploded. Cypress aggressively took me by the front of my
neck and gently squeezed while looking into my eyes.

"Give me another one," he demanded.

"I ca—ca—can't."

While he held my neck, he fucked me from the bottom.
Using his other hand, he pinched my nipples as his grip on my
neck slowly tightened.

"I want another one, baby. Give me another one," he repeated
sternly this time.

I saw the sun, moon, and stars when the dam broke a second
time. It was then that I knew I'd never have ownership of my vagina
again. She belonged to Dr. Cypress Boone, and if he ever decided
he didn't want her anymore, she'd be lonely and unsatisfied for the
rest of her days.

Cypress

I'D NEVER BEEN happier or more content with a woman until Tessa came along, not even Emery at any point in our relationship. I realize now I was never in love with Emery, although I did love and care for her. It was hard to believe I'd proposed to her, but I was grateful I'd come to my senses before it was too late.

A tiny part of me wanted to confront Rich because what he did was low-down and dirty; he deserved an ass beating. However, I decided to leave him in the past. Unfortunately, it took me half my life to realize he wasn't a good person or friend, and not having him in my life wouldn't change a thing for me. It was his loss, not mine.

I wouldn't be able to leave Emery in my past just yet, if at all. She didn't put up a fight when I sent her the date, time, and location of the paternity test. Once the test was done, I pushed the situation to the back of my mind because thinking about it made me anxious. The results wouldn't come any sooner just because I was stressed about it, so I chose peace.

Aside from the day I took the paternity test, if I could use one word to describe the days leading up to my father's surgery, I'd use blissful, and I had Tessa to thank for that. She was the first person I'd taken on a tour of Chicago, and seeing my city through her eyes gave me a greater appreciation. Of course, we visited the typical tourist places like Navy Pier, Willis Tower, Shedd Aquarium, Museum of Science and Industry, DuSable Museum, which she fell in love with, and her favorite, shopping on Michigan Ave., better known as the Magnificent Mile.

However, you haven't experienced Chicago until you've eaten at Harold's Chicken, Uncle Remus, Maxwell Street, and Giordano's. She had to admit that California's food didn't hold a candle to Chicago's dining options. We also drove down Lake Shore Drive and through some of the roughest and nicest neighborhoods. I wanted to make sure her first time in Chicago was memorable, and I believe I succeeded.

When we weren't out and about, we were at my condo whipping up gourmetlike meals, cozied up on the couch, watching movies, and talking. The only time we weren't up under each other was when I went to visit my family or when I was online teaching my classes. I couldn't seem to get enough of her.

Tessa helped me research what was required of me to become a landlord and also shared the idea for a new business venture she'd been thinking about, which I thought could be very informative and profitable. There was so much to learn about the history of Blacks in America and if Tessa created a means for people to learn, I had no doubt it would be successful. Every day, I learned something new about Tessa that increased my desire to keep her in my life. Based on her actions, her feelings matched mine, and I was excited about the possibility of a future together.

"I want you to come to the hospital with me," I said out of the blue.

It was the night before my father's surgery. We were lying in bed after sexing each other to exhaustion. Her head was on my chest, and my fingers were lost in her thick mane as I massaged her scalp.

"Okay."

"I'm serious, Tessa."

"I am too. I came here to support you, and if my supporting you requires my presence at the hospital, I'll go."

"But that means—"

"I'll have to meet your family. I know."

"Are you sure?"

Tessa sat up and turned to face me. It took some effort not to let her plump breasts distract me, but I managed to focus on what she had to say.

"In the past two months, I quit my job, ended a long-term relationship, and disrespectfully gave my mother a piece of my mind. None of that was normal behavior for me, but the only thing that has felt as good as leaving a job that no longer spoke to my soul, ending a relationship with a man who didn't value me, and finally expressing my true feelings to my mother, is the time I've spent here with you. We're moving fast, Cypress, but I don't want to slow down. I'd love to meet your family."

"C'mere."

"I'm right here."

My hand went around the front of her neck, and I pulled down until my lips could touch hers. While I gave her a sloppy kiss, I used my other hand to push the sheet from my waist, exposing my already stiff manhood. Gripping the base, I stroked until it stood at attention.

"Sit on it," I demanded.

With my hand still holding her neck, Tessa straddled my waist, and I guided my dick to its new favorite place.

"In matters of the heart, time means nothing," I mumbled against her lips. "Time can't tell me how to feel, and I feel like you're mine."

When I released her neck, she planted her hands on my chest and bounced up and down until her pussy began to contract, urging me to fill her with my seeds. We reached our climax quickly and simultaneously. The next thing I remembered was the sound of my alarm.

We met my parents and sister at the hospital. Tessa and I were running a little late because I insisted we shower together. She warned me not to try anything freaky, but when her ass brushed against my dick, there was no turning back. Three orgasms later, we finally left. They'd already put my father in a room when we arrived at the hospital.

"It's so nice to meet you. I hate that we're meeting under these circumstances," my mother commented after I introduced Tessa to everyone.

She crossed the room and embraced Tessa like they'd known each other for years.

"You're not seeing me at my best, but I'm glad to meet you. You can bring your pretty self on over here and give me a hug. I promise I won't break."

"Damn, Pops. Are you flirting with my woman in front of your wife and me? That's bold," I joked as Tessa went to the side of the bed to hug my father.

"We've kinda met on the phone, but it's nice to meet you in person," Jade said when my father finally released Tessa. They hugged as well, and it warmed my heart that my family had given her such a warm welcome.

"It's nice to meet all of you. Cypress has told me a lot about you all."

"Well, it sounds like Jade may be the only one who's heard about you, but that's okay. I know you now," Ma said.

"You know he can't tell you about anyone he's dating until it's serious—uh-oh, son. Does this introduction mean what I think it means?"

My father may have been teasing, but if I'd told him my true feelings about Tessa, he'd have the answer to his question. Before I could respond to him, two nurses entered his room and shooed us away. We all joined hands and said a quick prayer before leaving him and going to the waiting room.

Jade and my mother were so enthralled with Tessa that the four hours my father was in surgery flew by. They were so invested in their conversations a few times that they forgot I was there. It was cool, though. I wanted them to embrace Tessa, and I got what I wanted and more. My thoughts were solidified when my mother said, "I like her much better than Emery." Just the mention of Emery's name got Tessa and Jade fired up. Of course, Tessa had no problem expressing her dislike for Emery. However, Tessa knew I didn't plan to tell my family about the possibility of Emery being pregnant with my child unless it was absolutely necessary, so she couldn't communicate her disgust for Emery the way she wanted.

"Tessa, I assume, with all of your accomplishments and since you have a daughter who's almost twenty, you're around my son's age."

"Thank you, and yes, ma'am. I'll be forty at the end of this month."

The end of this month? Duly noted.

"Well, I had Jade around your age. Cypress was eighteen, and I couldn't have asked for a better big brother for her."

"Ma, can you not do this?" I pleaded.

"What? I'm just throwing it out there, just in case Tessa thinks she's too old to have another child," Ma defended.

Miriam Boone had absolutely no chill. She'd known Tessa for all of five minutes and was already discussing babies. I was so embarrassed I tuned them out and had no idea how Tessa responded. I was relieved for more than one reason when the doctor came out to tell us the surgery was a success. While in a group hug, including the doctor, I said a prayer of gratitude. The road to a full recovery would be long, but we were thankful Robert Boone was alive to start the journey.

We remained at the hospital for a while longer to see my father when he came out of recovery and was taken to the room he'd be in for the next seven days. As expected, he was groggy, sore, and tired but in great spirits. As Tessa and I prepared to leave, Jade offered to get my mother some lunch, and the three of us left together.

"I'm glad that's over," Jade said once we were on the elevator.

"Me too, but Pops has a long road ahead. I'm glad I can stay in town and be here for support."

"Me and Ma can handle it, but I'm glad you can stay for a while too. Do you have to go back soon?" she directed the last question to Tessa.

"I can stick around until a few days before Thanksgiving. I should probably start looking for flights."

"Or you can spend the holiday with us. My mom loves you and would love to have you," Jade offered.

I kept my mouth shut and watched the conversation unfold. As much as I didn't want Tessa to leave, staying had to be her decision.

"I wish I could, but I don't want my daughter to spend Thanksgiving alone."

Jade looked at me and said, "Bro, get the girl a ticket." Then she looked back at Tessa and said, "See? Problem solved. I'm gonna head over to Subway and grab a couple of sandwiches for me and Ma. I can't wait to tell her you and your daughter will be here for Thanksgiving."

Jade was gone before Tessa could object. I chuckled at how that whole thing went down but waited to hear what Tessa would say. She pulled out her phone as we walked to the parking garage where my car was parked. When the person on the other end answered, she said, "How do you feel about spending Thanksgiving in Chicago?"

I knew from her question that she was talking to Cyrah. Based on Tessa's end of the conversation, my Thanksgiving was shaping up to be more like Christmas. She ended the call when we stepped into the parking garage elevator. I could feel her eyes on me as I pretended to be focused on something on the ceiling.

"I guess you got what you wanted after all," she said. "Did you put her up to that?"

"I had nothing to do with that. I warned you about Jade when you said she was harmless. The girl knows how to get what she wants."

"I see. Cyrah was excited and asked for Jade's phone number. She wants to get to know her a little before she arrives."

"I can arrange that, but are you cool with all this? I'll understand if—"

"This will probably be the best Thanksgiving we've ever had. I'm cool with it."

Tessa had only shared that she didn't have a great relationship with her mother, but I didn't know the details. It was hard for me to imagine not getting along with my parents, and I hated that it was her reality with the only parent she knew. Hopefully, my family could change her perception of the holidays.

When we arrived at my car, I opened the passenger-side door for her. I stood there with the door open until she'd secured the seat belt.

"Thank you," I said before closing the door.

Tessa's eyes were on me when I entered the car on the other side.

"I should be thanking you—and I will later," she said seductively.

I liked the sound of that. As I drove through the busy streets of Chicago, I briefly wondered if I should apologize to Tessa. My mother and sister meant well, but could be a bit overwhelming.

"So, what do you want to do for the rest of the day?" she asked, interrupting my thoughts.

"I can think of a few things," I flirted.

"I bet you can, and I bet all of those things will put your mother's theory to the test."

"Her theory?"

"That I'm not too old to have another baby. We've been very careless."

"I pulled out a few times," I reminded her, and she responded with a questioning glare. "Are you worried?"

"I hadn't given it much thought until your mother said something, to be honest. Right now, I'm not worried, but that may change. Maybe we should be more careful from here on out."

"I'm pretty sure that won't happen."

"What do you mean?"

"Baby, we're at the point of no return. How can you ask me to wrap up after I've had you so many times with no barriers between us?"

"Cypress—"

"Nah, I don't want to talk about this anymore. It's making me depressed." I put on my best sad face and was sure I sounded like a ten-year-old.

"Are you really pouting at your big age?" she questioned with a laugh.

"You'll see me have a full-blown tantrum at my big age if you make me wrap up. I'll be kicking and screaming until I get what I want."

She laughed again, but I couldn't have been more serious. I'd go through my condo and throw out every condom I could find before I used one with Tessa again. She'd clearly lost her mind.

Tessa

"TESSA, YOU HAVE to tell him," Brianne shouted.

It had been a few days since I'd met Cypress's family, who were all very welcoming. I couldn't get over how much Cyrah looked like Jade, but I shouldn't have been surprised because they both looked like Cypress. He'd gone to visit his father, and I didn't want to intrude on their time together. I had spoken to Brianne sparingly since being in Chicago, so I used my time alone to call her.

"Bri, between his father's surgery and him finding out that for the past year, his ex-fiancée has been sleeping with his best friend of twenty years, *and* she might be carrying his child, I haven't found a good time to tell him."

"Hold up. Run that back for me. You said *what?*"

When I finished explaining the details of what was revealed to Cypress about his best friend, former fiancée, and the baby on the way, her mouth was on the floor.

"Girl, that sounds like some shit from one of those movies on Lifetime. That man needs a medal of honor for not beating both of their asses. You know I don't condone violence against women, but that was some foul shit."

"I agree, but he was more upset at the betrayal of his friend and the possibility of sharing a child with Emery than he was with Emery."

"I can understand that because they'd been friends for a long time. But still, he couldn't have really been in love with her because most men would have lost it over something like that. It's a serious blow to the ego."

"True, but he called off the wedding for a reason. I guess whatever feelings he had for her are gone."

"I'm sure a part of the reason is that he's falling for you, which is another reason why you need to tell him about Cyrah. The longer you wait, the harder it will be for him to understand why you didn't tell him much sooner."

"I know, but—"

"There is no but, Tessa. You're making the situation worse by not telling him. Do it, and do it soon. Hell, Cyrah will be there tomorrow. At this point, you may as well tell the whole family together."

"The thought of doing that terrifies me," I admitted.

"I'm not trying to scare you, but it's the truth."

Talking to Brianne always helped me put things into perspective. If I put off telling Cypress that he was Cyrah's father any longer, the potential for things not to go well increased.

"You're right, Bri."

"I know I am. I'm wondering, though, how do you feel about him possibly having a baby?"

"I've thought about this situation a lot, and if the baby ends up being his, I'm cool with it. The likelihood of me being able to give him one is very slim. At least, he'll be able to experience fatherhood from the beginning."

"That's true. Unfortunately, his potential baby mama doesn't seem like she'll be the easiest to deal with."

"Ugh. You know what? I'll keep praying for the best."

The thought of Cypress being a new father didn't bother me nearly as much as the thought of having to deal with Emery for the rest of our lives, assuming we spent the rest of our lives together.

I didn't have much time to dwell on the thoughts of Cypress, Emery, and the potential baby because my mother called a few minutes after I ended the call with Brianne. She'd called a few times since I'd been in Chicago, but I didn't have the mental capacity to take her phone calls. Today, I chose violence and answered the phone.

"Hello," I answered dryly.

"Finally! You've been ignoring my calls for days."

"Yet, you keep calling. How can I help you?"

"I wanted to see what was on the menu for Thanksgiving because I invited a few of my girlfriends over for dinner."

"Cyrah and I will be out of town. You're on your own this year."

I should've felt guilty for the joy I felt informing her of this, but I didn't. She knew I didn't like any of her presumptuous-ass friends, and I didn't know what possessed her to invite them to my house.

"Out of town?"

"Yes, so you may want to get something catered to your house."

"Tessa, why would you wait until the last minute to inform me of this? What am I supposed to do for dinner? I've been telling my friends how good of a cook you are and how it was a shame you'd never have a husband to cook for. One of them was going to bring her son for you to meet and—"

"You couldn't stop at me being a good cook? The knife wasn't in deep enough, so you had to turn it, huh? I don't care what you or your friends do for dinner. As a matter of fact, until you can learn how to communicate with me without putting me down and being disrespectful, I don't want to talk to you."

I ended the call without waiting for a response from her. Dealing with my mother had been the most challenging aspect of my life. Every form of abuse was horrible and unacceptable; no human being should have to suffer through it. Verbal abuse attacked your mind and spirit, and there were times when I'd rather be physically beaten by my mother than have her verbal tongue-lashings playing on repeat in my head. I was sick of her and finally was doing something about it.

"Mom, you didn't tell me it was this cold," Cyrah complained as she slid into the backseat of Cypress's car. We'd just picked her up from Midway Airport.

"Girl, every time I've talked to you, I mentioned how cold it is."

"It's much colder than I thought it would be."

"Forty degrees ain't too bad for late November, but it's supposed to snow later today," Cypress told her.

"I'm gonna need to get a bigger coat and some boots because I didn't bring anything for this kind of weather."

"I'm sure Jade has a coat you can borrow or won't mind taking you shopping. It's one of her favorite things to do," Cypress added.

While he drove us through the city, Cyrah talked about how different it looked in Chicago versus California.

"Like, where's the grass, pretty flowers, and leaves? Is it always this dreary?"

"This is what fall looks like around here. I know you Californians aren't used to four seasons, but we get them all in the Midwest. Hell, sometimes in one day. So, you can stop looking for palm trees around here, but don't talk too crazy about my city."

"It's really a beautiful city, Cyrah, and the food in Cali pales compared to the places Cypress has taken me."

"You sound like you want to move, Mom," she joked.

"Ha! Let's not get carried away. Chicago's a great place to visit, but I definitely don't want to live here."

"I'm gonna bring both of you back for the summer, and I guarantee you'll fall in love," he assured us.

"I doubt it's better than Black Elm in the summer, but I'm looking forward to it. That said, I guess things are going well between you."

Cypress and I glanced at each other and smiled, but neither of us responded.

"I'll take that as a yes. Let me start making my Christmas list. I'm expecting great gifts for creating this love connection."

The satisfaction in her voice couldn't be missed. I couldn't imagine how she'd feel if she knew she was truly responsible for bringing her parents together. I hadn't decided when or how I'd tell them or if I'd tell them together. Initially, I thought telling Cypress first would be best, but now that so much time had passed, I wasn't sure if that was still the case. Thanksgiving Day was my deadline.

"Are we headed to your place, Dr. Boone?" Cyrah asked, pulling me out of my thoughts.

"Please, Cyrah, call me Cypress. You don't have to be so formal."

"Cypress? Hmm, that seems a little weird. I'll stop calling you Dr. Boone when you propose to my mother."

Her response and the confidence with which she spoke took me by surprise. Cyrah had always been very forward, much like Jade.

"Propose? We've only been—" I began before Cypress cut me off.

"What did I tell you about time, baby?"

"Baby? Ooh, you've graduated to pet names. I'll text you my Christmas list, Mom. Back to my question, though. Where are we headed?"

"First, we're going to have some lunch at what might be your mother's favorite restaurant in Chicago, and then we're going to my parents' house, where my mother and Jade are waiting for us. We have to start prepping for Thanksgiving dinner," Cypress answered.

"Will some of your extended family be visiting for dinner?" Cyrah asked.

"Yes, more than our usual bunch will be here this year. We host either my mother's or father's sides each year. It's supposed to be my father's side this year, but my mother's sister, who normally hosts, is having her kitchen redone. Before my father's heart attack, my mother volunteered to host everyone."

"Wow, Cypress. I had no idea," I said, suddenly a little nervous about meeting so many people.

"It'll be fine, baby. They're good people and will love both of you."

"Is your father gonna be up for so much company?" I asked, not convinced everything would be fine.

"He wouldn't have it any other way."

"Well, I'm excited. I've never had a big family dinner like this. Thank you for inviting us."

"Jade is who convinced your mother to stay, so make sure you thank her," he told Cyrah.

We arrived at Peach's, and I quickly forgot about our conversation in the car. I was excited to try something else on the menu and anxious to see if Cyrah enjoyed the food as much as I did. After we placed our order, we conversed while waiting for our food. I watched Cypress and Cyrah interact, and aside from their physical similarities, they also had some of the same mannerisms. I was sitting on one side of the table while they sat across from me, so it was easy to pick up on them.

Since she was a child, Cyrah always tilted her head to the side when she listened intently, and I hadn't noticed it until then, but Cypress did the same thing. They both had a habit of randomly touching the tips of their noses and fiddling with their ears when they didn't know what to do with their hands. I didn't think mannerisms were hereditary, but now I wonder. The waitress returned with our food, and once she'd placed everything on the table, she lingered for a few seconds.

"You have a beautiful family," she commented.

"Thank you," Cypress replied without missing a beat.

"Your daughter is the spitting image of you," she added before walking away.

I happened to be taking a sip of water when she said it, and like the day I met Cypress, the fluid went down the wrong pipe, causing me to choke. This time, with a few pats on the back from Cypress, I recovered quickly. However, I was stuck on mute for the remainder of our meal.

Cypress

WE ARRIVED AT my parents' house a couple of hours ago, and after all the introductions and hugs, we sat in the family room and conversed. This was the first time I'd seen my mother outside of the hospital in several days, and it was good to see her in her element. Eventually, she assigned us duties in the kitchen, and we got to work.

Tessa was at the sink cleaning collard greens. She'd been unusually quiet since we'd left the restaurant, but I hadn't been alone with her long enough to ask if something was bothering her. Our eyes connected a few times as I peeled the yams for the sweet potato pies, and she'd smiled, but it didn't reach her eyes. Hopefully, it was just her nerves about meeting my extended family in a couple of days.

"That young lady looks very familiar to me, son," my mother whispered after summoning me into the pantry. "She looks like she could be your daughter."

I was slightly jarred by her words, but I wasn't completely surprised because I had the same familiar feeling about Cyrah. I hadn't considered that we looked alike until the waitress at Peach's mentioned it. Since it had been brought to my attention, I did notice our faces had similar bone structures and features, we had the same skin tone, and we both sported dimples. However, I chalked it up as a coincidence because what else could it be?

145

"You think so?"

"Hell yes. She and Jade look like they could be sisters, and you know how people always think she's your daughter."

The age difference between Jade and me had confused people for years. It was crazy how many times I'd been mistaken for her father.

"I don't know what you want me to say to all this, Ma. You know us Black folk tend to look alike. Maybe our families are from the same tribe."

"Did you see the birthmark on her arm?"

I shook my head. "No, I hadn't noticed."

"You need to be more observant. Are you *sure* you're not hiding something?"

"I just met Cyrah and Tessa when I moved to Cali. What exactly could I be hiding?"

She sighed. "I guess you're right. The resemblance is uncanny, though. My spirit is trying to tell me something."

"What are you two whispering about in here?" Jade said as she peeked into the pantry.

"Nothing. I think your mother's getting old. She can't remember what she needed me to get for her," I lied.

We returned to the kitchen, and my mother returned to her position at the kitchen table, picking up the conversation as if she weren't insinuating some pretty explosive things a minute ago.

"From what my son says, you know your way around the kitchen," my mother told Tessa.

"I love to cook. It's sort of a hobby of mine. My specialties are breakfast dishes and desserts, but I think I can hold my own with most things."

"I guess you and Cypress have that in common. Unlike Jade, he's always enjoyed being in the kitchen with me."

"Hey, I can cook," Jade defended.

"I didn't say you couldn't cook. I said you didn't enjoy it like your brother," Ma corrected her.

"Oh, that's true. I only cook when I have to, and since you got me in here peeling potatoes and snapping green beans, I guess this is one of those times."

"We need all hands on deck this year, Jade. Your father is lucky he's not a hundred percent, or he'd be helping us too."

"Will he be released before Thanksgiving?" Cyrah asked as she sorted the black-eyed peas.

"He's being released tomorrow," I replied.

"Tessa, if I'd known desserts were your specialty, I would've saved all the desserts for you."

My mother had just finished frosting a German chocolate cake and was standing in front of the stove stirring the caramel she'd made from scratch.

"But then I wouldn't get to taste any of *your* wonderful creations," Tessa responded.

"I think she'll be around awhile, Ma. We'll get a chance to taste all of her cooking. Isn't that right, big bro?"

"I'll see what I can do to keep her around."

About an hour later, my mother asked me to take a change of clothes to my father. She'd already visited and didn't want to make a return trip. I hadn't chopped it up with Pops alone for a minute, so I gladly left the ladies to hang with my father for a while. Before leaving, I cornered Tessa coming from the bathroom.

"You good?"

"Yeah, I'm fine," she replied too quickly without looking me in the eyes.

"Look at me." I waited until we made eye contact. "Nah, I'm not buying that, baby. Something's up."

"It's nothing, Cypress. Just my nerves, that's all."

"About meeting my family?" She nodded. "Like I told you and Cyrah earlier, they're good people. I promise you have nothing to worry about."

"I know. I'm sure I'll be fine by Thursday."

I pressed a soft kiss on her forehead, then did the same to her lips.

"Will you be good here while I go to the hospital?"

"I'll be fine. Take your time and enjoy your visit."

I'd been chilling with my father at the hospital for several hours. My mom had been with him almost nonstop, so catching him alone was almost impossible. He was in good spirits and ready to be released tomorrow. We'd talked about his road to recovery, my move to California, my new position at BEU, the breakup with Emery, and Rich's betrayal. He mostly listened, giving his input when he thought it was necessary. I appreciated these moments with my father and was grateful he'd been given more time on this earth.

"Tell me more about Tessa," he said. "I can already tell you're falling."

"Can you? How so?"

"I looked at your mother the same way you look at Tessa, and never did I ever see you look at Emery that way."

"If you knew Emery wasn't the one, why didn't you say something?"

"Son, you're a grown man. Some things you have to figure out on your own, and you did."

"Yeah, but if you'd said something, it would have saved me a lot of time and heartache."

"Possibly, but is your heart really aching? Because on the outside looking in—"

I chuckled. "Okay, maybe not heartache, but you know what I mean. I feel like I wasted some good years on Emery."

"You live, and you learn. Life is all about timing, and I've always believed things happen when they're supposed to happen and for a reason. Nothing is a coincidence. Remember that."

I nodded as he spoke, soaking in every word.

"Tessa is a breath of fresh air. I feel like she was made for me. We clicked right away, and it seems like I've known her for much longer than I have, but it still feels new. Does that make sense?"

"It makes perfect sense. It sounds like you've met your soul mate."

"You believe in soul mates?"

"Of course. I knew right away your mother was mine and vowed not to do anything to mess it up. We were young, so any number of things could have happened because we didn't know much about love and relationships."

"Yet, you're still together."

"From the moment we met, I couldn't imagine my life without your mother."

We sat with our thoughts for a minute before my father spoke again.

"I hear Tessa and her daughter will be joining us for Thanksgiving. How'd that happen?"

"Jade," was all I had to say for my father to figure out how it happened.

"Leave it to Jade to bully someone into doing what she wants. I don't know where she gets that from."

"I'd say you know exactly who she gets it from. You've been married to her for over forty years."

He chuckled. "I'm so used to letting your mother have her way, I don't think you can consider it bullying anymore."

"True, and I feel sorry for Jade's future husband because she's a mini version of Ma."

We laughed because we knew the man lucky enough to marry Jade would have his hands full. About thirty minutes later, visiting hours ended, and I left Pops to get some rest, promising to return tomorrow to pick him up. Before I reached my car, I'd received a text from Tessa saying Jade had given her a ride to my place, and she and Cyrah were going out.

When I arrived home, it was dark and quiet. It wasn't late, but it had been a long day, so I wasn't surprised Tessa had gone to bed. I began to disrobe as soon as I entered my bedroom. The light from the TV illuminated the room as it played softly. I chuckled quietly when I saw Tessa asleep right in the middle of my bed.

After a quick shower, I didn't bother putting on any underwear. I slid underneath the comforter, and when the front of my naked body touched the back of Tessa's, my dick instantly rocked up. However, I'd decided I'd let her sleep and wait until morning to indulge in her goodness. That was . . . until she began rubbing her ass on my erection.

"I thought you were asleep," I whispered in her ear.

"No, I was waiting for you."

She took my hand, sliding it down her body until it reached her honeypot. Her legs opened just enough for me to slide a few fingers between them.

"Damn, is all that gushiness for me?"

She moaned in response. I played with her pussy while she continued to grind her ass against my dick. When she cocked her leg open a bit more, I knew what time it was. I felt her hand grip my dick and guide me into her warm, wet, welcoming domain.

As I fucked her from the back, I massaged her clit with my index and middle finger while tickling her earlobe with my tongue. The sounds of her moans increased, and the louder she became, the closer I knew she was to her peak. Tonight, we'd be testing out my mother's theory because as we exploded together, the last thing I thought about doing was pulling out.

Tessa

I STILL FELT TIRED when I woke up, and it took me thirty minutes to get moving. It was almost ten o'clock when I looked at the time, and I typically didn't sleep that late. I thought I smelled bacon, so I dragged myself out of bed and took care of my morning hygiene. After throwing on one of Cypress's oversized T-shirts and leggings, I went to the kitchen to see what he'd made for breakfast. I'd forgotten my Cyrah was in town until I saw her sitting at the kitchen table.

"Good morning, sweetheart." I went to kiss her forehead before checking out the spread of food on the counter.

"Hey, Ma. You slept late."

"I know, and I could've slept longer. I think it's this depressing-ass weather. The sun doesn't shine much around here."

"The snow Cypress mentioned didn't happen yesterday, but I heard it will start soon. He went to pick up his father, by the way."

"I figured. What did you and Jade get into last night?"

"Nothing much. We went to a club, and I met some of her friends. They swore we looked like sisters."

"Nice. Did you have fun?" I asked, not acknowledging her last comment.

"Yeah, it was fine. She's been working half days since her father's heart attack and had to go in this morning. I don't know how she did it because it was close to three a.m. when she dropped me off."

"Really? I'm surprised you're not still asleep."

"Me too, but I smelled food, and my stomach started growling. Cypress can cook. Have you been eating like this the whole time you've been here?"

"Sadly, I have. I need to get home before I gain fifty pounds."

We talked a bit more while we ate breakfast. After we cleaned up the kitchen together, Cyrah got a phone call from Jade telling her she was leaving work at noon and would pick her up by one thirty. Cyrah showered and dressed in a cute pair of sweats and a matching hoodie. When she returned to the den, she sat beside me on the couch and laid her head on my lap.

"I missed you," she admitted. "But it sounds like you and Dr. Boone are really hitting it off. I love him for you."

"Me too."

"What's wrong?" she asked, sitting up and shifting her body to face me.

"Nothing. I'm fine," I lied.

I wanted to tell her who Cypress really was, but I needed to tell him first.

"Mom, you know I know you better than anybody. You've been acting strange since we left the restaurant yesterday. Jade is on her way to pick me up, but if you want me to stay and hang out with you, I can."

"No, sweetheart. I really am fine. Things are just moving a lot faster than I expected between Cypress and me. I'm just processing it all."

"I can understand that. Meeting his family so soon is a lot. I'm a people person, and I was even overwhelmed yesterday. I can't imagine what it'll be like tomorrow with his whole family."

"Yes, but we're here now, so no backing out. We're in this together now."

"I would never leave you hanging, Mom. Being around his mom makes me wish Nana was different. Mrs. Boone is so warm and welcoming, like a mother and grandmother is supposed to be."

"Well, if you ever decide to give me grandchildren, I promise I'll shower them with more love than they'll be able to stand."

"I don't doubt that because I've never felt I was lacking in that department. Sometimes, I wish I knew my father, but my life has been great. For all I know, my father is an asshole, and we dodged a bullet."

Your father is far from an asshole. He's arguably one of the best men I've ever encountered.

I couldn't find the words to respond to Cyrah because I knew Cypress was a great man.

"Oh, Jade is here. I'll see you later at the Boone's house, right?"

"Yeah."

We hugged and exchanged cheek kisses before she left. I remained in the den on the couch, trying to figure out how my life had become so complicated. When Cypress returned, I had to tell him. I had run out of excuses. To keep myself busy, I grabbed my laptop from the coffee table to do some research on my business idea. I hadn't done much since I'd been in Chicago, and I wanted this to happen, so I needed to put in some work.

As I opened the document where I'd been storing the information I'd found, Brianne's name flashed across the face of my watch. I rushed to Cypress's bedroom to grab my phone before the call dropped.

"Bri!"

"Tess, you good?"

"Yeah, my phone was in the bedroom, and I was in the den. What's up?"

"Nothing much, just calling to vent."

"Oh shit. What happened?"

She told me that Kendall, the guy she was dating, decided it would be best if they spent Thanksgiving separately. His excuse was that they hadn't been dating long enough for her to meet his family.

"I told him that was some bullshit."

"It sucks, but he has a right to his feelings," I told her.

"Tess, we've been dating for almost six months. You and Cypress went on one and a half dates, and he invited you—"

"Don't do that, Bri. Just because Cypress was ready for me to meet his family sooner than I expected doesn't mean Kendall isn't entitled to his feelings. Maybe he wants to make sure you're the one before he involves his family."

"Girl, that nigga met my parents and brother three months ago. You act like six months isn't a long time."

"That was your choice, though. You can't fault him for not being ready just because you are."

"I can and I will, but it's cool. Y'all got room for me in Chicago? I'm ready to catch a flight."

"Oh my God. Are you for real because I'd love that?"

"If I can find a flight, I'm there. Let me look, and I'll call you back."

"Okay. Don't forget your big coat," I said before ending the call.

I was excited about the possibility of my best friend coming to Chicago for Thanksgiving. With her presence, I'd have an ally just in case Cypress's family didn't like me, especially with the news I planned to tell him. My attention went back to my laptop, but before I delved into my research, I checked my email, and my heart stopped when I saw an email from Know Your Roots.

My hand quivered as I hovered over the email. I'd wanted to know who my father was for as long as I could remember. Now, I could have the information at my fingertips and was too scared to open the email.

"Just do it, Tessa," I encouraged myself.

I inhaled deeply a few times, and just as I was about to open the email, I heard Cypress frantically calling my name.

Cypress

BEFORE I LEFT the following day, I made breakfast, and the aroma from the food must have awakened Cyrah from her sleep. She entered the kitchen with a freshly washed face and her bonnet still on, stealing slices of bacon. We conversed while I finished preparing the food, and every so often, I'd catch myself staring at her a little too long. Thankfully, she was too busy scrolling on her phone to notice.

"Cyrah, have you ever met your father?"

Her expression didn't hide that she was confused by my question, but it was too late to take it back.

"No."

"What do you know about him?"

"Umm, just what my mother's told me."

"What did she tell you?"

"If she hasn't already shared that story with you, I don't think it's my place to do so. Maybe you should ask her."

"That's fair."

I left a little while later, hoping I hadn't made Cyrah uncomfortable with my questions. I didn't know what made me ask that question, and I regretted it as soon as it came out of my mouth. However, I didn't have much time to dwell on it. There were text messages from both my parents in the family chat when

I woke up, giving me my orders for the morning. I was instructed to pick up my mother by ten o'clock and take her to the hospital to pick up my father. When I picked up my mother, she talked nonstop about everything that still needed to be done to prepare for Thanksgiving dinner the following day.

"We should be home by noon. Once I drop you and Pops off and help get him settled, I'll go home and pick up Tessa. We'll go to the grocery store and pick up whatever you need. Jade and Tessa should be ready to help out by then too. I already set the tables and chairs up in the basement, and I'll set the garage up later today."

We had a big family, but my parents' house was big enough to host everyone. It would definitely be tight, but it'll be worth it.

"Thank you, son. Had I known your father would have a heart attack and need surgery, I wouldn't have volunteered to host both sides of the family."

"There was no way you could have known, so don't beat yourself up about it."

"Thank goodness Tessa and Cyrah are in town because nobody on either side of the family volunteered to help."

"Hold on now, Ma. In their defense, you only let certain people in your kitchen, which is why we host every year; they know this. Who would you have let help?"

I quickly glanced her way, and she was rolling her eyes because she knew I was right.

"That's not the point. Someone could've offered. It's the principle."

I knew better than to argue with Miriam Boone, so I simply nodded and agreed. Before we arrived at the hospital, she'd completed a grocery list with the items she needed from the store.

"I'm putting this list in your glove compartment. Don't forget because I need everything on this list."

"Yes, ma'am. I'll drop you off at the door, then go and park. I'll be up shortly."

I stopped in front of the hospital's main entrance, hopped out, and went around to the passenger side to help my mother out. Once she was safely inside, I found a parking space, then met her in my father's room. He was sitting on the edge of the bed while my mother moved around the room, gathering his things.

"You ready to blow this joint?" I asked my father when I entered.

"I could've left the day after my surgery," he said.

A nurse entered the room with some paperwork that needed to be signed. Shortly after my father finished signing everything, the doctor who performed his surgery entered. After the doctor shared the information and instructions about his postcare, I understood why my mother needed to be present when I picked him up. She was his primary caregiver, and I wouldn't have been able to relay everything the doctor said.

About forty-five minutes later, we headed to my parents' house. It had begun to snow, so the roads were a little slick. I was sure to drive carefully, but that didn't stop my mother from telling me to slow down every three minutes.

"We don't need another heart attack in this family. Will you slow down?"

"The roads ain't that bad, Ma. I'm only going twenty-five."

"Then go twenty," she fussed.

When I turned down their block, I could've jumped for joy. My father tried to refuse the wheelchair when we left the hospital, so I should've expected him to do the same when I tried to help him into the house.

"Did the doctor say I was handicapped? I can walk by myself," he griped.

I didn't even bother responding. I just stepped back and let him do his thing. He'd never been in a position that required him to need assistance from others, and he didn't like it. I felt sorry for my mother and Jade if he continued to be this stubborn. I had my own house to run away to and would eventually return to California. They lived with him and had nowhere to run.

"Do you need anything else before I leave?" I asked him.

"I can't have nothing I want, or I'll have to deal with your mother."

I nodded. "I wouldn't want to take that risk either. I'll be back in a little while. Call me if you think of something you need that won't get you killed."

"Be safe on those roads, son. I—"

The ringtone I had for Jade filled the room, interrupting my father.

"This is your daughter. Let me see what she wants. Hey, Jade," I answered the phone and put it on speaker.

"Cy, I need you," she cried hysterically.

"What's wrong? Where are you?"

"There was an accident. It started to snow and—and I was at a light. It—it turned green, and I went, but—but a big truck came out of nowhere. It—it—hit the passenger-side door. Cy, it was so bad. Please come. It doesn't look good. I'm scared."

If Jade could call me, she probably only suffered minor injuries and was distraught because she was scared. I was headed for my parents' bedroom door and heard my father shout my name.

"Keep me posted, and don't say a word to your mother until you know more details," he told me.

I nodded and rushed out of the house, not bothering to say goodbye to my mother, who was talking on the phone in the kitchen.

"Take a few deep breaths, Jade. I don't want you to have a panic attack."

"But it was bad, Cy. The truck hit her side—"

"Who's side? Cyrah was with you?"

"Yeah, and it was bad. Really bad. Please hurry."

"I'm on my way."

I almost busted my ass trying to get to my car, then realized I didn't know what hospital. I called Jade back, and it barely rang before she answered. Once she told me what hospital, I ended the call and headed toward Rush University Hospital.

Tessa!

I had to tell Tessa but couldn't tell her over the phone, knowing she had no transportation to the hospital. Picking her up would delay my arrival at the hospital, but I wasn't comfortable with any other options, and if Cyrah was hurt, Tessa needed to be there.

I arrived at my building and left my car running in front, telling the doorman the situation and rushing to the elevator. It was quiet inside, giving me little indication of where she might be.

"Tessa, where are you, baby?" I shouted.

She entered the kitchen from the den and looked like she had a lot on her mind.

"Did Jade call you?" I asked, wondering if she'd heard some news.

"No, but we need to talk."

The seriousness in her tone concerned me, but if she hadn't heard from Jade, I knew she didn't know about the accident.

"We can, but not right now. I need you to come with me."

"But—"

"Tessa, I can't go back and forth with you right now. We need to get to the hospital. Jade and Cyrah were in an accident."

She gasped. "Oh my God. Are they okay?"

"Get what you need, and let's go."

Thankfully, she didn't put up a fuss or ask more questions. A few minutes later, we were headed to the hospital.

"Tell me what you know. Are they hurt? Who did you talk to?"

"I talked to Jade. All I know is they were in an accident."

It was partly the truth. I didn't know enough details and didn't want to alarm her unnecessarily. The ride was quiet, but our nervousness filled the air. Tessa's leg bounced up and down as she nervously squeezed her hands together. I placed my hand on her knee and used my thumb to rub gently in a circular motion. It calmed her a bit, but not much.

"It'll be okay, baby," I assured her, hoping I wasn't telling a lie.

The ride took longer than it should've because of the snow, but we arrived safely, and I quickly found a parking spot. I called Jade to find out where she was located, and once inside, I told the attendant who I was there for and my relation to her and was taken to her room.

"Cy," she cried when she saw me.

Her face was swollen and bruised with a few cuts, but nothing else appeared to be wrong. When I reached her, she wrapped her arms around me and leaned into my chest as she cried.

"Where's Cyrah?" Tessa asked with fear in her voice.

Tessa

My HEART RACED all the way to the hospital. I tried not to think the worst, but when I entered the hospital room with Cypress and only saw Jade, I couldn't help but be worried.

"Where's Cyrah?"

Jade lifted her head from her brother's chest. Tears streamed down her face as she spoke.

"I don't know. They won't tell me anything."

"Oh God! What happened?"

She sniffled and gently dabbed her swollen eyes with the sleeve of her shirt.

"We were at a stoplight. I slowly pressed the gas when it turned green because the road was slick. As we crossed the intersection . . ." She stopped and took a few deep breaths before continuing. "A truck came out of nowhere and hit her side of the car. I called her name, but she—she didn't—respond. The ambulance came, and that was the last time I saw her. I'm so sorry, Tessa. I didn't—I didn't see the truck. The light—the light was green. It was my turn. I didn't mean for this—I'm so sorry."

I wanted to console her, but I needed some answers about my baby.

"The police have already been here to check on us and ask some questions. The person who hit us was arrested and is being held, but none of that matters if—"

"Don't think or talk like that, Jade," Cypress interrupted.

I didn't want to hear anything else unless it was about Cyrah, so I left the room and went back to the attendant who'd helped us before.

"Can you help me? I'm looking for my daughter. She was in a car accident and brought here in an ambulance."

"One second, ma'am. I'll see what I can find out."

Before the woman could give me any information, Cypress came around the corner and called my name.

"The doctor needs to speak to you."

He turned back around, and I followed him to Jade's room. The doctor was an older Black man with a welcoming spirit.

"Where's my baby? Where's Cyrah?"

"I'm Dr. James. Are you her mother?"

"Yes, please tell me she's okay."

He put his hands on my shoulders and said, "Calm down, ma'am. Take a few deep breaths."

As if I'd forgotten how to breathe, Dr. James demonstrated what he wanted me to do, and I mimicked him. When he thought I was calm enough, he removed his hands and began to speak.

"Your daughter is stable but has a broken wrist and ankle. I'll have to wait a few days for the swelling to go down before I cast them. Thankfully, no surgery is needed, but she lost an excessive amount of blood from a few of the wounds she received in the crash. We stopped the bleeding, but she will need a transfusion as soon as possible."

"Then do it! What are you waiting for?" I shouted.

"Her blood type is O negative, and unfortunately, that blood type is in high demand. If you, her father, or—"

"Cypress, you're a match. You can do it." I said it without thinking and knew I'd have some explaining to do.

"I, umm, I can. I'm O negative," he said with a bit of uncertainty in his voice.

"How much blood does she need? Can you check her blood type?" I asked, pointing at Jade. "She could be a match."

Jade was Cypress's sister, so she could also have O negative.

"I'll send a nurse in right away for you, sir," Dr. James told Cypress. "Do you know your blood type, Ms. Boone?"

"I don't, but if I'm a match, I'll donate."

"I'll have your file checked, and if you're a match, a nurse will come and get you."

He left, and I felt two pairs of eyes on me.

"How did you know I was a match?" Cypress asked quietly.

I couldn't avoid telling him any longer. This was not how I wanted him to find out, but I had no other option.

"Because you're her father."

"*What?*" Cypress and Jade exclaimed at the same time.

Before I could respond, a nurse entered the room and asked Cypress to come with her. His angry eyes stayed on me until he was gone. I was momentarily relieved I had time to gather my thoughts before diving into this long-overdue conversation with him. However, I'd forgotten about Jade. Her eyes were swollen, but that didn't hide the glare behind them.

"When were you planning to tell him?" she questioned, not hiding her displeasure with me.

"I don't owe anyone an explanation but him and Cyrah."

I couldn't talk to her about this before talking to them. Jade would have to wait.

"I think you owe a few more people explanations, but I can't make you talk."

"I planned to tell him today."

"Because telling him sooner wouldn't have made any sense," she replied sarcastically.

"I had my reasons for not telling him, but like I said, I don't owe you an explanation."

I didn't mean to have an attitude with Jade, but I matched her energy.

"Can I have some privacy?" she asked with the same tone I'd used with her.

I left the room but remained outside the door, pacing back and forth. It seemed like hours before Cypress rounded the corner, and when he did, I walked right into his chest.

"Cypress, I—"

"They should be coming to get Jade in a minute. She's a match, and thankfully, her injuries aren't severe, and she's well enough to donate. I need to call my parents," he said, continuing past me and entering the room with Jade.

I understood he was upset, but we'd have to talk eventually. I wouldn't worry about Cypress's or Jade's anger with me right now. I needed to see my baby and make sure she was all right.

"Dr. James," I said when I saw him round the corner, "can I see my daughter?"

"We have a couple more tests to run before we prep her for the transfusion. She was given some pain meds to control her pain levels, so she may be a bit groggy. After we start the transfusion, I'll have the nurses take you to her room."

"But she's okay, right?"

"She's fine, and I expect her to make a full recovery."

"Thank you, Dr. James. Is there somewhere I can wait so the nurses can find me?"

"Of course. Follow me."

I followed Dr. James to a waiting area and found a seat in the corner. My nerves wouldn't calm until I laid eyes on my baby.

When I sensed a pair of eyes on me, I looked up. Cypress and Jade had entered the waiting area and chose to sit as far away from me as possible, on the other side of the room. Their actions hurt my feelings, but my only concern at the moment was Cyrah.

"For Cyrah Howard?"

I shot out of my chair and damn near ran to the nurse. Cypress and Jade, although she was moving slowly, were right behind me.

"Follow me."

The nurse led us to the room where Cyrah was located. I almost knocked the woman down, trying to get to my child.

"Cy," I cried, startling her because her eyes were closed.

I went to one side of her bed and leaned down to kiss her forehead. Her face was bruised and swollen, much like Jade's, and she looked tired and weak. The rest of her body was wrapped in blankets, so I couldn't see her injuries, but I was careful not to touch her.

"Hey, Mom," she greeted with a weak smile, her voice low and raspy.

"Sweetheart, I'm grateful you're okay."

"Cyrah, I'm so sorry," Jade began, causing me to step away from the bed so the girls could see each other. "We had the right of way, and the truck didn't stop."

"This isn't your fault," she whispered. "I'm happy you weren't hurt."

Cypress quietly stood in the corner of the room. When Cyrah spotted him, her eyes shifted between the two of us.

"Why are you hiding in the corner, Dr. Boone?"

Cypress moved from the corner and approached the foot of the bed, folding his arms across his chest.

"No reason. It's good to see you awake, talking, and smiling. You had us worried."

"The doctor says I'm good besides the broken wrist and ankle. You guys can stop worrying, but unfortunately, I'll miss dinner tomorrow."

I'd completely forgotten tomorrow was Thanksgiving dinner. We were all supposed to be at Mr. and Mrs. Boone's house, helping Mrs. Boone finish preparing dinner.

"Don't you worry about that. I spoke with my parents, and they sent their love, prayers, and a message for you not to worry about anything but healing."

"Please thank them and ask your mom to save me a plate."

"Let me talk to the doctor to make sure you don't have any food restrictions first, young lady," I told her.

"It's just a few broken bones, Mom. I'm fine."

"I still want to check to be sure."

"Baby girl, your mother and I need to discuss a few things. Do you mind if we step out for a minute?"

"Umm, sure. Is everything okay?" she asked.

"Everything is fine. Jade, can you stay with Cyrah while Tessa and I talk?"

"I can't leave—"

"You can and you will," Cypress asserted. "We'll be right down the hall if you need anything."

He pulled the door open and held it. When I didn't move, he said, "Tessa, let's go."

His tone let me know that now wasn't the time to play with him, so I exited the room and headed toward the waiting area we'd just left. It was time for me to face the music.

Cypress

BECAUSE YOU'RE HER father.

Those words had been on replay in my mind ever since they left Tessa's mouth. I searched my memory for clues about when I could have conceived a child. Twenty years ago, I was like any typical male coming into his manhood, doing dumb shit and making poor decisions. However, if anyone who knew me back then were asked if I was irresponsible, they would tell you the exact opposite.

I actually prided myself on being the responsible one in my group of friends, and even when we did things we shouldn't have, I was the one with the level head, making sure things didn't go too far. My parents constantly reminded me that I was made up of the best parts of them, and they worked too hard to ensure I was afforded certain opportunities. There was no way in hell I would do anything to jeopardize their legacy.

Tessa's words threw me for a loop and left me questioning everything we'd built over the past few weeks. However, her words also helped me understand why our first time together didn't feel like the first time at all and why Cyrah and I seemed familiar to each other. Nonetheless, it was time for answers.

We left Cyrah's room and went back to the waiting area. Thankfully, it was empty, so we sat as far away from the nurse's station as possible. I didn't anticipate the conversation not going well, but just in case, we were far enough away that we wouldn't cause a stir.

"Start from the beginning," I stated as soon as we sat down.

She pulled out her phone, and I watched as she swiped the screen repeatedly. When she stopped, she handed me the phone. A picture of a beautiful, brown-skinned woman with straight, shoulder-length hair and a tiny waist with curvy hips was on the screen. She was wearing a bikini top with denim shorts, standing with her hands on her hips in front of the San Diego Zoo.

San Diego!

"A little over twenty years ago, I went to San Diego for spring break with my roommate and a few other girls. Going on that trip as a nineteen-year-old college sophomore was a big deal for me. I was big on following the rules, always on the straight and narrow path, and never bucking the system that my mother had put in place. She had me programmed always to do the right thing. I went without my mother's permission, and to this day, she still doesn't know."

As she spoke, I continued looking at the picture. I also went to San Diego for spring break a little over twenty years ago. There weren't many things from the trip I remembered, but I did recall a string of women, underage drinking, and weed.

"Anyway, on our last night in town, I met a man at one of the clubs. We danced with each other the whole night until, eventually, he asked me to go back to his room with him. I agreed, and the rest is history."

"Marie?" I blurted out when the memories began to flood my brain.

"That's me. Tessa Marie Howard. I guess I wasn't as memorable as you."

"Tessa, I was drunk, and you don't look remotely the same, and don't take that the wrong way. You were beautiful then, and you're even more beautiful now. There's so much I don't remember about that trip, not just you."

"I understand, but our one-night stand resulted in a baby being conceived. Since we didn't exchange full names or phone numbers, I had no way of contacting you. If you want to get a DNA test, I—"

"That's not necessary."

I told her my name was Cy, and she told me her name was Marie. No other information was exchanged. Now, here I am, twenty years later, with a kid I didn't know existed.

"Did you recognize me on our first date?"

She hesitated briefly before nodding.

"Why didn't you tell me then?"

"It's not that simple, Cypress. I couldn't just tell you I was the woman you slept with and impregnated twenty years ago."

"Why not? Isn't that what happened?"

"Yes, but it was our first date. I didn't know anything about you, and—"

"You knew enough to go home with me and, days later, fly to Chicago to be with me."

"So, you're judging me now?"

"No, I'm just stating facts. You didn't think this was a priority? You should've said something as soon as you recognized me. Why would you keep information like this from me?"

"When I tried to tell you, things kept happening that stopped me."

"Things? What things were more important than me knowing the truth?"

"Your life has been a little chaotic lately. I didn't want to drop something like this while you were dealing with your father's health, the betrayal of your fiancée and best friend, and the paternity of Emery's baby."

I thought about her reasoning and could admit she had a point. I'd been dealing with one thing after another, and it was definitely overwhelming. However, how could she not see that this news trumped everything else?

"I appreciate your concern, but damn, Cyrah is my daughter. I needed to know that," I told her.

"I planned to tell you on our second date, but you got the phone call about your father. After that, no time seemed like the right time."

"Does Cyrah know?"

She shook her head. "I wanted to tell you first."

"How admirable of you," I said sarcastically.

"She knows the whole story about how she was conceived, so she doesn't think you're a deadbeat, if that's your concern."

"It's nice to know she doesn't think I'm a deadbeat, but it doesn't fix the fact that I've been absent all her life. This is fucked up, no matter how you look at it. How the hell am I gonna explain this to my parents?"

"I understand why you're upset, but—"

"No, you don't. I don't think you have a clue. This whole ordeal has pissed me off, but do I have the right to be pissed? I did some irresponsible shit twenty years ago and didn't think about the possible consequences a single time since it happened. Today, you tell me this amazing young lady is my daughter, and I had absolutely nothing to do with why she's so fucking amazing. I didn't contribute a dime to her upbringing; I never gave her any words of wisdom or encouragement; I wasn't around to teach her how to ride a bike, tie her shoes, or how to spot a nothing-ass nigga. I don't even know her birthday. I could've lost her today and didn't know she was mine to lose. I'm nothing to her, yet already, she is everything to me. I'm happy my absence didn't fuck with her like it could have, but knowing she didn't need me in her life to become the person she is today . . . it's fucking with me."

I'd said a mouthful and wasn't surprised when Tessa didn't respond immediately. Hell, I was still processing everything I'd said.

"I'm truly sorry, Cypress. I was always hopeful that, by some miracle, Cyrah would have the opportunity to meet her father. I never imagined it would happen like this, but now that everything is out in the open, please don't reject my baby."

"You've known me long enough to know I'd never reject her. I'm hoping she won't be the one doing the rejecting."

"Cyrah was born on the eighteenth of December at six thirty-two p.m. She was seven pounds even and twenty-one inches long. She had a head full of hair and the deepest dimples I'd ever seen on an infant."

I wouldn't ask now, but I was sure Tessa had plenty of baby pictures, and I couldn't wait to see them.

"How did you choose her name?"

Cypress and Cyrah. Was that a coincidence, or was it intentional?

"I didn't know your last name, and I wanted her to have a part of you. Cy was the only thing I knew, so I chose a name that would allow me to honor you somehow."

It was intentional.

"Thank you."

"I know it's not the same, but I have pictures and videos of Cyrah from infancy up until recently. You're welcome to all of it."

"I'd like that."

We sat quietly for a while. I was still processing the fact that I had a daughter, and I was sure Tessa had some things on her mind that she needed to sort through as well.

"We should probably head back to Cyrah's room," she said.

"Every time I hear or say her name now, it'll have a whole new meaning."

She smiled, but it wasn't the big, bright smile I was used to. "When do you want to tell her?"

"After she's released. I don't want to drop something like this on her and leave her to unpack it alone."

"Whatever you want to do is fine with me. I'm gonna head back."

"Okay. Give me a few minutes."

Tessa left, and I remained in the waiting room for about thirty more minutes, trying to clear my mind. It was impossible. I have a daughter. A twenty-year-old daughter. I thought about the first time I'd seen her and thought it wasn't the first time. I recalled how she mentioned feeling the same way about me. If someone asked, I wouldn't be able to explain the connection I seemed to have with Cyrah, but now I knew why. We saw ourselves in each other.

I'm her father.

She's my daughter.

Tessa

"CYRAH, ARE YOU sure you don't want me to stay here with you overnight?"

The transfusion went smoothly, and Cyrah was already feeling better. The doctor wanted to observe her overnight to be sure there were no issues, but because her ankle and wrist needed to be cast, she'd be in the hospital for a few more days.

"I told you I'm fine. All you'll be doing is watching me sleep, so you may as well go back to Dr. Boone's house and sleep in a comfortable bed."

"If you're worried, I can stay here with her," Jade offered.

"You were in the accident too and need as much rest as I do. Nobody needs to stay," Cyrah objected before I could speak.

"What's going on in here?" Cypress asked as he entered the room. "I could hear Cyrah in the hallway; she shouldn't be getting so riled up."

I wasn't sure how Cypress felt about me, but seeing him flip into protective mode over his daughter warmed my heart.

"You're right. Sweetheart, if you don't want anyone to stay with you overnight, you have that right. I'll be back bright and early tomorrow morning, though."

"I'm staying," Cypress announced.

"Dr. Boone—"

"Save your breath and energy, baby girl. I'm staying."

I loved how Cypress wasted no time becoming the protective father, which made me admire him more than I already did. *Lord, I know I'm not perfect and didn't handle this situation the best, but please don't let this man be angry with me, at least not for too long.*

I looked at Cypress, who was looking at me. I couldn't handle his gaze, so I looked at Jade, who was looking back and forth between Cypress and me. It wasn't until Cyrah spoke up that I realized she'd been looking at all of us as we looked at each other.

"Okay, what's going on? And don't feed me a bunch of lies," she demanded. "Did the doctor give you some bad news? Am I dying? What is it?"

Her voice had elevated, although it remained raspy.

"Cyrah, please calm down. The doctor told us the same thing he told you. We're not hiding anything," I said.

"Oh, really?" Jade questioned.

"We're not hiding anything about your health, baby girl," Cypress added.

"All of you are acting weird. Jade, you've been in here speaking in riddles for the past twenty minutes. All of you are talking with your eyes, but I don't know what you're communicating with each other. And what is with this 'baby girl' stuff? I know you're dating my mother, but don't you think it's weird to call your student 'baby girl'? Somebody needs to tell me what's going on before I have security escort everybody out of here."

"He's your father, Cyrah," I blurted out.

"Tessa, I thought we agreed to wait," Cypress chastised.

I didn't look in his direction but could feel the heat of his glare.

Cyrah was confused and asked, "Who's my father?"

"Cypress is your father."

"Are you—Mom, are you serious?"

I nodded because fearing how she would react had stolen my voice. Cyrah looked at her father as if she'd been trying to solve an equation, and it was all coming together. Then she turned her attention back to me.

"I don't understand. How long have all of you known?"

"They found out tonight when we were told you needed a blood transfusion. I've always known our blood types didn't match, so I assumed you matched your father's. When the doctor said you needed blood—"

"How long have *you* known?" she interrupted.

"Since the night of our first date, but you need your rest. We can talk—"

"Oh, hell no. You think you can tell me something like this and leave?" If looks could kill, I'd surely be dead. I'd never seen my daughter look at me with such disdain. "I can't believe you knew and didn't tell me. We've lost enough time together. Every second counts, and you intentionally prolonged something I've wanted for my whole life."

Cyrah had a right to be upset with me, but it was a hard pill to swallow. I tried to think of another instance where my daughter's anger was directed toward me, but there was none. I could truthfully say we'd never had an argument of that magnitude.

"I'm sorry, Cyrah. I wanted to tell him first, and the timing was never right."

"The timing? The timing wasn't right? You've looked this man in the face for weeks and couldn't find the right time to tell him I was his daughter?"

Suddenly, a machine started beeping, and a nurse rushed into the room.

"What is going on here? Her blood pressure just shot up to dangerous levels. Honey, you need to calm down."

"I want to be alone. Can you make them leave?" Cyrah requested.

The nurse turned to us and said, "You heard her. She needs to rest anyway."

"Cyrah—"

"Please, Mom, just leave."

The coldness in her voice hurt me, but I didn't want to make things worse.

"I love you, sweetheart," I told her before entering the hallway.

Cypress was right behind me, and Jade caught up to us before we arrived at the elevator. She'd been giving me attitude since I broke the news to her and her brother, and I understood her displeasure with me, so I wouldn't hold it against her when all of this blew over. No one spoke as we left the hospital; it was the same in the car. When we arrived at the elder Boones' residence, Cypress turned off the car, and Jade quickly exited the vehicle, leaving me alone with her brother.

"You're not coming in?" he asked.

"No."

"My mother is going to ask why—"

"Can you tell her I don't feel well? Today has been a lot, and I'm drained."

"I'll tell her, but I doubt it'll work."

He started the car again, adjusting the heat before going inside. I reclined my seat, closed my eyes, and rested my head on the headrest. Not even thirty seconds had passed, and my phone rang. I ignored it because I assumed it was Cypress telling me his mother wanted me to come inside.

"Oh shit!" I cursed when I realized it was Brianne's ringtone.

Before I could call her back, she called again.

"My bad, Bri. I couldn't get to my phone."

"I'm in muthafuckin' Chi-Town!" she shouted.

I gasped as I adjusted the seat back to the sitting position. "Are you? Oh my God. I'm so glad you're here. So much has happened since I talked to you earlier. Cyrah was in a car accident; Cypress and his sister—"

"Tessa! Slow down. Did you say Cyrah was in a car accident?"

"Yes, it was scary for a while, but she's good. Where are you?"

"In an Uber headed to my hotel."

"Text me the name and address. I'll have Cypress drop me off. You don't know how happy I am you're here."

"Okay. Sending now."

Just as Cypress returned to the car, a text from Brianne came through.

"Would you mind taking me to this address?" I asked, handing him my phone.

"Why are you going to a hotel?"

"My best friend just touched down. I'm staying with her tonight."

He was surprised but tried to cover it up. "Umm, okay. Did you want to stop by my place to get some clothes?"

"I don't want to be too much of an inconvenience."

"It's not a problem."

"Okay. I'd appreciate it. Let me text her and tell her I'll be a little longer than expected."

I held my hand out and waited for him to place my phone in my hand, but he didn't.

"Cypress, can I have my phone?"

"I didn't tell my parents about Cyrah, and I told Jade not to say anything. I figured it would be best to wait until Friday."

"Okay."

"But my mother knows."

"What do you mean? How can she know if you didn't tell her?"

"Yesterday, she pulled me into the pantry and said Cyrah looks like she could be my daughter. She also noticed the birthmark on her arm."

"What did you tell her?"

"That maybe we were from the same tribe because, at the time, I had no other explanation."

"Well, soon, she'll know her intuition was right. Can I have my phone now?"

I held my hand out again, and he returned my phone this time.

"Thank you. Do you know when you'll drop me off so I can tell Brianne?"

"About an hour."

I texted Brianne my estimated arrival time before sticking my phone into my purse. The car was blanketed with silence, and I didn't want to engage Cypress in conversation. I wasn't lying when I said I was drained. Brianne was the only person I wanted to talk to, so I needed to save what energy I had left to update her on the mess that was my life. Cypress must have felt the same way because he didn't try to engage me either, at least not until we arrived at his place.

Cypress

HEARING THAT I was Cyrah's father messed up my head for a minute. I wasn't upset that I was her father; I was upset with how and when Tessa decided to drop the news. After taking some time to process everything, my anger dissipated, and all I wanted to do was find out as much as I could about Cyrah. I'd missed so much of everything, and I had a lot of questions. I was hoping to have some of the questions answered tonight, but Tessa had other plans.

"I didn't know your friend was coming to town," I told Tessa as she threw some stuff in a bag for her overnight stay with her friend.

"It was a last-minute decision. I'm surprised she was able to get a flight."

"Is she here to visit Cyrah?"

"I'm sure she'll visit her while she's here, but she decided to come to Chicago before we knew anything about the accident."

"Are you still planning to come to my parents' house for dinner?"

"Am I still invited?"

"Why wouldn't you be?"

She finally stopped moving and sat beside me on the edge of the bed.

"I don't know. I wasn't sure if we were good."

"Why wouldn't we be?" I asked.

She tilted her head to the side as if to say, "Don't patronize me."

"Look, Tessa. I don't like the way you handled this. I've tried to understand it, and it doesn't make sense. We're family now, so you're welcome wherever I am."

"But—"

"I think we should pump the brakes on us for a minute. I want to focus on getting to know Cyrah and learn how to be her father."

I didn't want to mention the paternity test results I was awaiting. Tessa wasn't wrong when she said I was dealing with a lot, although I didn't think it was a good enough excuse to keep vital information from me. She nodded in response before standing and dumping everything she'd put in the bag onto the bed.

"What are you doing?" I asked, wondering if she'd changed her mind about leaving.

"I'll just take all my things and stay with Brianne until she checks out. I have some stuff in your hamper that I planned to wash, but I can come back in a day or so to do that."

"You don't have to leave. I have plenty of—"

"No, it's fine and probably for the best. If you could take Cyrah a plate tomorrow, I'm sure she'd appreciate it."

Tessa was moving through my room like a Tasmanian devil, going from the bathroom to her luggage, to my closet, and then back to her luggage.

"Tessa," I called her name, but she didn't acknowledge me. "Tessa, baby, slow down. You don't have to leave. There's plenty of room here for—"

"No, I'd be more comfortable elsewhere."

I knew it was no use arguing with her, so I went to the den to wait. Thirty minutes later, I heard the door open and close. Tessa was nowhere to be found, so I looked down the hall and saw her waiting for the elevator. She didn't bother waiting for me when it arrived, forcing me to wait. When I finally got outside, I could just barely see her standing next to the trunk of my car, which I'd parked in one of the visitor spaces. I couldn't help but laugh at her stubborn ass, and I was willing to bet she wouldn't let me put her luggage in my trunk.

"This is Chicago, not Black Elm. You'll get snatched up standing your ass out here in the dark. Get in the car."

"I need to put my stuff in the trunk."

"Tessa, get your ass in the car before I put you *and* this damn luggage in the trunk."

She huffed and walked away, yanking open the car door.

"And don't slam my shit either," I shouted before she slammed it.

As soon as I got in the car, I tried to explain to Tessa what I meant by pumping the brakes. However, she wasn't in a place to receive my explanation—her words, not mine.

"I might be many things, but I'm nobody's fool. In my last relationship, I put up with the back-and-forth bullshit for too long. I won't do it again. You take as much time as you need to get to know Cyrah. I want that for you both. When you feel ready to explore us again, maybe I'll be available and interested; maybe I won't. Only time will tell."

I didn't respond because I didn't know what to say. When I told her I thought we should pump the brakes, I hadn't imagined she'd be dating other people or not interested in picking up where we left off. I hadn't told her, nor had I fully admitted to myself, but Tessa had a hold on my heart, and I didn't want her to let go.

We rode quietly to the hotel, and when we arrived, she tried to tell me she'd get her things, but, of course, I paid her no attention. I removed her luggage from the trunk and took it to the entryway, where she waited.

"Do you need a ride to the hospital tomorrow?"

"No, I'll manage."

"What about for dinner?"

"No, thank you. I'll figure it out if I decide to come. Can you text me your parents' address?"

"Sure, I'll do it when I get in the car."

Tessa reached out to grab the suitcase handle, but instead, I took her hand, pulled her into my chest, and wrapped my hands around her body.

"I don't know why you're acting like this is the end of us. I just need a minute to process some things."

"And I'm giving you as much time and space as you need. I gotta go."

I pressed my lips against her forehead before watching her walk away. When I couldn't see her anymore, I returned to my car. I wasn't sure if I'd done the right thing, but it was what I felt I needed to do.

A number from Rush University Hospital flashed across my dashboard as I headed home. My heart dropped because my first thought was something happened to Cyrah. I answered quickly but cautiously.

"Cypress speaking."

"I got your number from Jade," Cyrah whispered. "I hope that's okay."

"Of course."

"I can't sleep," Cyrah whispered.

"Are you in pain? Do you need something?"

"No, I'm fine. They gave me pain meds for my wrist and ankle, and I should be asleep, but it's not happening."

"What's on your mind?"

"What's not?"

"I understand. My mind has been whirling since I heard the news too. Are you upset or disappointed?"

"That you're my father? Not in the least. Finding out you're my father was shocking, but it also makes sense. It's weird, you know?"

"It's hard to explain, but I know exactly what you mean. From the first time I saw you, I thought I'd seen you somewhere before."

"Same. I'm upset and disappointed with how my mother handled this. I can think of a hundred different ways she could have told us, and me getting in a car accident and needing a blood transfusion would not make the list."

I chuckled because her sense of humor was needed during this time.

"I couldn't agree more. I've tried to understand your mother's reasoning, but I suppose it's not for me to understand. However, I don't want to dwell on it anymore."

"Yeah, you're probably right. This was the first time I've ever been angry with my mother. It might be hard to believe, but our relationship has been almost perfect."

"Don't let this situation mess that up."

"I won't, but I need a minute."

I didn't comment, but knew what she meant because I felt the same way.

"I'm sorry I missed the first twenty years of your life, but I promise I'll be here for the rest of my years if you allow me."

"I'd love that."

"Good because until you tell me something different, I'll be on you like white on rice. I want to know everything about my baby girl, even though you're far from a baby."

"I haven't been a baby for a long time, but since we got a late start, I'll make an exception for you under one condition."

"Anything."

"Can I retire Dr. Boone, skip right over Cypress, and call you Dad?"

The emotions I'd felt most of the day overwhelmed me when Cyrah asked that question. Tears gathered in my eyes, blurring my vision and causing me to pull over to the side of the road. For a moment, I couldn't find the words to respond because of a lump in my throat. My silence caused Cyrah some concern.

"If it's too soon—"

"No, that's not it all. I had to take a second to get my emotions in check. I'd be honored if you called me Dad, Daddy, Pops, Old Man, or anything that equates to me being your father."

We talked until I arrived home. Cyrah's voice began to drag, and I knew sleep was near. She didn't want to end our call, but I insisted, assuring her I'd see her the following day. It wasn't until I promised to bring her a plate of food that we said our goodbyes.

After I showered and slid between the sheets, it felt like something—no, *someone*—was missing. *Tessa.* The pillow she used held her scent, making me miss her even more. I'd gotten used to her presence and wondered how long it'd be before I was ready for us to pick up where we had left off. As she told me, only time will tell.

Tessa

"How is my niece?" Brianne asked as soon as she opened the hotel room door.

"Much better, or I wouldn't be here," I responded as I pulled my luggage into the room.

"Damn, girl, I didn't know you were coming with all your shit. Your man letting you leave for that long?"

I put my things in a corner, and we embraced like we hadn't seen each other in decades.

"I don't have a man," I told her.

"Excuse me? What hap—oh shit. You told him about Cyrah, and he put you out?"

"Kind of, but not exactly."

"Wait a minute. This sounds like it calls for pizza and wine."

She sat in the center of the king-sized bed with her legs crossed and a pizza box in front of her, then held up a bottle of wine she'd been drinking straight from the bottle. I kicked off my shoes, went to the bathroom to wash my hands, and joined her on the bed.

"Give me the bottle," I demanded.

I took a long swig and returned the bottle to her so she could place it on the bedside table.

"Start from the beginning," she requested.

"Cyrah and Jade, Cypress's younger sister, were in a car accident. A truck ran a red light and hit the passenger side of the door. Thankfully, the guy was arrested, but Cyrah suffered a broken ankle and wrist and a few wounds to her body. Those wounds caused her to lose an excessive amount of blood. She needed a blood transfusion immediately, and I knew I wasn't a match. I'd always assumed that she matched with her father since Cyrah and I didn't have the same blood type. So, I blurted out that Cypress was a match, and, of course, he's wondering how I knew his blood type."

"That was how Cypress found out he was her father?" I nodded. "Oh, damn. Continue."

For the next twenty minutes, while finishing a large pizza and an entire bottle of wine, I told her all that had occurred. One thing Brianne wouldn't do was sugarcoat a damn thing, and I wasn't ready for her forwardness.

"Right now, they're both pissed I didn't tell them sooner, and as an honorable mention, Jade's not fucking with me either."

"Damn, Tess. I hate to say I told you so, but I warned you this would happen. Sis, you fucked up."

"Tell me about it. Cyrah might never speak to me again, and Cypress wants us to 'pump the brakes.' You know what men mean when they say shit like that."

"Let's not exaggerate. Cyrah's upset, but once she calms down, she'll talk to you and maybe even understand why you didn't say something sooner. Cypress has a lot to process, and he may not want to do it while sharing space with you. If you had told them sooner, as I suggested, neither would be upset. You brought this on yourself."

I loved and hated that Brianne always kept it real. Of course, everyone needed someone in their life to be honest with them when honesty wasn't what they wanted to hear. However, this was one of those moments when I just needed her to listen. I knew I was wrong and didn't need her to double down on me.

"Kick me while I'm down, why don't you?"

"You know that's not what I'm doing. I believe it will all work out the way it should. In the meantime, don't rush or put any expectations on how long they should be in their feelings, okay?"

"I don't have a choice."

"I'm glad you understand that. What's going on for tomorrow? I know we'll see Cyrah, but do you still plan to go to her grandparents' house for dinner? I need some comfort food like nobody's business."

"You don't think it will be weird?"

"Didn't you say Cypress didn't plan to tell his parents until Friday?"

"That's what he said."

"Then why would it be weird—oh, you mean weird between the two of you?" I nodded. "It probably will be, but enough people will be around to make it not so weird. We can eat and run if you want, but I didn't come all the way to Chicago at the last minute to be eating restaurant food on Thanksgiving."

"Okay, we can go."

The following day, I woke up with a new outlook on the situation I'd created among my daughter, her father, and me. Brianne's advice seemed harsh last night because I was in my feelings. However, she was right when she advised me to give Cypress and Cyrah time to process their feelings.

My relationship with my daughter was strong, and I had no doubt we would bounce back from this. As for Cypress, my feelings for him grew quickly, and I'd been looking forward to possibly having a future with him. I was hopeful he'd find his way back to me before I moved on or lost interest, but if not, I'd be fine.

While Brianne slept, I went to the sofa in the corner of the room with my laptop in tow. With all that had happened, I'd forgotten about the email I'd received from Know Your Roots. I logged onto my computer and opened my email. After deleting several junk messages, the message from Know Your Roots stared me in the face.

"Just open it, Tessa," I whispered.

One click could change my entire life, and as much as I wanted to know about the other half of me, I was scared shitless. I hovered over the email for a few seconds before biting the bullet. I didn't know if I expected to see my father's name when I opened the email, but that was not the case.

The first few pages of the document were paragraphs about what to expect and how to read the graphs and diagrams. I was tempted to skip through all that, but I wanted to make sure I understood everything and let my nerves settle.

"What are you doing?" Brianne asked groggily.

"I got my results back from Know Your Roots."

If she wasn't fully awake a second ago, she was awake now. She jolted to a seated position and looked in my direction.

"Oh my God. What does it say? Hold on. Let me brush my teeth. Don't tell me yet."

"Okay."

At this point, I'd do anything to delay seeing the results, even though I was anxious as hell to know what they were. It didn't make any sense, but it was where I was at the moment.

"I'm ready," she said, plopping onto the space beside me.

"I haven't looked at them yet because I'm too nervous."

"You want me to do it?"

"Please."

She took my laptop, and I think I held my breath for the next minute. I watched her eyes as she scrolled through the information on the screen.

"Well, the first diagram tells you what parts of Africa your ancestors were likely from and what tribes they belonged to. Do you want to go over that, or do you want to get to the nitty-gritty?"

"I'll look at that later."

She nodded and proceeded to move through the document. When she stopped scrolling, her eyes widened, and her head snapped back.

"What? Why are you looking like that? Is it bad?"

"No, not at all. You matched with a few people, all with the last name Truth. When I saw the last name, I immediately thought of that bed and breakfast that you went to a few months ago that you raved about."

I didn't need Brianne to jog my memory. I'll never forget Truth Sanctuary. The odds of the people who owned Truth Sanctuary being related to me were slim. At least, I thought so.

"I'll never forget that place, but I highly doubt it's the same family. Are there pictures?"

"Unfortunately, no pics. You never know, Tess. Wouldn't that be wild? You could've been in the presence of your family and didn't know it. All three of the matches connect to email addresses. You should reach out."

"Yeah, I will. Not right now, though. I need time to think about what I'll say."

"Of course. If you need help, you know I got you. Let's go see my niece."

Cypress

I WASN'T SURPRISED WHEN I didn't sleep well. With all that I had on my mind and the absence of Tessa, there wasn't a chance a good night's rest would happen. Although I woke up feeling tired, I pushed through. After bathing and dressing for the day, I made breakfast for Cyrah. She seemed to enjoy what I'd cooked the morning before, and I had a feeling she wouldn't enjoy what the hospital served.

I cooked turkey bacon, scrambled eggs with cheese, and Texas toast French toast with sliced strawberries, pineapples, and honey dew. Once I placed everything in containers, I packed it in a portable food warmer and headed to the hospital. On the way, I received a phone call from my mother.

"Hey, Ma."

"Good morning, son. I know nothing can be done about it today, but I need you to go with Jade to look at her car. Someone called from the police station with the information, but I don't want her to go alone. With your father—"

"It's not a problem, Ma. We can go tomorrow. Why didn't she call and ask me?"

"She said something about you dealing with a lot and not wanting to bother you. What's that about?"

"Nothing. I'll be over in a few hours. Do you still have a lot to do?"

"Believe it or not, everything is just about done. I damn near had to pull an all-nighter, but I'll rest for the next few days. I'm good."

"Damn, Ma. I'm sorry you ended up having to do so much alone. Tessa and Cyrah were excited about helping, but—"

"Don't apologize, son. Accidents happen. This whole meal would've been canceled if Jade had been seriously injured. It almost was until you assured me my baby was okay and Cyrah was out of the woods."

"I'm glad you didn't. Everyone is fine. I'll see you soon. Love you."

"Love you too."

Our call ended as I found a parking spot. As I walked to the hospital, I thought about my conversation with my parents about Jade's accident. I was with my father when Jade called me, so he knew she was okay. However, convincing my mother was a bit more challenging. Between my father and me, we were able to calm her down, but she wasn't completely sold until she could speak to Jade. The past eighteen hours had been something out of a movie, but I was grateful there'd been no tragedies.

When I got to Cyrah's room, I tapped on the door a few times and waited for her to give me permission to enter. She was sitting up and seemingly alert when I entered. The smile that graced her face when she saw me touched my heart.

"Good morning, baby girl."

"I don't think I'll ever get tired of hearing that. Good morning, Daddy."

"And I don't think I'll ever tire of hearing that. I made you breakfast."

The excitement in her eyes let me know I'd made the right decision.

"Thank you so much. I thought I would be stuck eating the hospital breakfast and was prepared to starve until dinner."

"Well, now that's not necessary."

Cyrah's mobility was limited because of the brace she had on her broken wrist. Thankfully, she was left-handed, something else we had in common, and her right wrist was injured. I set up her meal on the mobile tray next to her bed. As soon as she took the first bite, she tried to do a little dance but was instantly reminded of the car accident.

"Ugh, the expression 'I feel like I've been hit by a truck' will have a new meaning for me. I've never been this sore in my life."

"I'm sorry you're going through this. If I could switch places with you, I would in a heartbeat."

She smiled. "But then I'd be the one making you breakfast, and I assure you, it wouldn't be this good. What do you put in the batter for your French toast?"

"It's a secret, but I guess I can tell my daughter. I use brown sugar and honey."

"Mmm, I can taste it now that I know. This is even better than my mom's, and hers is top tier, but please never tell her I said that."

"Scout's honor," I said, holding up my right hand.

I'd made a serving for myself, and we enjoyed our meal in a comfortable silence for a few minutes. Soon, a tap on the door caused us to look in that direction. Cyrah permitted whoever it was to enter, and a woman I'd never seen before entered the room.

Cyrah gasped before saying, "Oh my God. Auntie Bri, what are you doing here?"

"What do you mean? I heard my niece needed me, so here I am."

The woman went to hug Cyrah, and I automatically went into protective mode.

"Don't hug too tight; she's sore from the accident."

She gently embraced Cyrah, then turned her attention to me.

"Look at you, being overprotective already. You must be Cypress. I'm Brianne. We met twenty years ago, but I guess you don't remember me either."

"Umm, my apologies, but I don't remember. It's nice to meet you again, I guess."

"Where's my mom?"

"She stopped to talk to your doctor. It smells scrumptious in here. I know this isn't the breakfast the hospital provided."

"Nope!" Cyrah said confidently. "My daddy made this for me."

Brianne folded her arms across her chest, looking back and forth between Cyrah and me as her mouth curled into a grin.

"If that isn't the cutest thing ever. You said 'my daddy' with so much pride. I love this for you, Cyrah."

"Me too."

"And damn if you didn't steal his whole face. How did you two not see the resemblance as soon as you met?"

"In a way, we did," I interjected, although I wasn't sure Brianne was talking to me. "We both commented about the other looking familiar, but we couldn't place where we may have seen each other."

"How about every time you look in the mirror?"

Tessa walked in and stopped abruptly, probably not expecting to see me.

"Hey, good morning," she greeted nervously. "Sweetheart, how are you feeling?"

"I'm fine."

I could tell from how Cyrah responded that she was still upset with her mother.

"That's good. I spoke with your doctor, and he'll be in shortly to check the swelling on your wrist and ankle. If it's going down, he may be able to put the casts on tomorrow or Saturday."

"Will I be released then?"

"I believe so, but we can ask him when he comes in. This food looks great. Is this—"

Before Tessa could finish asking, Brianne interrupted her.

"Cypress made breakfast for his daughter and delivered it to her. Isn't that sweet?"

"Really? Yeah, that's really sweet. Did you bring enough for all of us?" she asked, eyes piercing my soul.

"I didn't think anyone would be here this early, but if you ladies want to stop by my place, I'd be happy to whip up something," I offered.

"No, thank you. We're good," Tessa responded.

"No, we're not. Everything is closed, and I'm starving," Brianne disputed.

"I told you to get something at the hotel. Now, you'll have to wait. Something will be open by the time we leave."

"Hotel? You stayed at a hotel last night? Is that why you arrived separately?" Cyrah questioned, eyes moving from me to Tessa, then back to me.

When we spoke last night, we only briefly mentioned her mother, so she had no idea what was going on between us, not that I would've told her.

"Yes. Your aunt Bri had a late flight, and I stayed with her. The restaurant in the hotel was open, but she was anxious to see you."

"I had to make sure my niece was all right. I guess I can survive another hour before my stomach starts scratching my back. Something better be open soon, though," Brianne said.

"I doubt it. I'm not sure how restaurants operate for holidays in Cali, but you probably won't find anything open around here except gas stations and liquor stores. Stop being stubborn and let me make breakfast for you and your friend," I tried offering again.

"Yeah, Tessa. Stop being stubborn," Brianne mimicked.

"Fine. If you don't mind, we'd appreciate it," Tessa agreed.

"It's not a problem. How about I head out now—wait, how did you ladies get here?"

"An Uber," they spoke simultaneously.

"Do you want me to wait or—"

"No, it's fine. We can take an Uber to your place. Can you text me the address?"

I hadn't had a chance to experience Tessa's stubbornness, but she definitely had it bad. Instead of trying to change her mind, I sent her my address, packed up everything I'd arrived with, and said my goodbyes, promising Cyrah for what seemed like the tenth time that I'd bring her a plate from Thanksgiving dinner.

Tessa

CYRAH MUST HAVE been waiting for her father to leave because he wasn't gone five seconds before she started in on me.

"Why are you giving him attitude?" she asked with more bite than she'd ever used with me.

"What are you talking about?"

"You know what I'm talking about, Mom. As soon as you walked in, the tension could be cut with a knife. You were giving him attitude while he was being nothing but nice to you."

"I wasn't trying to give him attitude, Cyrah. If that's the way it came off, it wasn't intentional. What goes on between me and Cypress—"

"You mean my daddy?"

Brianne had to cover the gasp that escaped her mouth when Cyrah interrupted me. I took a deep breath before continuing.

"Yes, whatever goes on between me and your father is our business."

"I think it's my business just as much as yours, but it's fine if you don't want to tell me. However, I will say, if anyone should have an attitude, it's him."

I couldn't believe the way Cyrah was talking to me. Her tone and demeanor were about to land her back in the emergency room.

"Little girl, I—"

197

"Tessa, let me talk to you in the hallway for a second," Brianne said, pushing me toward the door and not allowing me to answer.

"Why'd you do that?" I griped.

"Because I knew you were about to go off, and I couldn't have that. You know you aren't Cyrah's favorite person right now."

"I don't care. I'm still her mother, and she's not about to talk to me like I'm one of her little friends."

"I understand, but give her some grace. This is unlike her, but she's still very much in her feelings about everything. Now, the doctor is coming down the hall. We'll go back in there, hear what he says, and head out. Maybe you should give her tomorrow to process and come back Saturday."

"What? That doesn't even sound right. I'm her mother, and—"

"And she's not fucking with you right now. No worries, though, because her *daddy* will be here if no one else is."

I could have choked her for that last comment, but she pushed the door to Cyrah's room, allowing the doctor to enter while we trailed behind.

"Ms. Howard, how are you today?"

I tuned out while Cyrah and Dr. James conversed. My mind was on all that had transpired since I entered Cyrah's hospital room. Cypress being here surprised me, and I was shocked that he'd cooked and delivered her a hot breakfast. Neither the surprise nor the shock was in a bad way. I guess I should say I was in awe. Less than twenty-four hours ago, that man found out he was the father of a grown woman, and he stepped right into the role with no problem.

"The swelling has gone down quite a bit, so I will schedule your casts to be put on tomorrow. Are you ready?" Dr. James was saying as I tuned back in.

"I'm ready to be released, so yes," Cyrah replied.

The minute Dr. James was gone, Cyrah directed her attention to me.

"Look, Mom. I've never been upset with you, so this is a weird space for me. I apologize for being rude before. I'm dealing with a lot between the accident, broken bones, getting a blood transfusion, and finding out my professor is my father. I'm mad at you, and I need to be able to go through my emotions without being worried about our relationship."

"I respect that, Cyrah, but I won't allow you to disrespect me."

"Then give me a few days to miss you because seeing you upsets me right now."

It felt like I'd been stabbed in the heart, but I'd honor Cyrah's wishes. Without responding to her requests, I kissed my daughter on the forehead, grabbed my purse and coat, and left. Brianne remained with Cyrah for a few minutes before joining me in the hallway. Immediately, she embraced me, and I broke down in her arms.

"It's okay, sis. Cyrah loves you too much to be angry at you for long."

"I hope so," I mumbled. "Let's go."

"I don't think I've ever had French toast this damn good," Brianne praised.

"What about mine?" I asked, slightly offended.

"I said what I said, friend. This man must have the magic touch because I never thought I'd have French toast better than yours."

Brianne did not care about sparing my feelings as she stuffed her face. I should be mad at her, but she was right; Cypress's French toast was better than mine. I'd never admit that out loud, though.

"See if you ever get me to cook for you again," I threatened.

"Cypress, you'll have to give me your Cali address so I can hit you up when I visit. If Tessa won't cook for me, I'll pay you to do it."

Cypress laughed. "No payment would be necessary. I enjoy cooking."

"Really? So does Tessa, but I guess you know that already."

"Yes, we have that in common," he agreed.

"I see you still have that necklace. Do you remember giving it to me as insurance that I'd get Tessa back in one piece?"

"She told me her name was Marie, by the way. I don't recall giving it to you, but I remember panicking when I realized I didn't have it the following day. Eventually, it came back to me, and I ran from our hotel to yours, which was probably half a mile, to get it. If I'd come home and told my father I traded this necklace for some pussy, I wouldn't be sitting here today."

"Well, you got a lot more than pussy," she mumbled.

"Bri, chill out," I scolded and received a shoulder shrug.

"It's cool. She's not lying," Cypress said.

"You seem to be stepping into this role smoothly," Brianne continued.

"I haven't had to do much; it hasn't been a full day. Besides, Tessa did all the hard stuff already."

"You got that right, and don't you forget it. However, you're off to a great start. Cyrah already loves you."

"The feeling is mutual."

My best friend and my daughter's father conversed as if I weren't in the room. I had nothing to add, so I listened without interruption. Cypress looked alarmed when someone began banging on his door.

"He didn't look like he was expecting guests," Brianne said.

"Jade has the access code, so I doubt she'd be doing all that when she can simply let herself in. Anyone else would need to buzz him, or the front desk would notify him."

When we heard a woman's elevated voice, we looked at each other with wide eyes and hightailed it to the front door.

"I thought we were better than this, Cypress," Emery shouted.

"It's Thanksgiving, Emery. Do you *really* want to do this today?"

"Rich got his results two days ago and didn't waste a second sending me a picture of them. He's not the father, so it's you!" she shouted.

I didn't know how Emery's words affected Cypress, but they were like a gut punch to me, and it wasn't my baby. Cypress wasn't the kind of man who wouldn't take care of his responsibilities, but I knew he prayed Emery's baby wasn't his. Being connected to her for the next eighteen years was the last thing he wanted to do.

"I haven't gotten my results back yet. I'll reach out to you when I do."

Being the gentleman he was, Cypress didn't slam the door in her face, but his hand was positioned on the door, prepared to close it.

"You don't need to look at the results because if Rich isn't the father, this baby is yours."

"Considering I don't trust you or Rich, I'll need some medical proof. Until then, I refuse to assume the responsibility. Now, if you would leave, that would be great."

"Oh my God! I had no idea you were such an asshole. I can't wait to take you to court for child support. I'm taking you for every penny and then some," Emery ranted.

She finally left, allowing him to close the door. He leaned against it and released a deep breath. Cypress had been through so much since I'd met him, but the past twenty-four hours had been brutal. I wanted to console him but didn't know if it was my place.

"Cypress, are you okay?" I asked.

"No."

He pushed himself off the door and disappeared to another part of his condo. I assumed it was his bedroom. Brianne looked at me with expectant eyes, but I didn't know why.

"Go to him. He needs you right now."

"But—"

"Tessa, go check on that man."

Brianne was right. Cypress and I may not have been involved romantically anymore, but we were still friends, right?

Cypress

I COULDN'T—NO, I *WOULDN'T* believe God would deal me a hand like this. I made some bad choices in my younger years, but nothing I did warranted this kind of punishment. Emery was not the woman I thought she was. I loved, trusted, and gave her my loyalty, only for her to turn around and betray me in the most disrespectful way. The thought of having created a child with her made me sick to my stomach.

"Cypress," I heard Tessa whisper as I sensed her presence.

I was sitting on the edge of my bed with my head down, looking at my hands. I didn't feel like talking, but didn't want to be alone. When Tessa was close enough for me to reach her, I wrapped my arms around her waist and buried my face in her chest. She returned my embrace, lovingly caressing my head.

"I'm sorry you're going through this. I know this isn't what you hoped and prayed for, but you must look at the bright side."

I couldn't imagine a bright side. If I took Emery to court and fought for full custody, I'd have to raise our child alone. If we had equal custody, I'd have to figure out how to be a present father from halfway across the United States. Either way, I'd have to deal with Emery on some level, and right now, I could easily say I hated that woman.

"Have you checked your email?"

The last time I'd checked my email was before I got out of bed this morning, so I shook my head, indicating that I hadn't.

"Why don't you check it? I know Emery said what she said, but you need to confirm she's telling the truth."

I was hesitant to take Tessa's advice because I didn't want confirmation that Emery was, in fact, telling the truth. All I wanted to do was bury myself between Tessa's thick, warm, juicy thighs. The thought of being inside her had my dick rocking up. My hands moved from her waist to her ass, then back up to her waist before slipping underneath the sweater.

"Cypress, what are you doing?"

Tessa gripped my arms to stop them from moving. Begrudgingly, I adhered, but I wasn't happy about it.

"I don't mind supporting you, but you made yourself very clear last night. Pumping the brakes means you no longer have access to me in that way. I'm sorry."

I nodded in understanding, knowing I was wrong as hell for trying her but also knowing I would've been all in had she been on board.

"Where's your phone?" she asked.

I released my hold on her and retrieved my phone from the front pocket of my sweats. After unlocking it and opening the email app, I handed it to Tessa. As she scrolled through my emails, I held my breath.

"I don't see anything from the company. Did you check your junk mail?"

I shook my head. I hadn't even considered checking the email there because I assumed it wouldn't go to my junk mail since the company was legitimate.

"Here it is. Do you want me to open it?"

I nodded, becoming more anxious by the second. Tessa held my future in her hands, and I could not look at her as she prepared to give me my fate.

"Cypress, it says there is zero percent chance the child is yours."

I heard her, but it took a moment for me to process it.

"Say that again."

"The baby *isn't* yours, Cypress."

I shot off my bed and wrapped Tessa in my arms, lifting her from the floor and spinning her around. When I put her down, I cupped her face and pressed my lips against hers. I was grateful when she allowed me to kiss her, but when I got carried away, she put a stop to it.

"I'm sorry, baby. I—"

"It's fine, Cypress. I understand your excitement, but don't do that again," she warned.

"You sure? Kissing you is one of my favorite things to do."

"I'm positive. Hey, we should head to your parents' house. Your mother probably could use a few extra hands."

I studied Tessa for several seconds, wondering if putting our relationship on hold was the right thing to do. My gaze must have made her uncomfortable because she started heading for my bedroom door. I grabbed her wrist and pulled her body against mine, embracing her. She felt so good in my arms, but her body was tense. I knew I was sending mixed signals, but damn, my emotions were all over the place.

"Thank you for being here for me."

She looked up at me and smiled. "We're still friends and the parents of a great young lady, if nothing else, right?"

"Right. Let's get going."

"You ladies are a breath of fresh air," my mother commented, referring to Tessa and Brianne. "Cypress, which one of your cousins is suitable for Brianne so we can keep her around?"

"Hold on, Mama Boone. Are they fine? Because I'm shallow like that," Brianne said.

Tessa, Jade, my parents, and I were the only other people present, and we laughed at Brianne's honest comment. Dinner was set to start in two hours, so my family members would probably start arriving in about an hour. My mother and Jade were grateful when I showed up with the ladies. They had everything under control but welcomed the extra hands. Jade was feeling better, but her body was sore, much like Cyrah's, so my mother limited what she asked her to do.

"We got great genes on both sides as far as looks are concerned, but I can't lie to you; some of our nephews ain't worth a damn," my mother replied honestly.

"That's cold, Ma. How you gon' talk about my cousins like that?" I teased.

"I love my nephews, but I'm a woman first. I wouldn't set her up to have her heart broken with some of those buzzards."

Everyone broke out in laughter again. When we settled down, my father added his two cents while he relaxed in his recliner. The main floor of the house had an open concept, making it easy to communicate from room to room.

"Maybe you shouldn't try to play matchmaker, Miriam. If one of the boys catches her eye, or vice versa, just let it flow. You never know; she might be the one to make him want to do right."

"Preach, Papa Boone. All it takes is the right woman," Tessa commented.

Our eyes connected as she spoke, but she quickly looked away. There was no tension between us, but we'd been busy in the kitchen since we arrived.

"Tessa, can I talk to you for a minute?" I asked.

"Sure," she replied, drying her hands on a towel.

I led her into the hallway and to one of the guest rooms.

"What's up?"

"How do you feel about telling my parents about Cyrah today?"

"Right now?" I nodded. "You want me with you when you tell them?"

"That was always the plan, wasn't it?"

She giggled nervously, "Not if I had a choice."

"You planned to leave me hanging? Damn, Tessa."

"After the way you and Cyrah handled me after I told you, I don't think I can handle anyone else judging me like that so soon."

"My parents won't judge you. They aren't like that. I already know my mother will be ecstatic."

"What about your father?"

"Pops goes with the flow. They've already welcomed both of you into the family. Knowing that Cyrah is their blood granddaughter will just sweeten the deal."

"And the rest of your family?"

"My family is cool. They'll probably give me more shit about how this situation came about than you, and half of them shouldn't be judging anyway."

She released a deep sigh. "Are you sure?"

"I'm positive."

I could tell she wasn't in complete agreement, but she eventually gave in. I wasn't worried because I knew my parents well enough to know how they'd react. Tessa had nothing to worry about.

Tessa

"I NEED A MINUTE," I told Cypress after agreeing to tell his parents that Cyrah was his daughter.

"Okay, but if you take too long, I'm gonna think you snuck out," he joked.

"If I had somewhere to go, that would be a possibility."

He kissed my forehead before leaving me in the guest room. I thought about what could go wrong once his parents learned that Cyrah was their granddaughter. The Boones were nice people, and I didn't think they would kick me out of their house, but I couldn't help but wonder if they'd be upset that I didn't say something sooner.

"Well, I guess I may as well get it over with," I whispered as I returned to the kitchen.

"You good?" Brianne asked when I returned.

She could probably tell from my expression that I wasn't good, but I lied and told her I was okay.

"Pops, can you mute the TV for a few minutes," Cypress asked. "Tessa and I want to share something with you and Ma."

Mr. Boone did as his son asked without asking any questions. Mrs. Boone stopped what she was doing in the kitchen and gave Cypress her full attention.

"Are you having a baby?"

"Ma, why would you ask that?" Jade questioned. "Whenever someone says they have news, it's not always about a baby."

"Girl, hush. I ask what I want," Mrs. Boone clapped back at her daughter.

Jade had been standoffish with me, but not enough to alert her parents that something had gone awry between us.

"It's not that, Ma," Cypress told her.

"Well, somebody around here is pregnant. I dreamed about fish two nights in a row," Mrs. Boone announced.

"Oop!" Brianne exclaimed, covering her mouth.

"It's not me," Jade assured. "The doctors tested for it in the ER yesterday, not that I was worried."

Now, all eyes were on Cypress and me. I chose not to comment, and he redirected them back to why he asked for their attention.

"About twenty years ago, when I was a sophomore at UIC, Rich, and a few other of my classmates, and I went to Cali for spring break."

"I remember that trip. It was the first time you'd travel anywhere without us," Mr. Boone said.

"It sure was, and I was worried sick the whole time. I never did trust Rich, and it took a long time, but his true colors were finally exposed," his wife added.

Mrs. Boone expressed her long-time dislike of Rich at the hospital while Mr. Boone had surgery. She wasn't surprised at all when she learned he and Emery had been sleeping together.

"Can I finish?" Cypress asked.

"Go ahead, son. We won't interrupt you anymore," his mother assured.

"I'll get straight to the point. Tessa and I had a sexual encounter back then, and Cyrah is my daughter."

Neither of Cypress's parents responded how I expected. Mr. Boone was the first to say something.

"I guess you'll be getting that she-shed next summer," he said.

"Hallelujah!" Mrs. Boone praised. "I get my sheeee-shed. I get my sheeee-shed."

She pranced around the kitchen, singing and doing the happy dance. Only she and her husband knew why she was so excited. The rest of us stood by, confused, waiting for one of them to explain her excitement or address the news Cypress had just broken, which honestly seemed like an afterthought.

"Did either of you hear me?" Cypress asked.

Mrs. Boone approached Cypress and wrapped her arms around him. When she released him, she took his hands and looked up at him with the sweetest smile.

"Son, you're only confirming what I already knew. Your father has to build me a she-shed out back because I already told him Cyrah was your daughter."

"You went to Pops with your suspicions?" Cypress questioned.

"I sure did, and he thought I was crazy."

"I thought you were crazy before that, baby, but when you brought this to me, I knew you'd lost it."

"Really, Robert Boone?" Mrs. Boone put her hand on her hip and walked toward her husband. "You know you're in my care for several weeks. You're a brave man calling me crazy in front of company."

He grabbed her by the waist and pulled her onto his lap. Mrs. Boone was petite, so I doubt his actions would compromise his healing.

"It's your craziness that makes me love you more, baby," he told her before kissing her cheek.

"You'd better have cleaned that up, but you also better watch it."

She remained on his lap while he explained why he'd be building a she-shed next summer.

"Your mother proposed a pretty hefty wager when I dismissed her suspicions, and I should've known she was on to something because she was so confident she wouldn't lose. I'll admit, I noticed the resemblance between Cyrah and Jade right away, and your mother even pointed out the birthmark, but the whole idea seemed farfetched, and I chalked it up to being a strange coincidence. You couldn't pay me to believe you moved to California and reunited with the child you never knew you had. This woman is rarely wrong, but I thought I might've had her on this one. Congratulations, by the way."

"Thank you, Pops. That's not exactly how it happened, but yeah, I have a nineteen-year-old daughter. I thought there would be much more fanfare when I told you, but I guess your reaction could have been much worse."

"This is wonderful news, son. Tessa, you've been quiet. Are you okay?" Mrs. Boone questioned my silence.

Nothing was wrong, per se, but I was speechless during their whole exchange.

"I'm fine, Mama Boone."

"Can I ask you one question?"

"Of course. What would you like to know?"

"Have you known all along?"

I knew that was too easy. I didn't mean to start crying, but the tears began falling without my permission. Brianne started in my direction, but I held up my hand and shook my head because I didn't need consoling. I had no idea why I was crying and allowed the tears to flow as I spoke my truth.

"If you mean, have I known for the past twenty years, absolutely not, but I have known since our first date. To save you from having to ask, I recognized Cypress immediately, but I could tell he didn't remember me. Honestly, our first date didn't seem like the best time to tell him. Can you imagine one of your students setting you up on a date with her mother and having a woman you think you've never seen before tell you that the same student who arranged the date is the daughter you share?"

Mr. Boone spoke up, adding humor, saying, "Yeah, that would definitely ruin the moment."

"Robert, please," she scolded her husband.

"Papa Boone is right, though. I tried to tell him on the second date but was interrupted when he got news of Papa Boone's heart attack. I tried again on my first night in Chicago, but Emery paid him a surprise visit with more bad news. No time ever seemed like the right time, and I've apologized to him and our daughter for delaying sharing this information, and now I'm apologizing to the three of you."

I wanted to make sure Jade knew she was included in my apology. When I looked in her direction, she gave me a weak smile. It wasn't much, but I hoped it meant we were cool again. Mrs. Boone left her husband's lap to come and wrap her arms around me in the warmest and most loving hug I think I'd ever received, causing me to shed more tears.

"There's no need to apologize to us, Tessa. You handled it the way you thought was best, and the important thing is we know now. I don't like to dwell on the past because the future is so bright," Mrs. Boone consoled me.

"I'm fine, Mama Boone. I don't know why I'm crying."

"There's nothing wrong with shedding a few tears," she told me.

"Papa Boone said something that made me reflect on our situation. For the first time, I thought about the enormity of what happened. I knew nothing about Cypress, and he knew nothing about me. We unknowingly created a child and went our separate ways, only to be reunited twenty years later. I feel so blessed that God saw fit for us to cross paths again. My daughter will now have the opportunity to form a bond with the man who helped me create her. She has a loving family who has accepted her with open arms, no questions asked. This truly means everything to me, and I thank you from the bottom of my heart."

Our emotional moment was cut short by the arrival of the first guests. I went to the bathroom to get myself together, and Brianne was waiting for me when I opened the door to leave.

"You good, sis?" she asked.

"I am, but thanks for checking. My emotions got the best of me because I was expecting his parents to react much worse to the news. Mr. and Mrs. Boone are angels."

"They are some of the nicest people I've encountered in quite awhile. However, I can imagine how this feels for you because of your mother."

"Bingo. I wish Cyrah weren't in the hospital so she could be here to meet all her people."

"It sucks, but this is her family. They aren't going anywhere," she reminded me.

Yeah, this is Cyrah's family.

Cypress

MY FAMILY TOOK up every inch of my parents' house, but it was shaping up to be one of the best Thanksgivings I'd had in a long time. The food was so good I almost ate myself into a stupor. It had been nearly two hours since I ate my last bite, and my stomach still felt like it was about to explode. Tessa and Brianne fit in like they'd been a part of my family for as long as I had. The only thing missing was Cyrah.

While my cousins started a few games, I stepped outside to call Cyrah. It was nearing six in the evening, and I was sure she was hungry. Her cell phone was damaged in the car accident, and the only way to reach her was through the direct number to her hospital room. I became concerned when she didn't answer the first time, but I waited a few minutes before calling back and was relieved when she answered.

"Hello."

"Hey, baby girl. You sound tired."

"Hey, Daddy. I'm not tired, but the nurses were here helping me use the bathroom. I don't know how I'll manage once I'm released."

"It may be a challenge, but we'll figure it out. How's your day been?"

"Uneventful. Watching TV while going in and out of sleep."

"Your body needs the rest to help you heal. Are you hungry?"

"Starving."

"Okay. Give me about an hour, and I'll be there with your food. I'll have your mother tell me your favorites."

"Okay, and don't forget dessert."

"I gotchu, baby girl."

I ended the call and went back inside to find Tessa. When my eyes landed on her, she was cornered by my cousin, Darrin. Without hearing a word coming from his mouth, I knew he was trying to spit game. That was his MO, but he was harmless because we'd yet to meet a woman who took him seriously. My mother introduced Tessa and Brianne as Cypress's new girlfriend and her best friend, so I didn't know why Darrin was trying to shoot his shot with the woman who was supposed to be mine. Any woman who wasn't blood-related wasn't safe around him.

"Aye, cuz, move around," I told him.

"Chill, cuz. I'm thinking about moving to the West Coast and had a few questions for your girl," he lied.

"Nigga, your ass won't even move to the West Side of Chicago. Move around," I repeated.

He whispered something to Tessa I couldn't hear and went to bother someone else.

"Sorry about that," I said, apologizing for Darrin.

"I'm not even sure what *that* was, but thanks for the save."

"You seem to be enjoying yourself."

"I am. Your family has proven to be among the most likable people I've ever encountered. Granted, I don't have a lot of experience with large families. I wish Cyrah were here to meet them all, but I'm glad you didn't tell everyone about her today. It'd be a bit overwhelming."

"I agree, but I told you my family was good people. Of course, we have a few knuckleheads like Darrin, but he's not a threat.

Speaking of Cyrah, I spoke with her a few minutes ago, and she's hungry."

"I can make her plate if you're about to leave now," she offered.

"Can you? I'm leaving in about thirty minutes."

"I'll go do that now."

She slid past me and headed to the kitchen. Before I could follow her, my mother stepped in front of me.

"What aren't you telling me?" she questioned.

"About what?"

"You and Tessa. You've been acting strange with each other all day."

"There's nothing to tell, Ma."

"Don't lie to me, boy," she said, poking me in the chest. "I'm not blind. What did you do?"

"What did *I* do? Why does it have to be my fault?"

"Because it's *always* the man's fault in some way, shape, or form. Now spill it."

"Not this time. She's the one who waited until Cyrah needed a blood transfusion to tell me I was her father."

"Is that how you found out?"

Although my parents knew that Jade and I had donated blood for Cyrah's transfusion, they didn't know the details of how Tessa told me I was Cyrah's father.

"Yeah, but I don't want to get into all of that right now. Tessa is making Cyrah a plate for me to take to the hospital."

"Cypress—"

"Ma, I promise we're good. There's nothing to worry about."

"Fine, I'll take your word for it and let you two figure it out," she conceded.

"Thank you. Let me say my goodbyes because I'm unsure how long I'll be gone. She's been alone all day and—"

"You don't have to explain, son. Go take care of my granddaughter and tell her I'm coming to see her tomorrow."

"Will do."

When I found Tessa in the kitchen, she was putting some desserts in a container.

"Where does your mom keep the plastic bags?" she asked.

"In the cabinet in a plastic bag like every other Black person you know."

We laughed at what everyone knew to be the truth. Tessa opened a few cabinets, and sure enough, there was a plastic bag full of plastic bags in the third cabinet she opened.

"Bingo," she exclaimed as she pulled one out of the bag.

When she finished packing up Cyrah's food, she handed that bag to me.

"Here you go. Brianne and I will catch an Uber back to the hotel if you're not back before we're ready to go."

"You're not coming to the hospital with me?"

She shook her head solemnly. "No. Cyrah requested I not visit her for a couple of days. You can have her all to yourself."

I knew Cyrah was upset with Tessa, but I was still shocked she'd made such a request. Tessa couldn't hide the hurt in her eyes, and I felt for her.

"I'm sorry about the tension between you two. I'm sure it'll blow over in a couple of days."

"I hope so. Give her my love."

"Of course."

No one cared that I was leaving because their attention was elsewhere, so I managed to leave the house without answering any questions, telling a few people I had to make a run. Most of the men and a few women were watching the football game. Two groups were playing spades, one was playing dominoes, passionate conversations were being had in every corner, and kids were doing what kids do.

Thirty minutes later, after stopping at the lounge down the hall to warm her food, I tapped on Cyrah's hospital room door, entering when I was given permission. The excitement on her face let me know she was anticipating my arrival. Like this morning, I placed the food on the mobile tray next to the bed to make it easier for her.

"Oh my goodness! The smell alone has my mouth watering," she said excitedly.

"Well, dig in," I urged.

Like this morning, she thoroughly enjoyed her meal. We talked about her plans after she was released.

"Of course, you'll be staying with me. I wouldn't have it any other way," I told her.

"I appreciate that, but I've been thinking about how I'll get back home. Do you know how much of a pain it'll be flying in this condition?"

I hadn't thought about how Cyrah would get home. Classes didn't start until the second week of January, so we had plenty of time, but I was sure she hadn't planned to stay in Chicago for that long.

"Before she decided to stay for Thanksgiving and have you join us, your mother and I talked about driving back."

"Driving back to Cali? How long does that take? A week?"

I laughed at her exaggeration. "About thirty hours, but we'd stop along the way."

Cyrah looked at me skeptically, and I could understand her hesitance.

"I think I'd rather take my chances on a plane. At least I wouldn't have to be in a car for two days."

"Well, you don't have to decide now. At this point, I don't know if it's still in your mother's plans anyway."

She let the moment pass without addressing that comment, then changed the subject.

"So, when do you plan to tell my grandparents about me? I might be a little more excited about them being my grandparents than you being my father. No disrespect."

I knew she was teasing from the tone of her voice, but I didn't doubt she was excited about her new grandparents. Cyrah was their first grandchild, and even though she was a full-grown adult, they would still spoil her rotten.

"We told them earlier today."

"How'd it go?"

"A lot better than I expected, but let me clarify. I knew they wouldn't be upset and would accept you with open arms. However, my mother noticed the resemblance between you, me, and Jade as soon as she laid eyes on you. She also noticed the birthmark on your arm."

I pushed up the sleeve of my hoodie and showed Cyrah my birthmark, which almost matched hers perfectly.

"Wow, I never noticed," she expressed in awe, looking down at her left arm. "This is so crazy."

"Your grandmother was so sure you were my daughter that she and your grandfather made a bet. When we told them, she was dancing around the house about the she-shed he has to build her next summer."

"I know that's right, and I know she'll hold him to it."

"Most definitely. Now that I know you're mine, I can't look at you without seeing myself. You really did steal my whole face."

"I did, and thank God you're good-looking because I'd be pissed if you weren't."

I loved my daughter's sense of humor and couldn't wait to discover what else there was to love about her. Visiting hours ended, but Cyrah wanted me to stay, and I did until she fell asleep.

Tessa

IT HAD BEEN a very long day, and by the time the Uber dropped us off at the hotel, it was almost ten p.m. Although the time wasn't late, we'd been up and on the go for over twelve hours. I wasn't up for much conversation and was grateful Brianne wasn't either. We could recap the day in the morning.

After a nice, hot shower, I fell asleep as soon as my head hit the pillow. It seemed like I'd only been asleep for a few minutes when my phone began to ring. I ignored it for as long as possible, but I answered after the person called back for a third time.

"Hello."

"Tessa, it's me, Tisha."

Hearing her name caused me to sit up in bed. Tisha was the property manager for Tesrah, and if she was calling me in the middle of the night, it had to be important.

"Is everything okay?"

"No one is hurt, but there was a fire."

I was wide awake now.

"A fire? Oh my God. Thank goodness no one was hurt. Do you know what happened?"

"Not yet, but it looks like the fire was contained to the apartment where it started. No other parts of the building have been damaged."

"That makes me feel better, but I hate this happened. I'll see if I can find a flight out—"

"No, Tessa. You don't have to come back yet. I have everything under control, but I wanted to inform you of the incident."

"Tisha, I can't let you handle this on your own. I'm not even sure something like this is in your job description. I'll let you know when I get a flight."

"Okay, but don't worry. Right now, we can't do anything but wait for the fire department to do what they do and tell us how the fire started."

"Thank you, Tisha. I'll see you soon."

I ended the call and looked at the time. It was one a.m., which meant I'd only been asleep for a few hours, and it was eleven p.m. in California. I fell back on the bed and released a deep sigh.

"Do you want to look for flights now or get a few more hours of sleep?" Brianne asked.

"Sorry to wake you."

"Girl, I was awake after the first round of rings and could hear the whole conversation. I'm glad no one is hurt, and the fire was contained."

"Yeah, me too. I'll look for some flights now."

An hour later, Brianne had decided she'd come to Black Elm until the weekend after my birthday, which was exactly one week away, and we were booked for a nine o'clock flight. I was so tired I easily returned to sleep. When my alarm went off at five a.m., I could've cried. Instead, I got up and prepared to head back to Black Elm.

"Are you sure about leaving without seeing Cyrah?" Brianne asked.

We'd discussed it last night, and I would honor her wishes. Brianne argued that Cyrah said that because she didn't know I'd have to leave town, and I agreed, but I still chose to honor her wishes.

"I'm sure, but we don't have time, anyway. I'll let Cypress know what's going on, and he can update Cyrah. When she's ready to talk to me, she'll reach out."

"If you say so," she hesitantly agreed.

We were headed to the airport in an Uber two hours later. It was approaching seven a.m., and I figured Cypress was still sleeping, but I knew once I made it to the airport, it would be a madhouse, and I wouldn't have a chance to call.

"Hello," he answered sleepily.

"Hey, Cypress. I'm sorry to wake you. There was a fire in an apartment in one of my buildings, so Brianne and I are headed to Black Elm."

"Oh shit. Was anyone hurt?"

"No, no one was hurt, and the fire was contained to the apartment. No other parts of the building were damaged."

"That's good."

"Yes, it is. Can you do me a favor and let Cyrah know? It's a little early to call her, and she's not talking to me right now, anyway."

"Tessa, I'm sure she'll talk to you if you call her about this or anything. I think you're taking this a little too far."

"It's fine, Cypress. We'll talk when she's ready, but make sure you let her know I left Chicago."

He sighed. "I can do that. Let me know when you land, and keep me informed about the fire."

"Will do."

When I ended the call, I could feel Brianne looking at me. I looked in her direction, and her lips were curled into a smirk.

"What's funny?"

"Nothing. Just listening to you and your baby daddy converse. He still wants you, you know."

I shrugged, not wanting to talk about Cypress and me.

"He kept his eyes on you all day yesterday. No matter where you were in that house, he wasn't far away or focused on anything else for too long."

"I was a guest in his parents' home, and he wanted to make sure I was okay."

"That's probably true, but I guarantee you that since he told you he wanted to pump the brakes, he's questioned if he did the right thing multiple times."

I thought about the moments we shared in his bedroom after Emery's visit. Things would've gone much further had I allowed them, but it wouldn't have been for the right reasons.

"He needs a minute to sort through his feelings. You know firsthand what he's been through over the past few weeks. The same reasons you have for holding off telling him about Cyrah are the same reasons you shouldn't have a problem giving him the space he needs to process."

"I don't have a problem with it, and I'm giving him space. I'm also not going to sit around sulking and waiting for him."

"I heard that, sis. I need to figure out what I want to do with Kendall's ass. He's called me multiple times a day since I hung up in his face, but I think we've run our course."

"Seriously, Bri? You're ready to move on because he didn't take you home for Thanksgiving?"

"You damn right."

"Maybe he's embarrassed by his family and doesn't want you to judge him."

"What are we, in middle school?"

By the time we'd arrived at the airport, Brianne hadn't decided if she'd start answering Kendall's calls or block him, and I was out of reasons to defend the man. As I expected, the airport was as busy as ever, yet we managed to make it to our gate just before boarding. I slept most of the four-hour flight, which made it seem much shorter. The car service we ordered was waiting when we retrieved our bags from baggage claim, and I gave the driver the address for Tesrah.

When I turned my phone on, several texts and a voicemail came through. The texts were from Cyrah, which I thought was strange because her phone was damaged in the accident. I'd gotten her service turned off and wondered how she was texting me. However, once I read her message, the mystery was solved. Cypress had gotten her a new phone and somehow transferred her number to his plan. I texted her back, letting her know we'd just landed and when I had more information about the fire, I'd call her. She replied right away with a thank you. When we arrived at Tesrah, I went to our management office and found Tisha talking to a firefighter.

"Oh, perfect timing. Captain Norvell, this is the owner of the property, Ms. Tessa Howard," Tisha introduced me.

"Hello, Captain. This is my best friend, Brianne. I apologize for being unavailable, but I was out of town. Do you have any new information?"

"It's not a problem. Ms. Stepney informed me that she'd spoken with you right after the fire, so you're up to date with what we knew then, correct?"

"Yes, sir."

"We're still investigating and have to rule out a few things. The investigation will take a few days, but I will tell you, based on what we saw and gathered last night, we think a candle, cigarette, or something of that nature started the fire. I've been doing this for over twenty years and can see certain things immediately. I'll just say a man-made fire, whether intentional or not, looks very different from, let's say, a fire started from faulty wiring. Does that make sense?"

"Yes, it does."

"This is important to know because it means you will likely not be held responsible. Once we finish our investigation, I'm 99 percent sure that won't happen."

"That's definitely good news."

"As the property owner, you're probably anxious to remodel, but you can't until the investigation is closed. Your insurance company will probably conduct an investigation. It'll be a month or two before anything can be done."

"I understand, and thank you."

"You're welcome. Here's my card. Please reach out if you have any questions. Someone from the station or I will be in touch."

When Captain Norvell left, Brianne and I remained in the office with Tisha. She'd informed me that the tenant declined the offer for a hotel stay, stating she would stay with her boyfriend, but she accepted the $500 gift card, which didn't surprise me. After a thirty-minute phone call with my insurance company, Tisha graciously gave Brianne and me a ride to my house. The past few days had been much more eventful than I was used to, and it felt good to be home.

Cypress

W HEN CYRAH'S WRIST and ankle swelling went down, the doctor did more X-rays. Although she still ended up getting a cast on her wrist, she was able to get a boot for her ankle. Instead of using crutches to get around, she was given a knee scooter. I hired a nurse to assist her with her daily hygiene. She'd been released four days ago, and things were going well so far.

My mother managed to wait until Cyrah was released from the hospital to see her. It worked out better because my father was able to come as well. They loved on Cyrah so much that I was concerned she might become overwhelmed, but she soaked up every bit of it. Watching the three of them bond, one would never know they'd only met a few days ago. There weren't enough words to express the joy I felt.

Jade was used to being the baby of our crew, and I thought she might be a little jealous of the attention our parents gave Cyrah. However, she was almost as bad as them when it came to showering Cyrah with love. She said "my niece" so many times she sounded like a broken record. Part of it may have been her guilt about the accident, but I honestly believed the girls had genuinely bonded in a short time. When Jade came to visit, she came with luggage and had only left to go to work and visit our parents.

"This won't work for much longer," Cyrah stated as we sat down for dinner.

"What won't work?" Jade asked.

"This food. I can't keep eating like this. It's already bad enough I can't move around, let alone exercise. I'm gonna gain a hundred pounds before I go home."

I'd been cooking breakfast and dinner every day, and not once did Cyrah decline the food I'd served.

"You know you don't have to eat everything I cook," I told her.

She frowned before saying, "And turned down all this deliciousness? I think not."

We laughed as she stuffed the fork into her mouth. I kept it simple tonight, making Cajun chicken pasta and garlic bread.

"How often does Tessa cook?" I asked.

"She typically makes breakfast and dinner a few times a week, but never on the same days. It's always been just the two of us, and we usually had leftovers. We either go out for dinner or order in twice a week."

"My parents are old and old school. There's always a hot meal on the table. When I was growing up, I didn't think they believed in eating at restaurants. My friends used to talk about going out to eat, and I couldn't even relate until I was in my late teens."

I laughed at Jade's comment, but it was true. Miriam Boone thought she could cook everything better than they could at any restaurant.

"How are things between you and your mom? Y'all good now?" I questioned.

"We've been talking at least once a day and texting a couple of times a day. She's been busy getting things in order for the apartment that caught fire. Things are slowly getting back to normal between us. Once I go home, I'm sure everything will fall back into place."

"That's good. I hoped you wouldn't hold on to that anger for too long."

"Isn't that the pot calling the kettle black?" Jade remarked.

"Tell 'em, Auntie," Cyrah added, using her favorite term of endearment for Jade. "When was the last time you talked to my mom?"

The last time Tessa and I communicated was when she texted me to let me know she'd landed safely. I told her we'd talk soon, but soon had yet to arrive. Three or four times a day, I'd been tempted to reach out to her, but something always stopped me.

"It's been a minute," I admitted.

"You still mad?" Jade pressed.

"I was only pissed for a hot second."

"Then why haven't you called her?" Cyrah questioned.

"Because during the hot second I was pissed, I might have told her we should pump the brakes."

"You might have, or you did?" Cyrah continued.

"I did, and she's holding me to it."

"As she should," Jade pointed out. "You might be my brother, but I'm a woman first. You can't put a woman on ice one day, then act like shit is cool the next."

"Honestly, that might have worked with the old Tessa before she quit her job, but not anymore," Cyrah added.

"I figured I could fix things when I returned to Cali."

"Tuh, you can wait if you want to, big bro, but if I were Tessa, I wouldn't give you the time of day."

"You might be an afterthought by then, Dad."

Although I still loved to hear Cyrah call me Dad, I didn't like what she had to say this time. She knew her mother better than I did, the new and old versions of her, so I decided to get my act together if my end goal was to be with Tessa. I'd be sick if she moved on while I sat around twiddling my thumbs.

As I was about to respond, the buzzer sounded. I wasn't expecting any guests because my parents told me they weren't visiting today. The last couple of unexpected visits I had were from Emery, and I hoped it wasn't her disrupting our evening. This time, I looked at the screen on the intercom and groaned when I saw Emery. Luck wasn't on my side tonight.

"How can I help you, Emery?" I asked through the intercom.

"You know why I'm here, Cypress."

I felt a presence behind me and turned to see Jade. Cyrah was headed toward me on her scooter.

"I don't need any backup," I told them.

"You can't snatch her up if she gets crazy, but I can," Jade responded.

"You don't get cool points for beating up a pregnant woman, Jade."

"Pregnant?"

This was news to my little sister because Tessa and I had left that tidbit of information out.

I couldn't respond because Emery laid on the buzzer. If I refused to see her, I'd probably have to call the police to get her to leave, so I pressed the button, allowing her to enter. I opened the door and waited for her to arrive to keep her from banging on it. As soon as Jade saw Emery's protruding belly, she commented.

"Cypress, if that's your baby, Mama gon' disown you from the family," she said.

"This is definitely your nephew, so you better get used to seeing me around," Emery taunted.

"Actually, Emery. I forgot to send you a screenshot of my test results. Let me do that right now."

I took my phone from my pocket and swiped through it until I found what I was looking for. After unblocking her number, I sent her the text and waited for her phone to chime with a smug look on my face. Emery received a notification, and she dug her phone out of her coat pocket.

"I don't need to look at these results because I know this is your baby, but if it'll make you happy . . ."

I focused on her face as she opened the text and then studied the results, recognizing exactly when she read the results, stating I was not the father.

"Where'd you get this from? This can't be real."

"It's real. Now that we've cleared that up, I need you to forget Cypress Boone exists."

"But—"

"But nothing, Emery! If I never see you again, it will be too soon. I was loyal to your ass for three years while you were out here fucking my best friend and only God knows who else. Get the hell on and go figure out who fathered that demon seed of yours. If you come anywhere near me or my family again, I'm gon' let Jade beat your ass like she's been wanting to."

I didn't even bother to exert enough energy to slam the door, opting, instead, to close it quietly. When I turned around, two pairs of eyes were staring me down.

"You got some explaining to do, big bro."

"Yeah, Daddy."

The last thing I wanted to do was talk about Emery, but this would be the last time.

"Damn, Cy. You've been dealing with a lot. I'm sure finding out about Rich and Emery was devasting, but to know how long they'd been messing around, then for her to try and pin a baby on you . . . if I'd known all this ten minutes ago, I would've—"

"She's pregnant, Jade," I reminded her.

"Oh yeah. That's okay. After she drops that load, it's on sight."

I chuckled, but Jade was serious. "Leave that woman alone. I guarantee you her Karma is already coming."

"I think I owe my mother an apology," Cyrah announced. "After hearing all that, I can understand why she hesitated to tell you about me."

"Girl, I should apologize too because I was salty as hell with her at the hospital when she dropped that bomb," Jade agreed.

"I think we all owe her an apology."

It wasn't until I shared everything with Jade and Cyrah that I could see my situation from Tessa's perspective. She had no idea how I would handle the news of Cyrah being my daughter, especially considering what I'd been dealing with. She tried to protect me in her own way, and I dismissed her for attempting to do so.

"I think she'll forgive us easily," Cyrah offered. "But you . . . You need to do some kind of grand gesture."

"A grand gesture? I can't simply tell her I was wrong and—"

"No, sir. I'm sure you hurt her feelings, so you need to do more than admit you were wrong and apologize," Jade told me.

"I don't have a clue of what I can do."

"That's why we're here," Cyrah said with a grin, rubbing her hands together. "And I'll call Auntie Bri and see if she has any ideas."

Tessa

WHY DO I *feel like shit?* Today was my fortieth birthday, and I woke up tired and sluggish. *Is this a preview of what my forties will be like?* I'd heard things about what starts to happen to your mind and body once you hit forty, and nothing I'd heard was particularly good.

Maybe it wasn't the entering of a new decade that had me wiped out. For the past few days, I'd been dealing with the aftermath of the apartment fire at Tesrah. Between communicating with the fire department, who found that the fire was started by a candle the tenant left burning, my property insurance company, the tenant's renter's insurance company, and getting estimates for remodeling, I'd put in more work than I ever did at BEU. Brianne helped as much as she could, but my friend had no patience or business sense, so she wasn't much help.

It probably didn't help that I was up until well after midnight last night. Ever since I'd received the results from Know Your Roots, the possibility of being related to the family that owned and operated Truth Sanctuary had been in the back of my mind. I didn't want to get my hopes up, but I couldn't help but be a little excited. After Brianne had retired to the guest room for the night, I started researching on the internet and social media to find out as much about the Truth family as possible. However, aside from the history of how Truth Sanctuary was started and everyday business-related news and posts, there wasn't a lot of information available.

One other thing had been on my mind that I didn't want to admit, but I missed Cypress. While we hadn't been in each other's lives for very long, he was what I'd been missing, and I'd gotten used to his presence. We hadn't communicated since I told him I'd arrived home safely. He hadn't reached out to me, but I couldn't be mad at him because the phone worked both ways, and I hadn't called or texted him either. Although I had a lot of other things that could have dampened my mood and made me feel worn out, I was certain missing Cypress was the main culprit.

I yawned as Brianne barged into my room, singing the Stevie Wonder version of "Happy Birthday."

"Happy Birthday to ya! Happy Birthday to ya! Happy Birrrtthhdaaayy!"

"Girl, it is too early for your nonsinging ass to be up making so much noise," I griped as I turned over and pulled the blanket over my head.

"Tessa, it's your birthday, and we have plans. Get up and get dressed. You don't even have to shower."

Brianne telling me I didn't need to shower got my attention.

"Exactly *what* do you have planned that doesn't require me to bathe?"

"It's a surprise. You can shower if you prefer. I was just letting you know it's not necessary for where you're going."

"Woman, if you're about to have me doing something extra physical, count me out."

"Just get up! I made you breakfast, and it's getting cold."

I didn't uncover my head until I'd heard Brianne leave the room. It wasn't as early as I'd thought when I rolled over and looked at the clock on my bedside table. Granted, since quitting my job, I typically still woke up before nine a.m. I'd actually gotten seven hours of sleep.

"I need to figure out why I'm so damn tired," I whispered, followed by another yawn.

I was moving slowly, but eventually, I made my way to the kitchen. Brianne had the table set with cheesy eggs, turkey bacon and sausage, assorted fruit, grits, and a stack of pancakes in the middle with a single candle in the center.

"I see you decided to shower, anyway," she commented.

"Oh my God, Bri. This is so sweet of you," I cried. "Thank you, best friend."

"You're welcome. Turning forty is a big deal, and I know this is the first birthday you've spent without Cyrah since she was born."

I'd been trying not to think about that. I knew our lives would be separate sooner or later, and we wouldn't always be able to spend our birthdays together, but I wasn't prepared for it to be this year.

"At least she called to apologize and isn't mad at me anymore," I reasoned.

"Yes, and you'll be besties again when she comes home."

"Eh, I don't know about that. She has her father and her aunt Jade now. I might be an afterthought."

"Don't start that mess on the morning of your special day. Bless the food so we can eat and get your day started."

While we ate breakfast, Cyrah called, and while we were on, a special delivery from her of a dozen roses and an arrangement of chocolate-covered fruit arrived. I was brought to tears when I read the card, which let me know we were in a good place:

Happy Birthday to the world's most amazing mom. I can't thank you enough for all the love you showered me with and everything you sacrificed raising me alone. You will forever be the center of my heart. ~ Cyrah

I was disappointed when I didn't hear from Cypress, but I wasn't sure he knew today was my birthday. I didn't recall telling him the exact date, but I would've thought Cyrah had mentioned it. It wouldn't be right to hold it against him, so I didn't give it too much thought.

After breakfast, I was told to dress comfortably, so I slipped on some leggings and a BEU hoodie. Our first stop was Love Your Melanin, a Black-owned spa in Black Elm. If you were a person of color and needed a self-care day, LYM was the best place in town. They usually had a waiting list a mile long, so I wasn't sure how Brianne got us in, but by the time we left, I was grateful. I didn't realize how much my body needed to be pampered.

We started in the steam room before soaking in a warm bath filled with heavenly oils and an assortment of salts. The bath was followed up with a body scrub and massage, after which we showered. We had facials and pedicures done simultaneously, something I'd never experienced and would recommend to everyone in the future, followed by manicures. Finally, I had my hair silk pressed for the first time in fifteen years, which was when I began wearing my natural hair. I was amazed it reached the middle of my back even after trimming my ends.

"Brianne, thank you so much for today. It's truly been everything."

"You're welcome, and I must agree with you."

"How did you get us in on such short notice?"

"What makes you think this appointment hasn't been scheduled for months?"

"Because I've known you for over twenty years, and if last minute was a person, it'd be you."

"Oh, it's like that? After all the trouble I went through to make today special, *this* is how you treat me?"

"Girl, hush. You know I'm not lying. Where are we headed now? I'd be happy if we returned to my house and had wine, popcorn, and pizza."

"Umm, absolutely not. It's still your birthday, and we got shit to do."

"Besides eating, what else is there to do?"

"Sit back and relax," she ordered.

After a light lunch, we ended up at a Black-owned boutique called Twice As Good, run by twin sisters. All the gowns were handmade by the sisters and were one of a kind.

"Bri, what are we doing here?"

"What do you think? You need a gown for tonight."

"A gown? For what? What's tonight?"

"Don't worry about all that, ma'am. Let's just go," she ordered, hopping out of the driver's side and heading for the entrance of the boutique.

Brianne had been chauffeuring me around all day in my car, so she left me sitting on the passenger side, trying to figure out why I needed a one-of-a-kind gown. Eventually, I got out and went inside. Brianne was already looking through the gowns, and after I saw a couple I liked and then looked at the price tag, she had to beg me not to leave.

"Girl, I am *not* spending this much money on a dress that I'll only wear once, and before you offer, I can't let you do it either. Let's just go to Neiman Marcus or Bloomingdale's."

"Not a chance. Now, we can stand here and argue all day, or you can pick out a gown. Those are your choices."

Reluctantly, I browsed through the boutique, and there wasn't a gown I saw that I didn't like. Ultimately, the price tag helped me make my decision because paying thousands of dollars for any item of clothing seemed asinine.

The gown I chose was an A-line symmetrical style, high in the front, accentuating my legs, low and flowy in the back, sleeveless on one shoulder, and a deep purple. The shoes and jewelry I selected were gold and perfectly accented the dress. Brianne had chosen a gorgeous black, fitted, sequined gown for herself.

"You look beautiful, sis. Now, come on—"

"Hold on, Bri. We're leaving the gowns on?"

"Yes, ma'am. Let's go!"

I was just about sick of this woman barking out commands. However, instead of voicing my annoyance, I took a deep breath and followed her outside. When she went in the opposite direction from my car, I was confused but didn't ask any questions. We ended up in a makeup bar two doors down from the boutique.

"Brianne?" a young Black lady with flawless makeup asked when we entered.

"Yes."

"Then you must be the birthday girl, Tessa. Happy Birthday."

"Thank you."

"I'm Katina, and I'll take care of you today. I love your dress and can already imagine the colors I'll use. Come with me, and I'll get you covered up so we don't ruin that beautiful dress, and I'll get started."

While Katina took me to one side of the bar, another young lady led Brianne to the other side. I wore makeup occasionally but had never had it done professionally. I was excited about how I would look. Katina kept me entertained while she worked on my face. She had a very bubbly personality, and it was contagious. The time flew by, and before I knew it, Katina turned me around to face the mirror.

"Damn! I look amazing!" I exclaimed.

"You looked amazing when you arrived. I simply enhanced your beauty."

"Thank you very much. You have very skilled hands, young lady."

"You're welcome, and thank you."

When I saw Brianne, I was in as much awe as I was when I saw my face. We were beautiful, and I wanted to know where we were going.

"Bri, will you please tell me where we're going now?"

"You'll find out soon enough, sis. Let's go!"

"Let's go! Let's go! Let's go! That's all you've been saying today. I'm sick of you."

"You won't be in a few minutes. You will crown me as the best friend ever. I will remind you of this moment and expect an apology."

"I look too good to be dealing with you and your nonsense. Let's go!"

This time, I walked outside ahead of her and was stunned into silence. A Lincoln Continental limo was parked in front of me, and standing next to it was Cypress, holding a bouquet of at least two dozen roses. He was dressed in all black from head to toe, his tuxedo fitting him like it was custom-made.

"Cypress, what are you doing here?"

"Happy Birthday, beautiful. These are for you."

He gave them to me, and I admired them for a moment. "Umm, thank you. I love them, but why are you here?"

Cypress

"I APOLOGIZE FOR HOW I treated you after you told me Cyrah was my daughter. It took some time, but I realized your delay in telling me was your way of protecting me. You knew I was dealing with a lot, and instead of trying to understand your reasons for handling it the way you did, I pushed you away."

"Cypress—"

"I'm ready to take my foot off the brakes and drive full speed ahead into whatever is brewing between us. I hope there's still a chance for us to continue building the bond we started. Our paths crossed again for a reason, and this time around, I don't want to lose the opportunity to make you mine permanently."

Before Tessa replied, Brianne approached her, removed the roses from her grasp, and whispered loud enough for me to hear, "Go get your man."

I appreciated her support and hoped Tessa took her friend's advice. As I apologized, I hoped she felt I was sincere and genuine and meant every word.

"I accept your apology, and I'd love to see where life takes us this time around."

I reached for her, and she quickly entered my arms. I buried my face in her neck and inhaled the beautiful scent I'd missed so much.

"Don't you dare mess up that makeup!" I heard Brianne yell, ruining our reunion.

"I've missed you," I whispered against her ear before pulling away.

"I've missed you too. My stubbornness wouldn't allow me to call."

I smiled because I knew that was the truth.

"I've been busy planning this day for you, and I didn't call you because I didn't want to mention something and ruin the surprise inadvertently."

"You did all this?" she asked, astonished.

"I did, with the help of Brianne and a couple of other special people."

I stepped away from her and opened the back door of the limo. When Jade stepped out, Tessa was surprised, but before she could react any further, Cyrah made her presence known.

"Hey, Mom."

Tessa's eyes widened when she heard Cyrah's voice, and she leaned into the car.

"Sweetheart! Oh my God!"

Since Cyrah wasn't very mobile in her condition, Tessa scooted into the limo to hug her. I couldn't see her face, but if I had to guess, there were a few tears. If her makeup was ruined, Brianne couldn't blame me. After Cyrah told me this would be the first of either of their birthdays they hadn't celebrated together, I made it my business to make sure they were together.

As expected, Cyrah needed extra assistance at the airport but said it wasn't as bad as she thought it would be. Because she needed a wheelchair, the three of us could board the plane sooner, and since we flew first class, she had plenty of legroom. The extra effort it took to surprise Tessa was definitely worth it.

"We have dinner reservations, so we need to get going," Brianne announced.

Jade and I got into the limo with Cyrah and Tessa while Brianne drove Tessa's car. We had a party room reserved at a restaurant called Sea of Flames. I'd never been there, but Cyrah assured me it was one of Tessa's favorite dining places. They specialized in spicy seafood dishes and typically had a waiting list. God must have been on our side the day I called because someone had just canceled their reservation for one of the party rooms, making it available for us.

"I can't believe y'all pulled this off. This has been the best birthday I've ever had," Tessa proclaimed.

"And your day isn't over yet, Mom."

"Are there more surprises?" she questioned.

"That's for us to know and you to wait and see," I told her.

She looked at me with the most beautiful smile. I wanted to kiss her lips and regretted not taking advantage of the moment when I had her in my arms.

"Brianne about drove me crazy with all the secrecy and demands she threw out. She's lucky I love her because I was ready to call an Uber."

"Yeah, she sent me a few texts telling me to come and get my mama," Cyrah shared.

"When did you get here?"

"Last night," the three of us answered simultaneously.

The limo driver announced that we'd arrived at our destination. I stepped out and helped Tessa and Jade do the same while the limo driver retrieved Cyrah's scooter from the trunk.

"Look at you with your fancy scooter," Tessa commented.

Today was the first time Tessa had seen Cyrah in person since Thanksgiving morning. Cyrah didn't get the cast, boot, or scooter until two days later.

"Isn't it cute? It's way better than crutches," Cyrah responded.

It had been almost a week, and she'd learned to maneuver the scooter very well.

"Did Cyrah tell you this was one of my favorite restaurants?" Tessa questioned as we approached the door.

"I know it seems like we've known each other longer than we have. Cyrah has offered to be my cheat sheet when needed until I know everything there is to know about you," I confessed.

"Is that right? I guess I'll have to recruit Jade to do the same for me."

"I'm sure she'd be more than happy to tell you all my secrets."

Somehow, Brianne beat us to the restaurant and waited inside with the hostess.

"That limo driver was driving slow and easy like Sunday morning," she complained. "They're making sure the room is set up, and then she'll take us back."

"Granted, this is probably one of the most upscale and expensive restaurants in Black Elm, but I didn't need to wear a—"

"Don't say it, Tess," Brianne warned.

"What? I'm just saying. You know I'm a fairly simple, low-maintenance woman. This dress cost—"

"Baby, do you feel beautiful?" I asked, cutting her off.

"Probably more beautiful than I've ever felt in my life."

"Then I don't care if we would play in the dirt. I wanted you to feel more beautiful than ever, and it sounds like I succeeded. The cost of the dress doesn't matter, so don't mention it again."

"Okay, Cypress. Let her know wassup," Brianne cosigned.

"Dang, big bro, I see you," Jade teased.

Tessa gave me a smoldering look, and I winked.

"Umm, hey, Bri. Let's go to the bathroom and check our makeup," Tessa requested, pulling Brianne by the arm.

I knew her well enough to know I had her hot and bothered. She didn't need to check her makeup because she looked flawless; she just needed to cool off.

"Dr. Cypress Boone, the room is ready. Please follow me."

As we followed the hostess to the back of the restaurant, we ran into Tessa and Brianne as they left the bathroom. I took her hand in mine and allowed Brianne to walk in front of us. Tessa needed to be the last person to enter the room for the surprise waiting inside.

"Have I thanked you for all of this?" she asked.

"No, but you can thank me later," I said with a smile and another wink.

I held her eyes until we entered the room, and everyone yelled, "Surprise."

Tessa was so startled she gripped my arm tightly and slammed her body against mine as she looked around. This was the most challenging part of her surprise. Tessa's only real friend was Brianne, so when Jade suggested throwing a surprise party for her, Cyrah didn't think it was possible. Tessa had a great working relationship with Tisha, Sharon, and Mika, and although they weren't friends, the ladies didn't hesitate to accept the invitation to the party. However, it would be a very small and intimate party with only eight people.

Jade had an idea, but it seemed farfetched because of the short notice. The timing didn't deter her, though. She created a group text with as many of our family members as she could think of, shared our idea with them, and asked who would attend the party at their own expense. Jade didn't include me in the text, and I didn't know how many could attend, so I was almost as surprised as Tessa when I saw the number of people in the room. I scanned the room and counted six of my cousins with their wives or girlfriends. It looked like a pretty good turnout if we included the photographer, DJ, a few of Cyrah's friends from school, and the waitstaff.

"What is—who—how did you get all these people here?" Tessa asked, perplexed.

"You ask too many questions. Are you surprised?"

"Am I? I don't think this birthday will ever be topped. Thank you so much."

"This was not all my doing. We can talk about those details tomorrow, and you can thank everyone who helped. Right now, let's celebrate you. Happy fortieth birthday, baby!"

Tessa intentionally thanked everyone in the room, including those we'd hired at the last minute, for making her birthday memorable. I saw nothing but pure joy on her face for the remainder of the night, except when I spotted her crying with Cyrah, Brianne, and Jade in the corner. I could only imagine what they were talking about, but I was sure some of it was Tessa expressing her gratitude to them for everything they'd done. Luckily, those conversations occurred during the latter part of the party, and she'd already taken a ton of pictures because her makeup was pretty much ruined.

I thought by the time we made it to my apartment and sent Cyrah and Jade to Tessa's, my lady would be exhausted. To my surprise and delight, she was hot, bothered, and ready to show me thanks.

Tessa

I KNEW I MISSED Cypress, but I didn't realize how much until his dick was inside me, stretching my slippery walls. I was on cloud nine following today's events. Never in my life had I felt so loved, especially at this moment. Cypress was skilled at providing pleasure. His kisses were soft yet filled with passion. His touch was gentle yet filled with aggression. His strokes were slow and deep yet filled with purpose. His gaze was piercing yet filled with . . . love? Lust, maybe, but not love. *Is it too soon for him to love me or for me to love him?*

I shook those thoughts from my head because I didn't want to get caught up in the idea that this man might love me already and I might just love him back. I closed my eyes because looking into his was what led me down the love rabbit hole. His gaze was overwhelming, and I couldn't handle it.

"Open," he demanded.

I knew he was referring to my eyes but pretended he meant my legs and spread them further apart.

"Oh, you want me to go deeper? Look at me and tell me you want me to go deeper."

It wasn't possible for him to go any deeper when I could already feel him in my chest. My head shook, discouraging him.

"Don't tell me no, Tessa. I said open your eyes and tell me you want me to go deeper. I want your eyes on me while my dick penetrates your soul, baby."

"Cypress, I can't look at you," I confessed.

"You can and you will."

Each time I denied him, it seemed his dick grew stiffer, thicker, and longer. If I didn't give him what he wanted, his manhood would hit my tonsils, but not in the way I was accustomed to. My eyes opened, and a smirk formed on his sexy lips.

"That's it, baby. Keep those beautiful orbs on your man."

"Oh God," I moaned with pleasure.

My climax was building, and the intensity of Cypress's gaze took me to the edge.

"Now tell me how deep you want it."

This man had to be crazy. He would split my thick ass in half if he went any deeper. My brain knew this, but my mouth and pussy were clearly willing to risk my life.

"Deeper," I whispered against my own will.

It was apparent whether or not I'd told him to go deeper, this nigga was looking for the buried treasure.

"You feel that?"

"Mmm."

"Nah, I said do you feel that?"

"I feel it, baby."

"You feel that love growing between us?"

"Yes, Cy, I feel it."

"Give me what I want, Tess. Drown my dick in them juices, baby."

Now, *that* was something he didn't have to ask twice.

We came up for air when the sun began to rise. I should've been exhausted after having such a long day, but I couldn't come down from my high. Cypress probably had enough energy to go a few more rounds, but my vagina and I were tapped out. As we lay in bed wrapped in each other's arms, I replayed the day's events over and over.

"I don't remember if I thanked you."

My head rested on his chest, and I could feel it rumble as he chuckled.

"If what we just did wasn't a thank-you, I can't wait to see what is."

"I'm glad you enjoyed it, but that's not what I meant. I meant verbally."

"You did that too," he said, laughing again.

I sat up and turned to face him in all my naked glory.

"Cypress, be serious for one second. I'm trying to tell you how much I appreciate you."

"Okay, I'm listening."

"Thank you. It's crazy it took forty years to have my first birthday party, but it was well worth the wait. I appreciate you for going through so much to make it special. No one has ever done anything like that for me. Besides Cyrah and Brianne, no one has ever made me feel so loved."

"You're welcome. I—"

"Wait, there's more. I also want to thank you for asking me to come back to your hotel room over twenty years ago. That was the first and only time I'd ever done anything like that until our first date. It may sound unbelievable, but it's true. I know Cyrah wasn't planned, but I never considered her a mistake. She may not have been created out of love, but she helped me to understand what love is. Cypress, having her gave me so much more than you could ever imagine. For the past twenty years, she's been my reason to live, be happy, strive for greatness, and not allow my mother to steal every possible ounce of joy. God knew I needed her, and there hasn't been a day I didn't thank Him and you for blessing me with such an angel."

"Damn, Tess, I don't know what to say. I regret missing so much of Cyrah's life, not only because she's my daughter but also because you had to raise her alone. I know you didn't always have the greatest support system, and it wasn't easy. Even though I had no control over it, I appreciate you not holding my absence against me."

I leaned forward and tried to leave a quick peck on his lips, but Cypress pulled me on top of him and deepened our kiss. I thought it would lead to more, but eventually, we separated, and I returned to his side. Sleep finally paid us a visit, and it was the best I'd slept since I left his bed in Chicago.

It was midafternoon when my bladder demanded attention. I was freshly showered and wrapped in a towel when I returned from the bathroom. Cypress was still asleep, and I did my best not to disturb him. After dressing in one of his T-shirts, I went to the kitchen to see what I could make for breakfast but came up short. His refrigerator was damn near empty.

"If we were at my house, this wouldn't be a problem," I mumbled.

I could either have some food from the grocery store delivered or order something from a restaurant. It only took me a moment to decide to order something from Breakfast and More, my favorite breakfast spot. My phone had been charging on the kitchen counter overnight, so I unplugged it and went to the living room, making myself comfortable on the couch. Pulling up the app, I perused the menu, and just as I began to make my selections, I heard Cypress's voice.

"What are you doing out here?" he asked with sleep in his voice.

"I didn't want to wake you. What do you want to eat?"

He'd made it to the couch and stood in front of me with his erection standing loud and proud.

"You."

Before I could process what he'd said, he was on his knees in front of me, my legs were on his shoulders, and his face was buried in my honeypot.

"Jeezus!" I hollered.

This man woke up and chose violence. The tongue-lashing he put on my pussy had me trying to scoot up the back of the couch. Cypress wouldn't let that happen, though. He wrapped his arms around my upper thighs, and all I could do was pray the walls were thick enough for the neighbors not to hear me. I came all over his face and had the audacity to think he was done.

"Turn over and get on your knees."

As if I were on autopilot, I turned over, got on my knees, and gripped the back of the couch as best I could. When he entered me from behind, he groaned so loud it shook my soul.

"Argh!"

One of his hands held onto my hip while he used the other to slap my ass cheeks as he pounded me from the back. The sting of each smack went straight to my libido, and my juices dripped down the inside of my thighs.

"Come with me, baby," he ordered.

I didn't try to fight it; my pussy didn't listen to me anyway.

Cypress

TESSA TALKED ABOUT her birthday celebration for several days and thanked Cyrah, Brianne, Jade, and me numerous times. It wasn't until Jade and Brianne flew back to their respective cities that Tessa stopped finding random reasons to talk about a moment she recalled from that day. It may have annoyed the others a tad bit, but I loved seeing her genuinely happy.

Although the next trimester didn't start until after the New Year, I had a lot to keep me busy. While in Chicago, I found time to put most of my winter clothing in storage bins and store them in the basement. Before leaving Chicago, I packed and shipped the rest of my clothing and other items I wanted to have in California, and they arrived days ago.

After much thought and consideration, I decided not to rent my condo as a regular rental property but as an Airbnb instead. It was in a great location, and per the research Tessa and I did before her returning to California, I'd make a lot more money. I hired a company to assist me in the process, and thus far, things have been moving forward smoothly. I may be able to list it as early as February.

The last step to make the move to Black Elm feel permanent was having transportation. When I found out Jade's car was totaled in the accident, I gave her my car. She was ecstatic for a few reasons, but mainly because it was free. I'd paid it off almost two years ago, so she only had to assume the insurance payments. You'd think she'd won the lottery when I told her. When she decided to move to California, which she still planned to do, I'd fly to Chicago, and we'd drive to the West Coast together. I was looking for a new car, but Cyrah had been gracious enough to let me borrow hers when needed because her injuries prevented her from driving.

It was unbelievable to think I was a new father to a soon-to-be twenty-year-old daughter. The three of us had plans to go out as a family for the first time, but Tessa wasn't feeling well and urged Cyrah and me to go without her. She'd been fine all day and looking forward to our first family night, so I wasn't sure if the sudden stomachache was real or if she faked it to give Cyrah and me some time alone.

"I think your mom tricked us into having dinner without her," I told Cyrah as we drove to a popular burger spot.

"You know, I was thinking the same thing, but I heard her talking to Auntie Bri earlier, and she sounded like she was looking forward to it."

"Maybe she thought we needed to have some daddy-daughter time. We haven't had any one-on-one time since we've been back."

"True, but it's not like we haven't seen each other. You've barely left our house since you brought her home the day after her party."

Cyrah was telling the truth. I'd been stuck to her mother like glue. However, Tessa may not be aware of the conversations Cyrah and I had each morning. She was an early riser, like me, so while Tessa slept in, my daughter and I bonded while I made breakfast.

"I guess you're right. You cool with that?"

"Am I cool having my father in our house loving on me and my mother? What kind of question is that? I've been waiting my whole life for times like this."

This girl wanted to break me down. As a person with a sister almost two decades younger, I was in tune with my softer side, but I still wasn't prepared for some of the things Cyrah said. I appreciated how she spoke her mind and expressed her feelings, good or bad.

"Baby girl, you keep talking like that, and I'll mess around and move in," I teased, quickly glancing her way.

"I wouldn't mind, and I'm sure my mother wouldn't either. The guy she dated before you came along was the longest relationship she's had, and he rarely came to our house, and it took several months for that to happen. Before Mac, she dated a few men for two or three months tops, but I don't think they knew our address."

"That was smart. You can't allow people too much access these days because there are too many crazies out there. What do you think made the last relationship last so long?"

We arrived at the restaurant, and our conversation was put on hold until we were seated.

"Do you think she was in love with this Mac guy?" I asked, picking up where we'd left off.

"I think she wanted to be but ultimately became comfortable with settling. My nana was always in her ear telling her she wouldn't find anyone at her age and a bunch of other negative stuff."

"Yeah, your mom has mentioned not being very close to her mother. I can't say I'm looking forward to meeting her."

"You shouldn't be, and I don't even want to waste my breath talking about her. Back to my mom and Mac. At first, it was because he said and did all the right things. When he started showing his true colors, she was vested and didn't want to jump back into the dating scene. They broke up for one reason or another every few months. It'd only last a few days, maybe a week, and they'd be back together. I probably shouldn't be telling you all my mother's business, but I guess it's too late now."

We laughed at her candidness and ease in telling her mother's business. I told her that Tessa had shared some things about her previous relationship, so she wasn't violating her mother's trust.

"Did she tell you he approached our table on our first date?"

Her eyes widened in shock, and her mouth was open when I glanced her way.

"You're kidding."

"I wish I was. It was funny because he was actually on a date. We didn't let it ruin our evening, though."

"Good, because who does something like that? The audacity of some people blows my mind."

The server arrived and took our orders. When she left, I decided to pry into Cyrah's dating life. Since we'd been back, she hadn't had any male visitors, although I recall her seeming very cozy with a few young men in my class.

"What about you? Any knuckleheads sniffing around that I need to threaten?" I asked.

Cyrah thought that was funny and shared that her dating life was nonexistent. She had only one serious boyfriend, and they broke up after high school.

"I know you probably don't want to hear this, but I'm not disappointed you aren't dating. No father is ever prepared for their daughter to put their heart on the line only to have it broken. Most men are assholes until they're about thirty, sometimes longer."

"How do you think you would've reacted if my mother had been able to find you and told you she was pregnant?"

That was a great question and caught me off guard. Finding out I'd impregnated a one-night stand at twenty would've rocked my world.

"I don't know, baby girl. I want to think I would've handled it like a mature adult, but I was young. One thing I know for sure is I would've taken care of my responsibilities. Even if I didn't want to, my parents would've made sure of it. I wonder how things would've worked out between me and your mom."

"Thank you for being honest. Do you believe things always happen as they should or for a reason?"

"I've always felt that way, but since I found out about you, I can't think of a reason good enough for me to have missed your whole life."

Regardless of the reason, missing the first twenty years of my daughter's life will bother me until the day I die.

"I don't want you to beat yourself up about it, and you don't need to keep apologizing. It was out of your control."

Cyrah and I had talked about my absence, and she knew how much it bothered me. I'd probably be apologizing for the rest of my life.

"I'll work on it," I told her.

Our food arrived, and we continued conversing while we ate. We remained in the restaurant until they closed. Although it would've been nice if Tessa had joined us, I enjoyed the one-on-one time with my daughter.

Tessa

WHEN I WAS positive Cypress and Cyrah were gone, I slipped on a pair of jeans, a black sweater, and some booties. Our December weather was nothing like Chicago's November weather, but it was chilly enough for a jacket at night.

I'd finally drummed up enough courage to email the people listed as my possible relatives in the results from Know Your Heritage. I'd been extremely anxious for the past few days while waiting for a reply. A couple of hours before Cyrah, Cypress, and I were scheduled to leave for dinner, I got an email from a woman named Larisa asking if we could meet this evening.

The only excuse I could think of to get out of dinner was to pretend like I didn't feel well. Luckily, Cyrah and Cypress fell for it and agreed to go to dinner without me. I didn't want to tell anyone I'd finally contacted the family for some reason. Brianne had been on my ass about it since we'd left Chicago, while Cyrah had only inquired about it once. Cypress hadn't said anything, but I couldn't remember if I'd told him about it with everything that had been going on with him.

In the email, Larisa mentioned living in the Sonoma area, and I almost couldn't contain my excitement about the possibility of being related to the Truth family. We decided to meet at a diner in a city halfway between Sonoma and Black Elm. The closer I got to my destination, the more nervous I became. When I pulled into a parking space and turned off the car, I closed my eyes, took a few deep breaths, and prayed things would go well.

I entered the diner and looked around. It wasn't crowded, but enough people were dining that I couldn't single out who I was looking for. A gorgeous woman sitting in the back corner caught my eye, and when she spotted me, she waved me back. Before I reached her, she was on her feet, preparing to greet me.

"Tessa?" she questioned.

I nodded and said, "Larisa?"

When we confirmed our identities, she pulled me into an embrace that reminded me of the hugs from Mama Boone.

"Oh my God. You look just like Daddy. Let's sit down. There's so much we need to discuss," Larisa urged. "Are you hungry?"

"I'm too nervous to eat," I admitted.

"Please don't be nervous. I'm starving and don't want you to watch me eat."

Larisa didn't wait for me to answer and handed me a menu. We took time to decide what we wanted, and when the waiter approached our table, we placed our order. When the waiter left, Larisa reached across the table and took my hands. The smile she wore calmed my nerves, and I relaxed.

"I can't tell you how long we've been waiting for you to find us," she said.

"You knew about me? Who is 'we'?"

"Tessa, I'm one of your younger sisters. We have another sister and three brothers."

"Wait. I'm confu—did you say you're my sister, and I have other—I—I don't—wow."

"I know this is a lot to take in, which is why I'm here alone. I'm the oldest and had to make an executive decision. I thought it might be too overwhelming for you to meet everyone at once."

I didn't know I was crying until I felt something wet on my face. I've been an only child for my entire life and just found out I have two sisters and three brothers. It took me awhile to formulate the words to respond.

"How do you know me? Why hasn't anyone tried to find me?"

"I'm going to tell you everything as it was told to me, but—"

"But what?"

"There's something you should know before I begin, and it's not good news."

"I can handle it."

Larisa's eyes saddened as she inhaled and released it. "Our father passed away eight years ago. He was headed home from a quick trip to the grocery store and was hit by a drunk driver."

Hearing that my father died before I could meet him was devastatingly painful, but hearing how he died was worse. I looked at Larisa in disbelief because I was on such a high when I laid eyes on her, and now, I was a blubbering mess. She moved to my side of the booth and consoled me while I mourned a man I knew nothing about.

"I didn't want to tell you, but I couldn't keep it from you," she said as she rubbed my back. "I'm sorry, Tessa."

"I know, and thank you. I don't know why I'm so emotional since I didn't know him."

"Because you hoped to meet him someday, and now you know it's impossible. It's okay to let your emotions flow."

Larisa returned to the other side of the booth when the waiter brought our food. After she said a quick blessing over it, we began eating. I was still stunned by what I'd just heard and still processing. A few minutes passed before she continued.

"Are you and your mother close?" she asked.

It was a strange and unexpected question, but I assumed she asked because it concerned what she planned to tell me.

"No, we never have been."

"Some of what I share will include things about your mother that you may or may not know. Nothing I say is meant to be offensive or hurtful. When our father learned of your existence, he sat our whole family down and told us everything, but I'm aware he only told us his side of the story."

"I understand."

"Our father's name was Lawrence Truth. He met your mother the night before he was to marry my mother. His friends threw him a bachelor party and hired some . . . well, Dad called them 'women of the night.'"

"Prostitutes?"

Larisa nodded. "Your mother was one of them."

I gasped. "No!"

"Yes, and to make a long story short, Daddy drank a lot more than he was used to and ended up having sex with your mother."

"I—I'm still stuck on her being a prostitute. It explains a lot of things I saw during my childhood, but . . . damn."

"I know it's hard, but—"

"I'm good. Please continue."

"My parents had somewhat of an arranged marriage. Although nothing horrible would have happened to them had they refused, they were expected to go through with it. At first, Daddy was completely against it, so my grandparents made an agreement with him that if he were still single when he turned twenty-five, he had to marry my mother."

"What about your mother? How did she feel about marrying him?"

"Our father was a very handsome, popular, and well-liked man, and my mother had a crush on him throughout her teenage years. She would've married him as soon as she turned eighteen had he agreed."

"Wow."

"Yeah, I know. Anyway, Daddy turned twenty-five and was still single. He held up his end of the bargain and proposed to my mother. He didn't know she was a virgin when he proposed. While that sounds noble to many men, Daddy was used to a woman with more experience. Needless to say, Mama didn't know the first thing about pleasing a man."

"I think I know where this is going, but continue."

"The night of his bachelor party, he was drunk and sexually frustrated, and that was how his relationship with your mother began."

"It became an actual relationship?"

"Well, nowadays, we'd call it a 'situationship.' The following day, he married my mother but continued to sleep with yours. It went on for a few months before my mother began to put two and two together. It broke his heart to see her so hurt when she confronted him. He begged for her forgiveness and agreed to stop seeing your mother."

"Did he know he'd impregnated my mother before things ended?"

"This is where it gets tricky, and I question if Daddy was completely honest. They met up so he could end things, and she told him she was pregnant. He admitted he wasn't happy because, obviously, he wouldn't be able to hide his transgressions, but he didn't believe in abortion. He told us your mother was hell-bent on having the procedure done, even after he offered to take full custody and relieve her of any parental responsibility after you were born."

"He did that?"

"That's what he said. However, your mother was worried about ruining her body and being unable to take 'clients.' She asked him for money for the abortion, and he refused, so she said she'd pin the baby on another one of her regulars and get the money from him. When they parted ways for the last time, he thought the abortion was a done deal."

"How or when did he find out it wasn't?"

"I can't remember if he saw it in the paper or on the local news, but when you were hired as the youngest professor in the history of BEU, he saw your face and said he knew you belonged to him."

"Oh, wow!"

Cyrah came to mind as I listened. Our stories were so different, yet there were some similarities.

"Somehow, he tracked down your mother, and she forbade him to contact you. She told him you believed another man was your father for your entire life, and you and that man would be devastated if you found out the truth."

"Are you fucking serious?"

My mother was a piece of work. She lied to me about my father and lied to my father about me. If she were in front of me right now, only the hands of God would be able to pry my hands from her neck.

"Again, this is very one-sided—"

"She *did* that shit. I'd bet my life on it. My mother—ugh! I hate her. This is the first time I've said it out loud, but the feeling has been brewing inside me my whole life. I hate my mother. Do you realize what she did? I could've had two years with my father had she not lied to him and run him away. She never wanted me, and it was apparent every day of my life. Why didn't she just abort me or give me to my father? She kept me around to make me feel like shit."

I was damn near hysterical at this point. Tears were pouring from my eyes uncontrollably, snot was draining from my nose, and I was sure Larisa could barely understand my words. None of that mattered, though. Larisa came back to my side of the booth and, in that semicrowded restaurant, let me cry on her shoulder until my tears dried. When I'd calmed down, she reached into her purse and took out an envelope.

"Daddy wrote this letter to you after he met with your mother. No one had ever read it, but he made sure everyone knew where it was in case he never got a chance to give it to you himself. Read it when you're ready."

I took the envelope and stared at it for a long time. Eventually, we parted ways after exchanging all of our contact information. I didn't realize until I was halfway home that I had never confirmed if there was a connection to Truth Sanctuary. There was a lot I needed to process, and Larisa promised to give me a few days to do so before she came looking for me. I was prepared to explain myself to Cyrah and Cypress because I was sure they'd beat me home, but to my surprise, they did not. I may have lied about not feeling well before, but it wouldn't be a lie if they asked me when they returned home. I was physically, mentally, and emotionally exhausted when I climbed back into bed.

Cypress

TESSA HADN'T BEEN herself since she backed out on dinner. She didn't appear to be physically sick, but she'd been extremely quiet and distant. When I asked her about it, she told me she was fine and changed the subject. When I talked to my father about what could be wrong with her, he suggested she might need space. I'd been at her house consistently for several days, and it was possible, so I decided to go home after dinner.

"Cyrah, do you have plans for your birthday?" I asked as I rose from the table and prepared to help Tessa clean the kitchen.

"I asked her the same question two days ago," Tessa said.

"How much can I do with a broken ankle and wrist? Clubbing is completely out of the question."

"How about you invite some of your friends over?" I suggested.

"Dad, I'm turning twenty, not ten. Besides, this lady doesn't like people she doesn't know in her house."

"She's not lying," Tessa agreed.

"My options are limited this year, but next year, I'm doing it big for my twenty-first. You two better get those pockets ready," she warned.

We tossed around some ideas for Cyrah's twenty-first birthday celebration before Cyrah changed the topic.

"So, I think I know what I want to do," she announced.

"What to do when?" Tessa questioned.

"With my life. I'm 90 percent sure I'm ready to declare a major. Well, kind of."

"Oh yeah?" I asked. "What's that?"

"Jade and I were talking—"

"Oh shit. Don't tell me you took advice from someone who has no idea what she wants to do with her finance degree," I quipped.

"Don't talk about my auntie like that. She's great with numbers but doesn't like her job. So, we were talking, and I mentioned I was interested in real estate and contemplating getting licensed. Jade expressed some interest too and suggested if we both become licensed, we could become partners after we get some experience. When my trimester starts, I will finally declare myself a business major specializing in finance."

"I like that sound of that, sweetheart," Tessa beamed.

"If you got Jade excited about something, I like the sound of it too. Do you think you'll be able to study for the license while in school?" I asked.

"I believe so. School has always been easy for me. Hopefully, once I declare my major, that doesn't change, but I think I can handle doing both."

"I'm sure you can. Once Jade is here, you can help each other," Tessa suggested.

"How is your business idea coming along?" I asked Tessa.

"Great, actually. Black Elm has much more African American history than I could have imagined. It would be the perfect base location. I'm almost done with the proposal. After the holidays, I plan to reach out to this Black-owned charter bus company and discuss partnering with them. If they're not interested, I'll buy a bus and hire a few drivers, but I'd rather not do that to start."

"Have you thought of a name yet?" Cyrah questioned.

"I thought about using Tesrah Tour Company or Tesrah Tours, but I don't know. I'll use one of those if nothing else comes to me."

"I'm proud of you, Mom. You didn't know what you wanted to do a few months ago after quitting your job, but now it seems you've found your purpose. That's pretty dope!"

"Yeah, baby, it takes a lot of guts to quit your job without a plan. I don't think I could do it," I expressed. "However, you quitting your job was the catalyst that started this reunion of sorts. Everything happens as it should."

"Agreed," Tessa said, while Cyrah nodded in agreement.

We talked awhile longer before I announced I was leaving. Although Tessa looked surprised, she didn't protest.

"You're leaving?" Cyrah sang.

"Yeah, I don't want to wear out my welcome."

"You're not wearing out your welcome. What are you talking about?" Cyrah questioned.

I looked at Tessa again, waiting for her to ask me to stay; it never happened. Instead, she busied herself with wiping off the counters.

"I figured I should utilize my space since I'm paying rent. Besides, I need to do laundry and get more clothes."

I left them in the kitchen, and before I was too far away, I heard Cyrah mumbling something to her mother. Tessa responded similarly, but I couldn't understand what they were saying. I grabbed my duffle bag, where my dirty clothes were already packed, and glanced around the room. It wasn't as if I wouldn't be back, so I wasn't pressed about leaving anything behind.

"I'll see you later, baby girl," I told Cyrah before kissing her forehead. "Baby, come walk me out."

Tessa nodded and followed me to her front door. I turned around to face her, and she couldn't look me in the eyes.

"You keep telling me you're fine, but I can tell something's up. I'll give you some space for a few days, but if you're still in a mood in a couple of days, you need to tell me what's going on with you."

"Okay."

She lifted onto her toes, and we kissed softly before we embraced. We remained that way until her doorbell chimed, startling us.

"You expecting someone?"

"No."

I turned around and looked out of the stained-glass window on the door. I couldn't see who it was, but I could tell it was a male figure. When I opened the door, the man I knew to be her ex was on the other side.

"You lost?" I asked.

It only took a second for him to recognize me, and when he did, his expression hardened.

"Is Tessa here?"

"Mac, what do you want?" Tessa questioned, stepping next to me.

"Can we talk in private?"

"Nah, she ain't got shit to say to you in public or private," I interjected.

"This ain't your business, man."

"She's my business. You got a problem with that?" I challenged.

"I understand Tessa may have led you to believe she was single, but—"

"Mac, stop with the nonsense and get the hell off my property. I told you it was over, and I meant it."

"We can get married if that's what you want. Look, I even got you a ring."

He pulled a little black box from his pocket and opened it. Sure enough, there was a diamond ring inside. It took some effort not to laugh at his last-ditch effort, but it was quite humorous. Tessa, however, had no problem laughing in Mac's face.

"Was that a proposal?" she managed to ask through her laughter. "You've clearly lost your mind if you think I'm marrying you."

"What do you want me to do? Get on one knee? I'll do whatever you ask. I've been miserable without you and didn't realize how much I needed you."

Mac started to get on one knee, but Tessa stopped him.

"No, please, don't. I don't care how many ways you propose. I wouldn't marry you if you were the last man on earth. I wasted three good years with you, and not once did you make me feel as loved as this man did in three weeks. You can take that ring and that proposal and shove it up your ass. Now, get the hell away from my house, and don't come here again."

Tessa marched away, leaving me at the door with her ex. He seemed stunned and didn't leave immediately.

"Why the fuck are you still on her doorstep?" I barked.

"We have history—"

"Nigga, don't make me beat your simple-minded ass in front of my woman's house!"

I stepped outside, but Mac didn't want the smoke. He turned and rushed to his car, speeding away from the curb. I went back inside, shaking my head at what occurred.

"I always knew Mac was a punk," Cyrah said as I walked past the family room, causing me to chuckle.

Tessa was in her room, sitting on the edge of the bed. She looked up when I walked in and offered a weak smile.

"You good?"

"I'm fine. I thought you were leaving."

"Do you want me to leave?"

She shrugged. "It's up to you."

"That's not what I asked you."

"If you want to leave, I can't stop you," her stubborn ass replied.

"That's still not answering my question, but it's cool. I said I'd give you some space, so I'll keep my word."

I turned to leave and was headed down the hall before I heard, "Wait."

I paused and turned around.

"Something has been bothering me, but I needed to sit with it for a few days before I shared."

"Is it something I can help you with?"

"No. This situation is beyond help. Let's go to the family room because Cyrah needs to hear this too."

When we entered the family room, Cyrah looked in our direction. Our expressions must have looked serious because she muted the TV and asked, "What's wrong?"

"Your mother has something she needs to talk to us about."

"Oh my God. Are you pregnant?"

My mind hadn't gone down *that* road, but with the way she'd been acting, it was a legitimate question.

"Oh shit! Is that why you've been so moody?"

"No, I'm not pregnant and haven't been moody," Tessa denied.

Cyrah and I gave each other a knowing look because her mood had certainly been up and down.

"What is it?" Cyrah pressed.

Whatever it was, Tessa had a hard time getting it out. She began to pace back and forth and started and stopped talking five times before she blurted out the last thing Cyrah and I expected.

"My mother used to be a prostitute, and my father was one of her customers."

"Oh shit."

"Excuse me, *what*?" Cyrah exclaimed.

"Yeah, I was shocked too. I finally reached out to the contacts given to me in the Know Your Roots email."

I knew Tessa didn't know her father but wasn't aware she was waiting for any results from Know Your Roots. I'd always thought the idea of using your DNA to trace your ancestry was great, but I'd also heard some horror stories about it.

"Let's sit down, baby."

I ushered her to the love seat and sat beside her. I wasn't prepared for any of the information she'd shared with us, and from Cyrah's facial expressions and comments, neither was she.

"I don't understand why I'm so sad about my father's death. I didn't even know him," Tessa cried.

"He was still your father, baby. You wanted to meet him one day, and now you know it will never happen."

"That's what Larisa said. It seems weird to cry over a man I've never met."

"This whole story is crazy. I knew Nana's spirit was dark, but I had no idea how dark it was."

"My sister gave me a letter that my father wrote after he met with my mother. I haven't read it yet."

"Are you afraid of what it might say?" I questioned.

"No, because based on what Larisa said, my father wanted me from the moment he found out I'd been conceived. I don't think he said anything bad. I just . . . I don't know. This has been a lot."

"Don't read it until you think you're ready, Mom," Cyrah suggested.

"I should probably read it soon. Larisa said she'd hunt me down if she didn't hear from me in a few days."

"I hate that your father passed away before you could meet him, but there is an upside to this. You've been an only child your whole life and now have five siblings. How does that feel?"

"I'm excited, anxious, and nervous to meet them."

Sometimes, great things come from the oddest situations. The three of us were examples of that fact. A few months ago, I would've never believed I had a nineteen-year-old daughter and would reunite with and fall in love with her mother. Life was strange that way.

Wait, what did I just say? Am I in love with Tessa Howard?

I thought about how much I missed her when she wasn't in my presence. After I told her we should slow down, it didn't sit right in my soul, but my pride forced me to roll with it. When she returned to California, my spirit was unsettled because we hadn't smoothed things out between us. I was nervous that too much time would pass and she would lose interest, even though I could have easily picked up the phone.

My feelings were very clear, and it hadn't taken very long. *I love Tessa Howard . . . but does she love me?*

Tessa

WE ARRIVED AT Brianne's home in Fresno yesterday and were waiting for the food we'd ordered from Cyrah's favorite locally owned restaurant, Triumphant African Restaurant, to be delivered. Since Cyrah couldn't do anything significant for her birthday, we decided to make the four-hour drive to Fresno to visit Brianne and have an intimate celebration with just the four of us. My monthly visits hadn't happened since I'd quit my job, and even though we'd seen each other, Brianne wouldn't let me forget I'd been slacking on my visits.

Brianne decided to give Kendall another chance, and we met him last night. Because of a prior work obligation, he couldn't attend Cyrah's birthday dinner, but he seemed cool and very much into Brianne. I believed she liked him more than she wanted to admit, and it'd be interesting to see how their relationship played out. He invited her to spend Christmas with his family, but she refused to get excited because he did the same for Thanksgiving . . . and then backed out.

"I can't believe my baby is twenty years old," I cried.

"Mom, are you crying? It's *not* that serious," Cyrah teased.

"It *is* that serious. You're my only baby, and you're not a baby anymore. Yes, it's *that* serious."

"I'm feeling a little emotional myself, so I can't say too much about your mother," Cypress added.

"Aww, Dad. I understand why you're emotional because this is a first for us. When I get out of this boot and cast, we'll do something fun. This lady is doing too much, though."

"Don't talk about me like I'm not here. I can't help how much I love you."

"I know, Mom, and I appreciate every ounce of your love. However, I hate to be the one to tell you, but you've been overly emotional for the past week or so. I don't know if I've ever seen you like this."

"There's been a lot to be emotional about. It's not like I'm sitting around crying for no reason."

When I thought about the past month and a half, it was hard to believe all that had transpired. Our lives had changed drastically but for the better. Witnessing Cyrah bond with her father was one of the things that had me in my feelings most of the time. He doted on her every chance he could, and in just a few weeks, she became the epitome of a daddy's girl. Anyone watching them together would never know they'd only discovered the nature of their connection a few weeks ago.

It took me a few years to build up the courage to order the kit from Know Your Roots. The results I'd received still seemed unbelievable, and a week later, I hadn't processed it all. Since I'd met with Larisa, we hadn't seen each other again, although we communicated daily through text or phone calls. She was very understanding about giving me the time to process the information she'd shared, and I appreciated her patience.

She'd suggested that Christmas Day would be perfect for me to meet my other siblings and family members, and I agreed. Larisa told me not to worry about the details of the day, and once she had everything planned, she'd share them with me. In the meantime, I had to work up the courage to read the letter from my father. From what Larisa shared about him, he made some mistakes as a young man, hence, his relationship with my mother, but he learned from them. I didn't necessarily think the letter would say anything hurtful, but once I read it, it would make his death and the fact that I would never meet him final. I knew it was true, but a part of me still held on to the fantasy of meeting him.

"That's true, best friend. Your life has been a Lifetime movie lately," Brianne commented. "I still can't believe the shit about your mother. The way she dogged you when you told her you were pregnant with Cyrah, you would've thought she was the Virgin Mary."

"Was it that bad?" Cypress asked.

"Tuh! It was worse. I'm guessing you still haven't had the pleasure of meeting Ms. Deloris Howard."

"Not yet, but she sounds like a piece of work."

"That's an understatement," Cyrah added.

"The last time I spoke with her was when she found out I wouldn't be home to cook Thanksgiving dinner for her and her friends. I told her I didn't want to talk to her until she learned to communicate without putting me down and being disrespectful."

"Since you haven't heard from her, I guess she's still working on being respectful," Cyrah commented.

"Her absence from my life has done wonders for my anxiety. I don't miss her at all. It's sad to feel that way about my own mother, but it is what it is."

"Did she call you on your birthday?" Cypress asked.

"If she had, you would've heard about it because I'm sure she would've found a way to ruin my day."

"Has she texted or called you today, Cyrah?" Brianne asked.

"You're funny, Auntie Bri. I can count on one hand how many times she's told me happy birthday and have a whole hand and a few fingers left. You know Nana isn't the well-wishing, gift-giving kind of grandmother."

"Damn," Cypress grunted. "I can't imagine that type of relationship with either of my parents. I'm sorry it's been this way for y'all, but I swear, my parents will make up for her absence. Pops was so excited his doctor cleared him to travel for Christmas."

"This will be the Christmas of all Christmases. I can't wait," Cyrah expressed with excitement.

Holidays had never been anything special in our family. The only time we had fun was if we celebrated with Brianne's family, which wasn't often because my mother always made me feel guilty for leaving her to fend for herself.

"Oh, the food's here," Brianne announced as she headed for the door.

"I'll go with her in case she needs a hand. You two go wash up," I told Cyrah and Cypress.

As I helped Brianne prepare the food, I felt nauseated when the aromas hit my nose. Thankfully, I could get it under control with a few deep breaths. Twenty minutes later, we were all sitting around Brianne's dining room table with the food in the center. After everyone had what they wanted on their plate, Cypress offered to bless the food.

"Thank you, Lord, for the food we're about to receive, and thank you, Brianne, for allowing us to celebrate Cyrah's birthday in your home. God saw fit for me to be reunited with a beautiful woman from my past who happened to give birth to my only child twenty years ago today. I'm grateful to be here, breaking bread with you, because our being together is nothing short of a miracle. Amen."

I tried to hold back my tears, but it was a lost cause. When I sniffled, three sets of eyes were on me.

"What?" I asked defensively. "That was sweet."

"It was very sweet but not tear-worthy," Cyrah said.

"Be quiet, and let's eat," I dismissed as I patted my eyes with a napkin.

They found humor in my high emotions, but I ignored them. I couldn't help that everything made me cry these days. Maybe it was something that happened when women turned forty. I ate my first forkful of spiced jollof rice, and almost as soon as it hit my tongue, the nausea I'd felt earlier returned. I hadn't eaten since breakfast, so I thought the feeling stemmed from my hunger and just ignored it and swallowed.

I shouldn't have done that!

"Oh my God!"

I slapped my hand over my mouth, hopped out of my seat, and ran to the powder room that, thankfully, wasn't too far away. As soon as I lifted the lid to the toilet, I emptied my insides into the ceramic bowl.

"Mom, are you okay?"

"Baby, what's wrong?"

"Sis, are you pregnant?"

My period!

Brianne's question caused more vomit to exit my body because why would she ask me something like that? When my stomach was empty, I flushed the toilet and turned around to find the three of them at the door. After pushing through them, I went to the guest room Cypress and I used to brush my teeth.

"Are you good?"

This time, only Cypress was at the door. He looked concerned while he waited for me to reply, but I didn't know how to answer. I didn't feel sick until I tried to eat the spicy jollof rice. Now, I felt like crap because I'd just thrown up my insides.

"I'm okay. I guess my stomach didn't like the spices in the rice."

"So, you don't think you could be pregnant?"

"I hadn't thought about it until Brianne asked. My period was due two weeks ago, but with all the shit that's been happening, I didn't realize it hadn't come until now."

That sounded crazy coming from someone my age, but it was true.

"I'll go pick up a few tests," he offered.

"Okay."

Cypress pulled me into a hug and kissed my forehead before sliding his index finger under my chin and lifting my head.

"How do you feel now?" he asked.

"Empty," I replied truthfully.

"That's understandable. I'll be right back."

He kissed my lips before getting the keys to my truck from the dresser and leaving. A few minutes later, Cyrah and Brianne entered. I was still stunned by the possibility of being pregnant and hadn't moved.

"Where's Dad going?"

"To pick up a pregnancy test," I whispered.

"Hold on. I bought a pack of three and didn't use one of them."

Brianne disappeared for a minute and returned with a box in her hand.

"I'm gonna ignore the fact that you got pregnancy tests lying around," Cyrah commented, taking the words right out of my mouth.

"Do that and mind your own business," Brianne told her, handing me the box.

My nerves were all over the place as I returned to the bathroom and closed the door. I leaned against it and took several deep breaths.

"I don't know what my old ass will do with a newborn," I whispered.

Instead of prolonging it, I peed on the stick and placed it on the counter. I didn't look at the test while I washed my hands, leaving it on the counter.

"Well?" Cyrah and Brianne asked.

"It says three minutes, and I couldn't look," I told them when I opened the bathroom door.

"Oh my goodness. You were the same way with Cyrah. Move out of the way."

Brianne gently pushed me out of the doorway, and not a full second later, she screamed.

"Tessssaaaaa, you're pregnant! You're pregnant! You're pregnant! You're pregnant!"

I heard her, but I had to see for myself. Cyrah and I looked at each other, then rushed into the bathroom. The test was still on the counter, and the word *pregnant* was on the little screen. I was at a loss for words. The moment seemed surreal.

"Mom, you're giving me a sibling after all these years," Cyrah said excitedly.

"You gotta give me a nephew to spoil this time," Brianne said.

I couldn't respond to either of them because . . . *What the fuck?*

"How do you feel?" Cyrah asked.

"Are you excited?" Brianne pressed.

"I need to sit down."

Cypress

DRIVING TO THE pharmacy around the corner, I prayed Tessa was pregnant. We'd discussed children very briefly and generally, and aside from thinking her eggs were too old, she hadn't expressed being opposed to it. When my mother mentioned being around Tessa's age when she had Jade, Tessa requested we be more careful but never forced me to use condoms. *Can I assume she's okay with having another child?*

I made it to and from the pharmacy in record-breaking time and was grateful I didn't get pulled over. When I arrived back at Brianne's house, I realized I'd left so quickly I hadn't closed the garage. I didn't see anyone when I entered the house, so I went straight to the guest room. As I approached the door, I heard Brianne ask Tessa if she was excited, causing me to pause to listen to her answer.

"Bri, I just turned forty. What the hell do I look like with a newborn? People will think I'm the grandmother picking them up from school."

"First of all, fuck everybody who thinks that bullshit because you and Cyrah can pass for sisters. Second, forty is not old. If Kendall knocks me up, we're having a damn baby, and that's all there is to it."

"Yeah, but neither of you has children, and he's five years younger than you," Tessa reasoned.

"So, you're not happy?" Cyrah pressed, and I could hear the sadness in her voice.

"It's only been a few minutes, but my initial reaction isn't happiness or excitement. It's more like panic, fear, and what the fuck."

"I can understand the panic and what the fuck, but what's there to be afraid of? You're a whole grown-ass woman who supports herself and lives a very comfortable lifestyle with a man who will be right by your side," Brianne said.

"The last time I did this, I was a teenager, and from what I can remember, pregnancy was no walk in the park. I can't imagine what the next nine months will be like."

"Maybe this time will be different," Cyrah said.

"I should've been more responsible, but I truly thought the odds of me getting pregnant were slim to none. Maybe the test is wrong, and it's a false positive. I could be going through menopause or something."

I've heard enough!

If I had never had more children, I would have continued living a happy and joyous life. Even though I missed her childhood, Cyrah filled a void I didn't realize existed. However, the disappointment I felt knowing Tessa could be carrying another child of mine and wasn't excited about it tore me up inside.

The possibility of experiencing Tessa's pregnancy from beginning to end, watching my seed grow in her womb, seeing our child enter the world, and watching them grow and mature excited the hell out of me. It messed me up to know Tessa didn't feel the same way.

"I'm back," I announced as I entered the room.

"Hey, umm, Bri had an extra test," Tessa said nervously.

"And?"

Of course, I pretended I didn't eavesdrop on their whole conversation.

"It says I'm pregnant, but let me take this one to see what it says."

"I bought two of them; take them both," I encouraged.

She took the bag from my hand and headed for the bathroom but stopped short in front of the door.

"I need some water," she said when she turned around.

"We'll go get a couple of bottles. Come on, Cyrah," Brianne said.

"How do you feel?" I asked.

"Physically, the same as I did before you left. Mentally, I'm shocked."

"Are you? We haven't been careful, so you shouldn't be that surprised."

"You aren't?"

"I wasn't expecting it, but I'm not surprised. I haven't used a condom since you straddled my—"

"Here you go, sis. Guzzle it down so we can get those results," Brianne said as she handed Tessa two water bottles and disappeared again.

I was glad Brianne understood Tessa and I needed some time alone. I closed the door behind Brianne to give us some privacy because we needed to have a serious conversation after she took the pregnancy tests. She didn't mention abortion, but I had to make sure she wasn't considering it. I busied myself with my phone while she drank the bottles of water and anxiously waited when she went into the bathroom ten minutes later. I stood when the door opened and looked at her expectantly.

"Well?" I asked when she hadn't said anything.

"It only took them five seconds to read positive," she replied.

I wouldn't say her tone was solemn, but she definitely wasn't excited.

"C'mere," I summoned.

When she reached me, I sat on the edge of the bed and pulled her onto my lap.

"Can I be honest?" I asked and received a nod in response. "I overheard your conversation with Cyrah and Brianne."

Her body tensed as she spoke. "You listened to our private conversation?"

"I did, and—"

Tessa tried to get up from my lap, but I tightened my hold.

"Chill out, baby. My intention wasn't to eavesdrop, but your lack of excitement about the possibility of being pregnant kinda stopped me in my tracks."

"Can you blame me? I'm forty with a twenty-year-old. I'm closer to grandparent age than the parent of a newborn age."

Cyrah told me she wasn't dating, so I knew Tessa was only trying to make a point and didn't even bother addressing her comment.

"Are you saying you don't want this baby?"

She sighed. "No, I'm not saying that at all. I didn't expect to find myself in this predicament at my age. I should've—*we* should've been more responsible. We've been dating a short time and almost called it quits when—"

"I was with you until you started talking about us calling it quits. Don't you think you're exaggerating a bit?"

"Did you not say you wanted to pump the brakes? What if you wake up and feel that way again?"

"Come on, baby. You know why I asked for space. It had everything to do with needing a minute to process having a grown daughter and you not telling me sooner and nothing to do with not wanting a future with you."

"I've always said I wanted to be married if I had any more children. This isn't—"

"Then let's get married."

"Cypress, you're only asking because I'm pregnant. I don't want this baby to be the reason you propose. I want you to do it because you love me—"

"I *do* love you," I blurted without even thinking about it.

"You . . . what?"

"I love you, baby. This child has nothing to do with how I felt about you an hour ago, yesterday, or a week ago. Believe me when I tell you I loved you before those sticks told me you were carrying my seed . . . again."

"Oh, I, umm, I didn't know."

"Now you do, and—"

"I love you too, Cypress. I realized it the night of my party— well, before that, but I thought it was too soon. I've been in denial since, and—"

"Tessa, we're too old to act like teenagers and be scared to express our feelings. I apologize for not professing my love for you the moment my mind and heart were in one accord. With everything I had going on—never mind, I won't make any excuses. I love you, you love me, and we're about to have another baby. The next time I propose to you, don't dismiss me like I'm that punk-ass nigga you wasted three years with. You understand?"

She nodded.

"Nah, open that pretty-ass mouth of yours and tell me you understand."

"I understand, Cy."

"When we get back home, you're going to make an appointment to find out when our old asses will be the parents of a newborn. I heard everything you said and understand your reservations, but we got this. I'm excited, but I'm nervous as hell."

"That makes two of us."

"Are you excited, nervous, or both?"

Ten minutes ago, she was everything *but* excited, giving every excuse under the sun about why her being pregnant wasn't the blessing I knew it was. I prayed our conversation helped ease her fears and changed her feelings.

"Both."

My smile reached from ear to ear from that one simple word. I was on top of the world, and nothing could take away my high. I deserved this kind of joy, and I wouldn't take it for granted.

Tessa

My dearest Tessa,

I am your biological father, Lawrence Truth. If you're reading this letter, I am no longer among the living, you've met your sister Larisa, and she's shared everything that led to me not being a part of your life.

I loved you as soon as I knew you were conceived and mourned you when I thought you would never be. You are my firstborn. The circumstances surrounding your conception were not ideal, but you are a part of me, and I love you as much as I love your sisters and brothers.

I'm sorry, baby girl. I'm so very sorry. I never hugged you, kissed your cheeks, read you bedtime stories, tucked you in at night, or wiped your tears away. I missed every single second of your life, and my heart breaks a little every time I think about it. I longed to look into your eyes, the ones shaped just like mine, to tell you all these things, but unfortunately, it wasn't meant to happen that way.

Tessa, I begged Deloris not to abort you because I wanted you. I wanted you, baby girl. Please, don't ever forget that. I'm happy your mother changed her mind, but I wish I'd known sooner. Even though I had nothing to do with your success, I am so very proud of you, your accomplishments, and the woman you've become. I pray that your life has lacked nothing physically, mentally, spiritually, or emotionally and remains that way for the rest of your days.

Although it will not make up for my absence, I have left you a portion of our family estate and a monetary amount that our family attorney will discuss with you. Please accept this as a token of my love.

With love from the depths of my heart,

Your father

IT WAS CHRISTMAS morning, and after reading the letter from my father, I was a crying, blubbering mess. However, I wouldn't care if I never received another gift for Christmas for the rest of my life. Nothing could top reading words written to me by the man who helped create me. Knowing he wanted me, begged for me, and loved me shifted something in my soul.

My mother made me feel unwanted and unloved my whole life, as if my mere existence was an inconvenience. There were no hugs, no words of encouragement, nothing that led me to believe she liked me, let alone loved me unless it was for something that would benefit her somehow. Yet, my father, who didn't know I existed until I was almost thirty and never had a chance to meet me, wrote me a one-page letter and damn near healed all the brokenness I'd felt my entire life.

I folded the letter to put back in the envelope, and some other papers fell onto my lap. At first glance, it looked like something from a newspaper. I picked them up and gently unfolded them. What was revealed to me caused another round of tears. My father had newspaper clippings of articles written about me when I became a professor at BEU and a couple of other times when I'd been in the paper for some research I'd done for the university and the African American Studies department.

On the back of each article, he'd written short messages like, "I'm so proud of you, baby girl," and "Brains and beauty all in one." I was so touched by his sentiments that I cried hysterically, causing Cyrah to come to my room.

"Mom, what's wrong?"

I couldn't stop crying long enough to get my words together, so I handed her the letter and articles and let her figure it out. By the time she'd finished reading, I'd managed to calm down.

"This is—this is—I don't have the words, but I understand the tears," Cyrah said as she used her scooter to get as close to me as she could before wrapping me in a hug.

"He gave me everything I didn't get from my mother in one letter and some newspaper articles. How is that possible?" I cried.

"That's pure and genuine love, Mom. Don't question it. Soak it up and carry it with you for the rest of your life. You've always been worthy of the love your father expressed in his letter."

I looked at Cyrah and became overcome with emotion again.

"I can't believe my life right now. If I didn't believe in miracles, the past few months would've made me a believer. Everything I've prayed for has come to fruition, so excuse me ahead of time for my random bouts of tears."

"You've been doing it for a couple of weeks, Mom. I'm used to it."

"You know what? I think I'm gonna take back the gifts I bought you," I threatened.

"That would be rude, but honestly, I'd be cool without getting any gifts. Nothing can top having both of my parents, my paternal grandparents, aunts, uncles, and cousins. Today is about to be lit!"

Her excitement brought tears to my eyes. They were happy tears, but tears, nonetheless.

"Merry Christmas. Is somebody cooking breakfast, or are we starving ourselves until dinner?" Jade questioned groggily as she leaned against my bedroom door frame.

Cypress's family arrived yesterday morning. We hung out at my house, eating, drinking, and talking until late in the evening. Initially, Cypress planned to stay at his apartment with his parents, but no one wanted to leave last night, and there was plenty of space at my house.

"Merry Christmas, greedy. Cypress went to the store to pick up a few items for breakfast. He should be—"

"I'm back, and I think Jade and Cyrah should make breakfast for everyone," Cypress announced as he entered my bedroom.

"That's not what I had in mind, but if you're suggesting it, I know I don't have a choice," Jade replied.

"Wait a minute! How'd I get involved? I only have one good arm and leg," Cyrah objected.

"Niece, you move around on that scooter better than people with two good legs. Come on!" Jade ordered.

Cyrah mumbled as she rolled her scooter out of my room.

"In case you needed a reminder, you're cooking for six people," Cypress shouted after them before closing and locking the bedroom door.

"What are you doing?" I asked when I noticed him removing his hoodie.

"You fell asleep on my last night."

"I was tired."

"I know, and I didn't bother you. However, right now, you're wide awake."

He pushed his sweats and underwear down, stepping out of them along with his socks. Seeing his naked body sent chills through my body, and his thick, long dick, standing at attention, made my mouth water.

"Your parents are here," I reminded him, licking my lips.

"You'll have to be quiet. Besides, they're still in their room, probably doing the same thing I'm trying to do."

"Oh my God."

"We can be quick," he reasoned.

"Fine, c'mere," I summoned, licking my lips again.

I moved to the edge of the bed with my legs open and hanging over the side. When Cypress stepped between them, his manhood lined up with my mouth. I wrapped my hand around the base and leaned forward, licking the tip before taking as much of him as I could in my mouth.

"*Sss*," he hissed.

Cypress's hands palmed the back of my head as I slid my mouth up and down his length.

"Just like that," he whispered.

As saliva gathered and my mouth became slicker, Cypress tried to suppress his groans but failed.

"Argh, fuck!"

His knees buckled slightly when the suction of my jaws tightened, and I used my tongue to tickle the head.

"Tess, baby, I'm—"

He lost control and began to fuck my mouth as if it were my pussy. My eyes watered, but I didn't stop. I knew he wouldn't last much longer.

"Baby, I'm about to—"

That was all the warning he could give me before his seeds hit the back of my throat. I kept sucking, draining him dry, until he had enough strength to remove himself from my mouth.

"That wasn't fair, baby," he told me before collapsing on the bed beside me.

I figured Cypress would nap for about ten minutes, so I hopped in the shower. However, two minutes later, he joined me.

"No nap?" I asked.

He turned me around and lifted me onto his dick as he pressed my back against the cold shower wall.

"Oh my God, Cy."

"You gotta be quiet if you don't want anyone to hear you," he whispered against my ear.

I did my best to quiet my praise and moans, but I wouldn't doubt if someone heard me. My body knew we didn't have much time, and it wasn't long before my toes tingled. The sensations traveled through my body, stopping at my center and stripping me of my juices.

"That's it, baby. Come on this dick," he ordered, filling me with his seeds.

Ten minutes later, when we were almost dressed, someone knocked on the door.

"I hope y'all done being nasty. Breakfast is almost ready," Jade shouted through the door.

"Hurry up before they think we were in here doing something," I huffed.

"We were," he said with a chuckle.

I couldn't go out there with dick on my breath, so after getting dressed, I rushed into the bathroom to brush my teeth. Cypress stood behind me when I finished, staring at me through the mirror.

"You read the letter from your father?"

I nodded.

"You okay?"

"Better than okay. I'll let you read it later."

"That's personal, baby. I don't need to read it, but I wanted to make sure you were good. Let's go before Jade's impatient ass comes knocking again."

"Merry Christmas," I sang when I entered the dining room and went directly to Mama and Papa Boone to hug them. "I hope the room was to your liking and you were comfortable."

"Everything was great. You'll have to let me know that mattress company. It was heavenly," Mama Boone told me.

"Of course. I'll make sure you have the info before you leave."

"This woman always finds a way to spend my money," Papa Boone griped.

"First of all, it's *our* money. Don't act like you didn't wake up raving about how comfortable that mattress was."

I loved watching the elder Boones go back and forth. Some might have seen them and thought they were fussing or arguing, but it was so wholesome and sweet.

"Was that the doorbell?" Mama Boone asked.

Cypress and I looked at each other as he approached me and asked if I was expecting more company.

"Everyone who should be here is here," I told him.

I followed him to the front door and wanted to crawl under a rug when he opened it, and I saw my mother standing on the other side.

"Mom, what are you doing here?" I asked, stepping next to Cypress.

"You're letting strange men answer your door?" she replied instead of answering my question. "Is *he* the reason you didn't accept Mac's proposal? I know I raised you better."

Cypress slid his arm around me and pulled me to his side.

"What do you want?"

"It's Christmas. I let you slide for Thanksgiving but knew you wouldn't let me down twice. Have you finished making breakfast? I'm starving. Aren't you going to let me in?"

Deloris rambled on and on as if I hadn't told her I wanted nothing to do with her.

"I thought I told you—"

"Don't be like that, baby. Like your mother said, it's Christmas." He stepped back, taking me with him and giving my mother room to enter. "Come on in, ma'am."

"Oh, at least he has manners," she commented as she stepped inside.

I looked at Cypress angrily, and he mouthed, "It's fine."

My mother continued into the house and stopped in the dining room. I was sure she was surprised to see someone at the table, let alone multiple people.

"Who the hell are these people?" she barked, turning toward me.

Embarrassed wasn't enough to describe how I felt, but I refused to let this woman come into my house and disrespect me and my guests. I was prepared to unleash forty years of pent-up anger and resentment on her and didn't care if it ruined our relationship forever.

Cypress

I COULD TELL BY the look in Tessa's eyes she was ready to let her mother have it, so I interjected before she could respond.

"I don't think we've met. I'm Cypress, Cyrah's father and your future son-in-law."

Tessa's mother was a fair-skinned woman with a sharp nose, beady eyes, and lips that were more on the thin side. She was very unattractive, and Tessa looked nothing like her, which meant she probably looked more like her father. I wouldn't doubt if Tessa's beauty was a part of why her mother mistreated her.

I knew Tessa questioned why I invited her mother inside, but I hadn't officially met her, and I wanted to give her the benefit of the doubt. If she were as horrible as Tessa, Cyrah, and Brianne claimed, she would undoubtedly say or do something offensive, and I wanted Deloris to meet her match: Miriam Boone. My mother was born and raised on the South Side of Chicago and wouldn't hesitate to set Deloris straight. She maintained her control in most situations, but Miriam hated disrespect and wouldn't stand for it from anyone, whether toward her or someone else.

"*Excuse* me? Cyrah's *father*? Is this some kind of joke? What lies did Tessa tell you to make you believe she has a clue who fathered her bastard child? I hope you got a DNA test because you are one of many options."

"Why would you say that? You know it's not true," Tessa shouted.

Before I could open my mouth to defend my woman and child, my mother was in Deloris's face.

"I know damn well I didn't just hear you call my grandchild a bastard," Miriam chastised. "I don't know you, and I don't want to, but if you let one more disrespectful word fall from those crusty lips, I will beat you like you stole something. How dare you come into your daughter's home and insult her and my granddaughter like they don't have feelings?"

"Grandchild? Tuh! You believe her lies too? You all have to be the dumbest people in the world. Tessa told me herself that she didn't know who Cyrah's father was, so I'm not saying anything that's not true. And you can get out of my face. I don't have to explain myself to you or anyone else. Tessa is *my* daughter, and Cyrah is *my* granddaughter. I'll say what I want about them and—"

Smack!

Everyone in the house reacted differently. I heard everything from "oh shit" to "damn" to "oops," but what got me was my father shouting my mother's name before her hand landed on Deloris's face. Robert knew his wife, and he knew what was coming before it happened. He couldn't get to her fast enough, but when he did, he pulled her away from Deloris.

"I can't believe you just did that," Deloris said, covering her cheek.

"Say one more disrespectful thing, and I'll do it again," Ma promised because I knew it wasn't a threat.

"Tessa, call the police. I'm pressing charges."

"No one here will corroborate your story, so don't waste your time," Cyrah told her. "And at the moment, you're trespassing, so I'd suggest you leave before *we* call the police."

"Little girl, I—"

"I hate you! I hate you with everything in me!" Tessa shouted. "You wanted me to be like you, didn't you, Deloris? You wanted to paint the narrative of my story to make it look like yours, but there was only one problem. I'm not a whore. I have never sold my body to the highest bidder."

The look on Deloris's face was one of utter shock. Her beady little eyes bounced around the room to find all eyes glued on her. She opened her mouth to speak, but Tessa wasn't done.

"Everything you've ever told me about my father is a lie. You wanted me to think he wasn't ready for a family and didn't want me, but I know otherwise. He begged you not to have an abortion and offered to take full custody of me, but you refused. He thought you went through the procedure, but lo and behold, thirty years later, he found out I was alive. When he came to you about me, it was the perfect opportunity for you to right your wrongs, but instead, you lied to him and forbade him from reaching out to me. It's okay, though. I know everything I need to know to sever all ties with you and not feel an ounce of guilt. Get the hell out of my house, and don't ever come back."

"Tessa—"

"You heard her," I interjected. "It's time to go."

I gently gripped Deloris's elbow and guided her toward the door. On her way out, she resisted as she spewed profanities and damned all of us to hell. When I finally got her outside, I waited until she drove away before going back inside. I returned to the dining room to find everyone surrounding Tessa in a group hug. I gave them a moment to shower her with love and give her words of encouragement, and when they went back to the table, she ran into my arms.

"I had to get that off my chest," she said.

"I know, and I'm glad you did. How do you feel?"

"A hundred pounds lighter."

"I'm proud of you for standing your ground."

"Me too. I love you, Cypress."

"I love you more, Tessa."

I couldn't believe it was only noon when I looked at the time. It seemed like it was much later in the day because the morning had been very eventful. After Deloris left and the mood shifted back to a happy place, we enjoyed the breakfast Cyrah and Jade prepared as if Deloris had never been there. I'd never seen Tessa smile as much as I did after the incident with her mother, and I was happy she didn't allow it to ruin her day.

"Have you heard from Larisa?" I asked Tessa.

"No. She was supposed to text me her address last night, but I haven't gotten anything."

"You think something happened?"

"I don't know. I believe dinner is at four, so maybe she's just running around getting things ready and forgot to call or text me. I'll give her about thirty more minutes before I—oh, this is her calling now.

"Merry Christmas," she greeted, answering her phone on speaker.

"Merry Christmas, big sis. What time are you all headed this way?"

"I was actually going to call you in about thirty minutes to see if you forgot to send the address."

"What? I sent it last night. Hold on. Let me check my messages. Oh, damn, Tessa. I forgot to send it. I'll send it now. I'm so sorry."

"It's no problem. I've done that hundreds of times and wonder why someone isn't replying."

The text came through, and when Tessa opened it, her mouth flew open, and her free hand covered it.

"Tessa, are you there?"

"Huh, oh yeah. What did you say?"

"Did you get the text?"

"Oh yeah. Umm, is this the address of Truth Sanctuary?"

"It is. Have you been here before?"

"Your family owns Truth Sanctuary?"

"*Our* family owns Truth Sanctuary. Have you visited?" Larisa asked again.

"Back in September, I visited for a week. It was the best experience I've ever had."

"Oh, wow. You probably already met some of our cousins. Four main families run the grounds, each working three months a year. We can talk more about it when you arrive, or some other time. Did you read the letter from Daddy?"

"I did."

"Good, then you know he left you some things in his will. We don't have to talk about it today, but you own a portion of Truth Sanctuary."

"This is unbelievable."

"Believe it. I'll see you soon."

The call ended, and Tessa remained motionless, staring into space. Based on what she'd told me about Truth Sanctuary, she fell in love when she visited. Her visit was what inspired the idea of African American history tours. I was sure the news she'd just learned was a lot to process.

"Life keeps getting better and better, Cypress. This is huge," she said, finally coming out of her daze.

"It is, and very exciting."

"Speaking of exciting, are you ready to share our news?"

"I'm waiting for you."

"Let's do it."

When we made it to the family room, everyone was waiting. None of us were big on gifts, so it took no time for everyone to open what they'd received. Gift cards for favorite stores, jewelry, spa treatments, clothing, cigars with accessories, and cash were popular among our group.

"Cyrah and I have something special for the Boone family," Tessa announced.

I was a bit confused because I thought she and I had some big news to share, but I guess it would have to wait.

"Daddy, can you sit on the couch next to Jade, please?" Cyrah asked.

I did as she asked and anxiously waited to see what this mother-daughter duo had for us.

"Everyone knows how Cyrah was conceived, so I won't bore you all rehashing it. Unfortunately, the three of you missed almost twenty years of Cyrah's life. We'll never be able to make up those years, but we wanted to share some memories with you," Tessa said.

"We made you all photo albums with pictures starting from Mom's pregnancy. Mom did a great job capturing every birthday, milestone, activity, and big event. In the back of each photo album are a couple of USB drives with videos."

While Cyrah spoke, Tessa gave my parents an album to share. Jade and I had our own. Immediately, my mother began to *ooh* and *ahh* over each picture, commenting on how much Cyrah and Jade looked alike. However, I couldn't open my album.

"Daddy, what's wrong? Why aren't you looking at the pictures?"

"I think I'll wait until later," I told her.

"But why?"

"Because I want to take my time, studying and enjoying each one."

"And he doesn't want to cry in front of us," Jade added. "Oh my goodness. This looks just like me, and I had this *same* dress."

I didn't acknowledge Jade's comment, but she was partially correct. I had a feeling looking through the album would make me very emotional.

"This was so thoughtful of you. Thank you for these memories," Ma said, sounding like she was on the verge of tears.

"Yes, I love this," Jade agreed.

"Cyrah, I have one more gift for you," I announced as I stood from the couch.

"There's nothing else under the tree," she said.

"I know."

I reached up, and behind my neck, I undid the necklace I'd worn every day since I was eighteen.

"This necklace has been in our family for generations. It is given to all of the firstborn children beginning with your great-great-great-grandfather, and now, it's my turn to give it to my firstborn."

She gasped. "Daddy, I don't know what to say. This means everything to me."

"You don't have to say anything, baby girl. Turn around so I can put it on."

There wasn't a dry eye in the room, including mine and my father's. This was a proud moment because there was a time I didn't think I'd be able to pass this necklace along. Once the necklace was secured on Cyrah's neck, she turned around and wrapped her arms around my torso, burying her head in my chest.

"Thank you so much, Daddy. I will cherish this forever."

"You don't have to thank me, but I appreciate it. I love you, Cyrah."

"I love you too, Daddy."

We hugged for a while longer before I remembered we had one more thing we needed to do.

"Okay, Ma, Pops, Jade, we have one more gift for you," I announced as I stood from the couch.

"Oh, you are full of surprises today," Ma said.

Tessa handed each of them a small gift bag, and we watched as they looked inside. Cyrah did the honor of recording their reaction. Inside the bags were onesies she'd had custom-made, each with a personalized quote. The onesies were gender-neutral because when we went to the doctor a few days ago, we found out Tessa was approaching eight weeks, and it was much too early to find out the gender. She wanted to wait another month to tell anyone just in case something happened. I refused to think that way and put negativity into the universe. It took a little convincing, and we compromised, agreeing only to tell my parents and Jade. Everyone else had to wait until she was in the second trimester.

"I knew it! I knew it! I knew it!" my mother shouted as she held up the onesie.

She and Jade hopped from the couch to ambush Tessa. I thought they'd forgotten about me, but they eventually showed me some love. My father made his way over and put his hand on my shoulder.

"You've had a helluva year, son. Congratulations!"

"Thanks, Pops. That means a lot."

My father was right; this year had been one for the books. In January, I would've never imagined I'd be living this life, and the past five months had been incredibly surreal. It was as if I'd been given a second chance at happiness, and I was grateful to be blessed with the opportunity. This time around, I'd cherish every moment.

Tessa

W HEN THE SIX of us finally piled into my truck and headed to Truth Sanctuary, I was a ball of nerves. I kept thinking about what could possibly go wrong. Larisa was very welcoming, but what if my other siblings and the rest of the family weren't? I'd be devastated, so I didn't want to get my hopes up. While everyone else in the car conversed about one thing or another, I was too caught up in my thoughts to engage.

"You've been quiet," Cypress said while the others talked amongst themselves.

"I'm nervous as hell."

"That's understandable. I think everything will be fine, but if it isn't, just say the word, and we're gone."

I nodded, then became lost in my thoughts again. The hour-long ride seemed to go by in a flash, and before I knew it, we were turning onto the property.

"Wow, this is beautiful," Mama Boone cooed.

"It is. Wait until you see the rest of the property. I visited for a little getaway back in September and fell in love. I didn't want to leave."

"Wait one darn minute. You didn't tell me the Truths we're related to are the Truths that own this place. Are you kidding me?"

"I didn't know for sure until a few hours ago, sweetheart."

"You probably met some of our people and didn't even know. This is wild."

We parked in front of the bed and breakfast, and before everyone had gotten out of my truck, a crowd of people was standing on the porch waiting.

"Come on," Larisa shouted. "Everyone is excited to meet you."

I looked at Cypress, still on the driver's side of my truck, and he mouthed, "I told you."

"Let's go, Mom," Cyrah urged when she rolled up next to me on her scooter.

As we headed toward the porch, members of my family came down the stairs and formed a line. Larisa was at the beginning, and when I reached her, she hugged me. Of course, I was overcome with emotion and began to cry. When she released me, she looked at Cyrah.

"This must be my niece."

I nodded but couldn't find the words to introduce them officially.

"I'm Cyrah. You must be my aunt Larisa," Cyrah said.

"I am, and you are absolutely gorgeous. What happened here?" Larisa asked, pointing to Cyrah's wrist and ankle.

"A little fender bender, but I'm okay."

"Good. You ready to meet your family?"

"As ready as I'll ever be," I replied.

It took at least thirty minutes for us to be introduced to my siblings, their significant others, and their children. Tasmyn was married to Ray, and they had a son and daughter. Lawrence Jr. was married to Sasha, and they had two daughters and a son. Tashawn's wife's name was Tisa, and she'd just had a baby girl two months ago. Finally, I met Lawson and his fiancée, Nya, and they had no children. Before we got to the extended family, I introduced Cypress and his family to my siblings and their families.

After all the introductions, I was sure it would take several months to remember all the names. I was relieved we received a warm welcome from everyone, and I didn't feel any negative vibes among the group. When it was time to go inside, Cypress assisted Cyrah up the stairs before he and Papa Boone were whisked away by some of the family men. Mama Boone went directly to the kitchen to see what was cooking and if she could help. I spotted Jade flirting with one of my cousins in the corner while Cyrah and I stood back and took it all in.

"This is unreal," she said.

"Isn't it? I can't believe the majority of these people are our blood relatives. I'm in awe right now."

"Me too. Every holiday from here on out will be so much different than what we've experienced."

"Definitely," I agreed.

"Hey, there you are. My mother's in the back. She's been waiting to meet you," Larisa said.

"Your mother?"

Whenever we talked, I wanted to ask Larisa about her mother. She never brought her up, so I thought she may have also passed away.

"Yes, and I can tell by the look on your face you're worried. Don't be."

"Umm, okay."

Cyrah managed to maneuver her scooter through the pockets of people, and we made it to the back of the house.

"She's out here on the back porch," Larisa said as she stepped outside. "Ma, this is Tessa and my niece, Cyrah."

Larisa's mother stood from the rocking chair and took a few steps toward us. I didn't know what to expect from this woman. After all, I was the product of an affair her husband had.

"My goodness, you are Lawrence's twin," she declared with a smile. "I'm Bernadette, but everyone calls me Nettie. It's wonderful to meet you both."

"It's nice to meet you too, Miss Nettie," I said.

"Yes, ma'am. It's nice to meet you," Cyrah added.

"Risa, would you mind taking Cyrah back inside? I want to speak to Tessa alone."

I knew this was too good to be true. This woman was about to take out all her anger about my father's affair on me. I guess I couldn't blame her, though. I was the closest person to my mother, and since she couldn't curse Deloris out, I was the next best thing. Cyrah and Larisa went back inside, and I froze.

"Come have a seat, Tessa. I promise I don't bite."

I slowly sat in the rocking chair beside hers and waited for her to unleash her wrath.

"I know you're probably wondering what I could possibly have to say to you," she began.

"It crossed my mind."

"I was furious when I found out your father was having an affair. When I confronted him, I was prepared to leave him, and we'd only been married a few months. He promised he would end it and never cheat again. I decided to forgive him, and I believe he was faithful from that point forward. After he ended things with your mother, he came home and told me everything. Knowing he was sleeping with a prostitute and wasn't madly in love with the woman softened the blow a bit, but not much. I could see the hurt in his eyes when he told me she was pregnant with his child and getting an abortion. We never discussed the affair again until he saw your picture in the paper. He wanted to go to the university and tell you who he was, but I advised him not to do that. Not because I didn't want him to meet and have a relationship with you, but because we had no idea what you'd been told about your father. He decided to track your mother down first and was crushed when she told him about the other man you thought was your father."

"There was no other man. Well, I take that back. There were several men. Her bedroom was like a revolving door. Some stuck around longer than others, but most were there one minute and gone the next. None of them acted as a father figure. My mother lied to him because she knew meeting him would mean the world to me."

"Larisa told me your mother lied about that. I hate that I talked him out of going to the university. Do you understand why I thought that was a bad idea?"

"I do. If what my mother had said was true, my father showing up at my job would've turned my world upside down, and the man who thought I was his child."

"Tessa, I welcome you into this family with open arms and heart. I love you because you are a part of my husband, and I will treat you no differently than my other children."

Of course, her words brought me to tears. We stood to our feet, and she embraced me like a mother would her child. This woman genuinely loved me; I could feel it flowing from her spirit.

"When are you due?" she whispered as we separated.

"Huh?"

"You're pregnant, right?"

"Oh, I, umm, how did you know?"

"Not a woman in this family has been able to keep their pregnancy a secret from me. Sometimes, I know before they do. Just a gift I was blessed with, I guess."

"Wow. I'll have to introduce you to my boyfriend's mother. She claimed to know as well. Maybe she has the same gift."

"Is she here?" I nodded. "I can't wait to meet her. So, when are you due?"

"In August. I can't believe I'm about to have a newborn at forty."

"Your son will be blessed to have you. This time around, pregnancy and motherhood will be a joyous experience. You'll see."

"My son? You think it's a boy?"

"I *know* it's a boy. Come on. Let's go inside. It's almost time for dinner."

The ride home from Truth Sanctuary was much different from the ride there. While everyone else was exhausted, I talked nonstop. Thankfully, everyone understood my excitement and let me ramble for the whole hour. I still found it hard to believe I was a descendant of Joseph Truth. When I visited Truth Sanctuary for the first time, I felt a strong connection. I would've never guessed there was a reason I felt that way.

I went from being an only child to having two sisters, three brothers, nieces and nephews, and a boatload of cousins. Instead of dwelling on the fact that I missed the opportunity to meet my father, I focused on all the other blessings that stemmed from him being my father. Knowing he loved me without knowing me healed all the scars my mother left on my heart. I'd never felt as whole as I did right now. It felt like I was getting a second chance at life. This time around, I was surrounded by people who loved me. I loved that, and I wouldn't take it for granted.

Epilogue

A YEAR AND A HALF LATER

TESSA

CYPRESS WAS A patient man. After he proposed to me almost a year and a half ago, the first New Year's Eve we spent together, he wanted to get married immediately. He suggested we go to the courthouse, but I nixed that idea immediately. I'd waited a long time to get married and only planned to do it once. He wasn't happy about waiting so long to make me his wife, but he let me plan the wedding of my dreams, and the day had finally arrived. As I prepared to meet my man at the end of the aisle, I thought about the past eighteen months. They'd been the most eventful months of my life thus far.

With the money my father willed to me, I didn't have to work another day of my life. However, I spent most of my pregnancy getting Truth African American History Tours up and running. When I shared my ideas and research with my siblings, I discovered my youngest brother, Lawson, had a charter bus company. My family approved of the company's name, and Lawson and I became partners. We'd been running the tours for the past eight months, and business was booming.

As Mama Nettie predicted, I gave birth to a bouncing baby boy after experiencing the most joyous pregnancy I could've imagined. Aside from a few bouts of morning sickness, I had nothing negative to say about the thirty-nine weeks I carried Cypress Lawrence Boone. His delivery was smooth, and the first ten months of raising him were a breeze. I couldn't have asked for a more perfect baby.

Cyrah graduated two trimesters early from Black Elm University with honors and a degree in business. Three months later, she passed the exam to become a realtor in California, and a month later, she became licensed in California. Jade moved to California and into the apartment Cypress had rented. It took her awhile to convince Cyrah to move in with her because my daughter was in love with her baby brother, and sometimes, I think she suffered from separation anxiety when she was away from him for too long. Eventually, she agreed to move in with Jade, but they spent a great deal of time at our house with baby Cypress.

Mama and Papa Boone visited us so frequently Cypress and I had a bet about how long it would be before they moved to California. Mama Boone would've moved months ago if she'd had it her way, but Papa Boone wasn't completely sold yet. It was only a matter of time before she'd convince him. She hated being so far away from her first grandson, and if Papa Boone didn't come around soon, I wouldn't have been surprised if she moved without him.

I was seven months pregnant when I saw my mother again after the Christmas incident, and thankfully, I hadn't seen her since. We were having dinner as a family at one of the local restaurants, including Mama and Papa Boone, because they were in town visiting. Initially, she pretended she didn't notice me, even though we made eye contact as soon as she entered the dining area. When her friends pointed me out, she had to acknowledge my presence. It would seem strange if she ignored me because she had to keep up appearances, and I was sure she didn't tell them we were no longer speaking.

Her eyes landed on my stomach, and she couldn't hide her shock or keep her mouth from spewing nastiness. However, she didn't get to say much because Cypress shut her down, and Mama Boone was locked and loaded. To avoid being embarrassed in front of her friends, she put her tail between her legs and almost ran to her table on the other side of the restaurant. I almost felt guilty for how much I enjoyed the whole scene, but then I remembered who Deloris was and didn't feel bad at all.

"Mom, are you ready?" Cyrah asked, peeking into my private room.

"Give me two more minutes."

"You better not be in there crying and messing up your makeup," Brianne shouted behind Cyrah. "You know how those pregnancy hormones have you."

Imagine my surprise when I learned I was ten weeks pregnant last week. Actually, I shouldn't have been surprised at all because my soon-to-be husband refused to wear condoms, and at my age, I had no desire to get on any birth control. However, Cypress agreed to get a vasectomy after this baby, so I wouldn't have to worry about any more surprises like this.

My wedding party was much larger than it would've been had I married a few years ago before I met my family. Of course, Cyrah was my maid of honor, and newly married Brianne was my matron of honor. She and Kendall had been married for six months and were expecting their first child in six months. Brianne was ecstatic when she learned she wouldn't be going through her pregnancy experience alone. Jade, Larisa, and Tasmyn were my bridesmaids, while three of my nieces and two of my nephews were the flower girls and ring bearers.

As I stood and looked in the full-length mirror again, my cell phone rang with Cypress's ringtone.

"Oh no! Why is he calling?" I rushed over to my phone and quickly answered. "Hello."

"Baby, what's taking you so long? You should've been walking down the aisle by now."

The desperation in his voice was adorable.

"I just needed a few minutes to myself. I'm coming."

"I've waited way longer than I wanted to make you my wife. Hurry your ass up, or I'm coming to get you."

He ended the call before I could respond, but I had nothing to say anyway. I tossed my phone on the bed and made a mad dash to meet my man at the end of the aisle. History did have a way of repeating itself, but this time around, I was writing my own ending.

Cypress

WHEN I TOLD my father that Tessa was a breath of fresh air, I had no idea how true it was. Every time I laid eyes on her, it felt like she gave me a new lease on life. I often wondered how I lived before we were reunited. She was the yin to my yang, the ups to my downs, and the sunshine to my rain. No one could tell me we weren't made for each other. I proposed, thinking we'd be married within three months. However, Tessa had different plans. My baby chose a wedding date and began planning the wedding of our dreams. I still hated that she made me wait so long to make her my wife, but when I saw the results of her planning, I knew it was worth it.

Experiencing fatherhood for the first time from two different ends of the spectrum was an adventure. I had Cyrah, a full-grown adult, completely spoiled, but because I missed so much of her life, she may as well have been a toddler. She could ask me for anything in this world, and I would probably die trying to make it happen for her, and I didn't see that changing any time soon.

Watching Cyrah with her brother reminded me a lot of how I was with Jade. He was surrounded by immeasurable amounts of love because none of us could get enough of him. He even had Jade and my parents attached. Baby Cypress was the joy none of us knew we needed. The light in his eyes, the innocence of his giggle, and the pureness of his love gave life a new meaning. I wasn't surprised when Tessa told me she was pregnant again because I couldn't keep my hands off her. Every time we made love, conception was my goal, and thankfully, her "old" eggs were on the same page.

Emery reached out to me from an unknown number shortly after she showed up at my house, and I gave her the paternity test results. It was a long text message, full of nonsense, but somewhere in there, she apologized. After reading it, I didn't bother replying to her message and blocked the phone number. As for Rich, I hadn't seen or heard from him since the day I saw him in the grocery store with Emery. I didn't wish him any ill will, but Rich was dead to me. I had no reason to think or speak of him, and I didn't. Samuel and Omar brought his name up on occasion, but the last time they spoke of him, I made it clear not to bring his name up in my presence again.

My whole life changed when I accepted the job at BEU. It was unbelievable to think the position wouldn't have been available had Tessa not resigned. I was recently promoted to African American Studies department chair after Dr. Stephens retired, which surprised me as much as it did everyone else since I hadn't been at the university very long. Who would've thought a one-night stand over twenty years ago would lead to the life I have now? I'd heard my father say many times, "Greater comes later," and I couldn't agree more.

Finally, I looked up and saw my wife at the other end of the aisle. Immediately, my eyes became blurry. Tessa's beauty took my breath away and forced me to breathe simultaneously. I felt something brush against my arm but couldn't look away from my future wife as she seemingly floated down the aisle.

"Son," my father whispered, placing a handkerchief in my hand.

He was my best man, while Omar, Samuel, and Kendall stood in as my groomsmen. Omar, Samuel, and I remained close after my move. They'd visited a few times, and we connected when I went to Chicago. Because Brianne was Tessa's best friend, Kendall and I became friends by default, but he was a good guy.

I took the handkerchief from my father and dabbed my eyes. When Tessa reached the front of the aisle, I didn't wait for the minister to give me instructions. I stepped in front of Tessa, lifted her veil, and pressed my lips against hers.

"Hold on, young man. We haven't gotten to that part yet," the minister said.

"You look so beautiful, baby," I whispered when I pulled away.

"Thank you, but if you don't get back in your position, this man might not marry us," she told me.

I returned to my position beside my father and waited for the minister to start the ceremony.

"Who gives this woman to this man?" he asked.

Lawrence Jr., the oldest of Tessa's brothers, offered to walk her down the aisle, but she chose to walk alone. However, all of her siblings were seated in the front row and stood at the same time.

"We do!" they shouted.

"And me too," Cyrah added.

Tessa told the minister to take out that part of the ceremony since she was walking down the aisle alone, and no one would give her away. However, Cyrah suggested her aunts and uncles do the honors, and it looked like it was a great idea because Tessa was pleasantly surprised.

I was excited to take my place next to my beauty and move the ceremony along. The minister babbled on and on about some things I was sure were important, but I didn't hear a word he said until he told us it was time to recite our vows. We turned to face each other with our right hands joined.

"Tessa, you may recite your vows."

"God did his thing when he made you. Cypress, you are everything I could've imagined in a life partner. You know what I need without asking; you know the perfect words to lift my spirits; you know when to give me space or smother me with love. You know me, and I love you for that and so much more. Thank you for showing me what it is and feels like to be loved. Thank you for being the man I dreamed of and the father our children need. You gave me hope when I'd almost given up, and I promise to love you until the end of time."

"Cypress, you may recite your vows."

"They say no one is perfect, but, baby, you are perfect for me, and we are perfect for each other. Tessa, you've made life worth living, and I can't see myself doing this with anyone but you. Thank you for being the woman I prayed for and the mother our children need. I am in awe every time I think about how the universe conspired in our favor to have us cross paths again, and I am grateful. It may have taken twenty years for us to get here, but it only took twenty minutes for me to know you were special. Thank you for loving me, and I promise to love you until the end of time."

THE END

AFTERWORD

Dear Readers,

Thank you for reading Tessa and Cypress's love story. I had no idea where this story would go when I began writing, but I love how it unfolded, and I hope you did as well. A one-night stand came full circle, and although there were some unexpected twists and turns, Tessa and Cypress's reunion was everything they didn't know they needed.

If you enjoyed this time around, please leave a five-star review. Thank you again!

Kay Shanee

ACKNOWLEDGMENTS

I would first like to thank God for blessing me with creativity and allowing me the opportunity to share it with others.

Thank you to B. Love and my pen sisters at B. Love Publications. Your continuous support, inspiration, motivation, and encouragement means everything to me.

Thank you to LaSheera Lee and everyone at Black Odyssey Media for trusting me with this opportunity and giving me more avenues to share my work.

Last but not least, I thank my husband, Tommy. He sees all the behind-the-scenes efforts of my creative process, supporting and loving me through it all. I love you, babe!

WWW.BLACKODYSSEY.NET

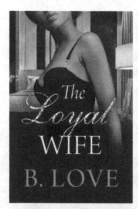

The *Loyal* WIFE

B. LOVE

EVERY BLACK GIRL DANCES

a novel by candice y. johnson

COURAGE to *Love* AGAIN

KIMBERLY BROWN

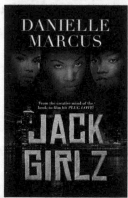

DANIELLE MARCUS

From the creative mind of the book-to-film hit *PLUG LOVE!*

JACK GIRLZ

A THRILLER

INNO CENT INTENT

K.C. MILLS

SOLDIERS OF LOVE

BEAUTIFUL SCARS

N'TYSE & UNTAMED

Love ON THE NINTH Floor

Aries Skye

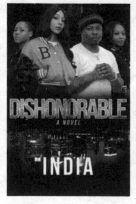

DISHONORABLE A NOVEL

INDIA

OUTRAGED

A TOPHER DAVIS THRILLER

BRIAN COPELAND